THE DUKE'S DEAREST DILEMMA

Willful Wainwrights
Book 1

BY
WENDY LACAPRA

ARE YOU SIGNED UP FOR DRAGONBLADE'S BLOG?

You'll get the latest news and information on exclusive giveaways, exclusive excerpts, coming releases, sales, free books, cover reveals and more.

Check out our complete list of authors, too!

No spam, no junk. That's a promise!

Sign Up Here

www.dragonbladepublishing.com

Dearest Reader;

Thank you for your support of a small press. At Dragonblade Publishing, we strive to bring you the highest quality Historical Romance from some of the best authors in the business. Without your support, there is no 'us', so we sincerely hope you adore these stories and find some new favorite authors along the way.

Happy Reading!

CEO, Dragonblade Publishing

ADDITIONAL DRAGONBLADE BOOKS BY AUTHOR WENDY LaCapra

Willful Wainwrights Series
The Duke's Dearest Dilemma (Book 1)

The Lyon's Den Series
Marked as a Lyon's Marchioness

To Marilyn,

I miss your smile.

and

To Monte.

He has crossed the Rainbow Bridge, but his doubleganger lives in this story.

Thank you, dear Richard P, for your permission to model Mercy on your best little boy.

CHAPTER ONE

MARSDEN, THE DUKE of Harbury's valet, entered Harbury's bedchamber. *"Ahem."* He made a show of clearing his throat. "Her Grace is prepared to receive His Grace at His Grace's convenience."

Harbury laid aside the anonymous letter delivered while he'd been taking his wedding vows—a letter warning of anger building among his tenantry, frustration centered on Harbury Hall's longtime steward, Anderson.

He would turn his mind to the matter tomorrow.

Tonight, he had other ducal duties to attend. Duties more terrifying to him than vague threats from an unidentifiable source. In moments, he would be expected to bed his wife. A wife he barely knew.

"You may retire," Harbury replied, hoping Marsden's smugly knowing expression would be the final wedding night ribbing he'd have to endure.

He rewrapped his heavy, brocaded banyan over his lawn nightshirt then strode across the chamber to the connecting door.

Should he knock first? Or should he just enter?

Enter the duchess's…

Er, his *wife's*…

No, Cassandra's—*Cassie's?*—bed chamber.

Blast.

Only fools vacillated. *Dukes*—he heard this charge in his father's voice—were *never* indecisive.

Harbury had been decisive about Cassandra, alright. Decisive at exactly the wrong time.

A few months earlier, he had swept Cassandra into a waltz at Almack's even though he'd known the patronesses had strict rules against young ladies waltzing without their permission. He'd been distracted. *Distressed.* He'd just seen the lady he'd loved for over a decade, Vivianne, dancing in the arms of her new husband, Lord Pennington.

But instead of creating a soothing diversion, his dance with Cassandra had catapulted both of them into scandal.

Countess Lieven had ordered the music to cease and then skewered Cassandra with one of her infamous dead-eyed glares. Next, the countess had publicly revoked Cassandra and her twin sister Eliza's vouchers, setting off a series of events leading to Eliza's marriage to Harbury's friend, the Marquess of Redver—a genuine love match—and his own, more Faustian bargain with Cassandra…a marriage of polite convenience, but for the necessity of begetting an heir.

Reparation toward Cassandra was Harbury's duty, and her sweet nature suggested she'd be a comfortable, biddable wife. But, having loved his older sister's one-time governess from the dawn of his manhood, he did not believe he could ever fully eradicate Viv, now Lady Pennington, from his heart. So, he'd promised Cassandra all he thought himself capable of giving—his name and his home.

Now, however, standing in front of his wife's door, his thickening blood forced him to acknowledge an alarming physical attraction to his wife, one he'd only become aware of today, when he'd taken her hand, and she'd placed herself forever in his keeping. Since then, his very inconvenient attraction had only increased. Desire weighted his legs, shrunk his lungs, and tore at the already gaping hole in his chest.

Want left him terrified. Terrified and yearning. He knew this feeling, this needy, possessive yearning. He *hated* this feeling.

Early this morning—so early the sun had yet to impose a

patina of pink over night's dark vault—Marsden had awoken him from a brandy-drenched slumber. Humbly, Harbury had submitted to all manner of preparation and pampering. He'd been shaved, buffed, scented, and then pressed into his starched finest, good as new—according to Marsden.

"New?" His friend Adrian had countered. "He looks like a peacock."

"Never you mind him." Marsden had side-eyed the marquess—an impertinence tolerated since Marsden had known them both their whole lives. "The *foremost* duty of a man about to wed is to be pleasing to his lady."

His. Lady.

"Excellent advice!" Adrian had exclaimed. "Remember, Harbury—*be pleasing.* Even you should be able to manage congeniality for *one* day."

And so, making a sincere attempt, Harbury had skated through a dizzying whirl beginning with solemn exhortations from a stern-faced bishop, and stringing through the well-wishes of a disconcerting number of ladies with painted faces and an equally bewildering number of men giving hearty, male back-slaps, before ending in one, sumptuous breakfast lasting well into the afternoon.

But, in his efforts to render himself acceptable to his lady, he'd become aware of her in a new way. She was kind, lovely, and desirable. She deserved his heart—a heart he had given someone else long ago.

Now, the guests had all departed, the brandy had worn off, and other kinds of spirits whispered in the shadows. Ghosts, perhaps, of the formidable dukes who had preceded him. They urged him to plant his seed, complete the deed.

Several hundred years ago, he wouldn't have had a choice. Wedding guests would have been waiting below, or even *inside* the bedchamber, for proof of consummation. As a lad, he'd even sniggered over a woodcut of a priest leering over a couple in bed in *The Romance of Melusine*. Then, of course, he'd been young and randy and made thoroughly stupid by *anything* associated with rutting.

Rutting. He frowned.

Could one *rut* with a wife? The word felt wrong. Vulgar.

What did one call marital consummation, apart from consummation, which surely only applied the first time? Amorous congress, perhaps?

Amorous. His mouth further tightened. He *should* love his wife.

His sweet wife.

His gentle, biddable, careful wife, with her dark, thick chestnut hair, her long, soft fingers, and her wide, perceptive, intelligent blue eyes. His wife, whom he had known for mere weeks. His wife, whom he *did not* love but had still bound to him until death they would part.

He did want her, however.

His breath had caught when she'd appeared on the threshold of the church's open doors. His throat had further constricted as she'd advanced toward him, her gown's silver cloth shimmering and swishing over a champagne-pale chemise. Her contained bearing, her pale skin, and her faint-but-gracious smile created the impression of otherworldliness, inviolability.

Except now, he—in the name of ducal dynasty—was tasked with breaking the spell.

After tonight, she would be inviolable no more.

Well—he took another deep breath—he would begin as he meant to go on. Dutifully. Honorably. She was his, under the law and in God's eyes. And, for better or worse, he would, as promised, worship her with his body.

He nodded to himself, banished the ghosts, and knocked on the door to his wife's boudoir.

"Enter," she called out in a voice almost too quiet to hear. After a beat she added, "please."

Just like her to say "please." She was always so very polite.

He entered. The sconces on either side of the bed were

aglow, further softening the already delicately elegant interior. He was alien inside her bedchamber. Hard, large, and male. He knew how to demand, how to choose an aim and bluster his way to the end. But to petition? To entreat? To lure? What did he know of such things?

Tonight, the skills on which he had been taught to rely were useless.

"Well…" his voice trailed. *Well, what?* He couldn't simply ask, *Fancy a tumble?* He chose a simple greeting. "Good evening."

"Good evening," she replied with a blush.

The physical sign of her responsiveness sent another, overwhelming surge of desire washing over him—want, keen and focused. The wave withdrew, leaving him with increasingly leaden limbs and a tight, uncomfortable feeling in his groin.

His gaze dropped from her averted eyes to her lips. He contemplated kissing her as he wanted to kiss her—open-mouthed and passionate.

The location of his stomach shifted, leaving him queasy.

In the nascent years of his manhood when he was no longer a boy but not yet of age, he'd spent hours clandestinely kissing Vivianne—who, by then, was employed as his sister's companion. Experience made him bolder, and soon he'd taken to whispering outrageous suggestions into her ears. Suggestions which left her giggling and sighing and promising him all once they were wed. But she'd married another.

Twice.

The first, after taking a bribe from his father. The second—more painfully—of her own volition.

He couldn't kiss Cassandra in the same manner he'd kissed Viv. It wouldn't be right. Even when church consecrated, lust without love felt like sin.

Like disrespect.

In silence, his wife pulled back the coverlet. She shifted her position, creating more space on his side of her bed. Even in the dim flicker of candlelight her white night rail merely muted her long, shapely legs, the dark patch of her womanhood, and the hints of color around her nipples.

She was lovely. Not overtly alluring like Viv, but still—

He shuttered the disloyal thought.

To be thinking now of Vivianne was not just unkind, but a betrayal, both to his wife and to his future children.

Cassandra lifted her hand. Her first finger stretched toward him while the others draped as if curling over an invisible balustrade. He knew so little about her, but he liked her hands. Her features she kept schooled, her posture erect, but her hands were nearly always in motion. Those hands hinted at deeper secrets. Secrets she might never trust him enough to reveal.

The thought made him want to try harder to know her. Perhaps even…

But no. Vivianne had cut a groove in his heart no one else could fill.

He grasped Cassandra's palm and raised her fingers to his lips. She held his gaze as he placed a kiss on the heavy gold band he'd fitted there just hours ago, and then into each of the four soft valleys between her knuckles.

Honored.

And he was. Truly.

He wanted to tell her. But he hadn't given her any reason to believe him.

Instead of speaking, he took off his wrap, sat down on the bed, then extended his impossibly large legs beneath the sheet. Beside him, she was warm and sweet-smelling. Each time she took a breath, the rise and subsequent fall of her chest made interesting contours in the fabric of her chemise.

Inviting contours.

The importance of proceeding "the right way" slowly ceded to more primal urges. He shifted onto his side and cupped her neck. He placed a closed-mouth kiss on each of her cheeks and then brushed his lips over hers. Even brief contact burdened his breath.

She blinked up at him, bewildered.

He bent down again, moving his mouth along her jaw, following a dab of scent to a spot just beneath her ear. She sighed and placed a hand on the back of his neck. Every hair on his body stood straight.

He rested his forehead against hers and heard her breath quicken.

Encouraging.

Hesitantly, at least at first, he palmed her breast. But when he moved to stimulate her nipple, she made a sound of protest. He glanced up, searching her face.

She stared at him, a wild, desperate look in her eyes. Then, she dropped her gaze and threaded her fingers through his, returning his hand to the same spot he'd abandoned.

"Go on," she whispered.

Lud, this was awkward.

Every time he'd been…*amorous* with Viv, she had mewed and simpered, undulated and encouraged. Not so, Cassandra.

His wife did not push him away, but neither did she draw him close. Still, beneath his ungainly hand, her heartbeat fluttered faster than a fledgling's wings. Her skin was heating. From what he remembered, warm skin was a sign of desire, wasn't it?

He glanced beneath the tented sheet to where their legs mingled.

Yes, even her thighs had pinked.

She whimpered as she took note of his perusal, not with desire, but with what sounded more like deeply rattled mortification.

Perhaps he ought to have doused the lights?

His gaze flicked back to her face, seeking guidance. But she had turned her cheek into her pillow. The one eye visible to him was firmly closed.

"You are beautiful," he murmured reassuringly. Whatever their reasons for marrying, this much he could truthfully offer. "I find you…enchanting."

Her lids barely opened. She studied him in silence.

Wife. *His wife.*

He caressed her cheek, then moved his hand back to her breast, holding her gaze as he stimulated the peak. This time she did respond. Her back arched, her lips parted, and her breath deepened. Another small whimper escaped, this one leaving him light and woozy.

"Do you know what is to come?"

After a moment's hesitation, she nodded.

Without him asking—thank heaven—she parted her legs. They'd skipped a step—*or ten*—had they not? But what did he truly know?

Would she mock him if she knew he, too, had "saved" this act for his wedding night?

Damn his romantic soul.

Yesterday, after all the ladies in the household had taken themselves off to bed, Harbury—slightly tipsy—had posed a question to his closest friend, his sworn brother: How *did* one bed a virgin?

Adrian's answer? *Good God, man.* And then, a moment later. *You're serious, aren't you?*

He'd only nodded.

Adrian had swallowed roughly, shrugged, then suggested, *gently?*

Not comprehensive as instructions go.

Harbury's explorations with Viv constituted the sum of his carnal experience. Viv, whom he'd loved, and who had allowed his hands and lips, but nothing more, to wander freely. On the shameful times he'd given into temptation and pleasured himself, he'd only had images from what he'd seen in forbidden books.

Thank God there'd been no witnesses present then, either.

How disconcerting to have what had been off-limits now presented to him without restriction—a living, breathing, willing, *beautiful* lady. How was bedding her not only permitted but his *duty?*

As tenderly as he could, he drew up her rail. He caressed her mound, causing her to make another, unintentional *yip*, but his fingers came away damp and glistening. He couldn't help himself. He took in the scent.

"Harbury!" she gasped.

Fire burned in his cheeks. "I need to make certain you are ready…"

Her gaze fixed on his hand. He knew she hadn't understood, but she answered, "I'm ready."

"Yes," he agreed. "But this may still hurt."

"I *know*." She sighed. "Please, just…just…*go on*."

Her "encouragement" landed as an accusation. But why should he feel wounded? Of course, she wanted the first time over and done with. She was embarrassed.

So was he.

Very well. He'd a task to complete, and, truth be told, a cock more than eager to participate. He might as well *go on*.

Careful to support as much of his weight as he was able, he positioned himself. Then, murmuring a soft apology, he thrust his way into a tight, slick passage fiercely protesting his invasion. Even so, a spasm of pleasure briefly blanked his mind.

Good God, St. Michael, and all the bloody dragons that ever lived.

The warm, wet sensation engulfed and shocked him, but nothing could have prepared him for the unbelievable experience of being joined. He was *inside* a lady—*his* lady. A visceral, spontaneous bond slipped into place. Instinctively, he set his cheek against hers, crooning unsummoned words, words of comfort, assurances the pain would soon be over.

Her limbs grew pliant. Was her body merely accepting the inevitability of surrender?

His was vibrating with song.

Her breasts caressed his chest as she adjusted herself beneath him. Hesitantly, she placed her hands on his shoulders.

"That's better," she said against his neck.

Yes. So much better.

He withdrew, only to thrust into her again—ungracefully, at first, but soon enough he found the rhythm. Her fingers trembled against his shoulders, then pressed harder, as if she couldn't decide whether to push him away or pull him closer.

Her hot breath fanned his ear. Her eyelashes tickled his cheek. More, he thought, *more*—while teetering on the edge of…what? Oblivion?

Fulfillment?

Words failed, so his body spoke soundlessly of need, want, and delight. Then, he lost awareness of everything but the staccato release of his seed. He came back into his mind with a full body exhale, a profound sense of gratitude and…

Well, more than a little chagrin.

What now?

He kissed her cheeks again before withdrawing, rolling onto his back and then taking her hand in his. The floodgates had broken, washing him in relief, exhaustion, and…*happiness?*

Yes. Happiness.

He'd done something right.

He squeezed her hand.

In fact, bedding Cassandra may have been the "rightest" thing he'd ever done.

THANK HEAVENS.

He'd moved. Cassie could finally breathe. The worst was over, and, while the bedding had not been *quite* as painful as she'd anticipated, more than anything in the wide world, the Duchess of Harbury wanted the Duke of Harbury out of her bed.

Now.

But demanding Harbury leave would be unforgivably rude, what with him collapsed at her side and his fingers threaded through hers. Annoyingly, he'd begun dragging his thumb repeatedly along her forefinger, as if, even though he'd withdrawn, he did not want to fully break their curious, alien connection.

That doesn't mean he genuinely cares for you!

So, you break it! Snatch back your hand. Turn away. Bid him—in no uncertain terms—good night.

She worried her bottom lip.

She'd wanted him. Even after his outrageous behavior at Almack's, she'd wanted him for her own. And yet startling, volcanic, and violently angry directives were erupting in her mind, splashing fury and heat in every direction.

What fiery, internal force had caused the disturbance?

Certainly not *her*! Everyone knew Cassandra Wainwright was the most dutiful and kind of the five Wainwright sisters, always accommodating and sweet.

Taradiddle and bilgewater.

She was no longer Cassandra Wainwright, but Duchess of Harbury. And Cassandra, Duchess of Harbury was currently hedgehog prickly and more bad-tempered than Eliza and Millie, her two most outspoken sisters.

And she didn't *want* to be nice, even though she *should* be nice.

He'd been gentle, patient, and *devil take him*, tender…which made her fury even more unacceptable. She had even, for an involuntary moment, been deeply joined to him, at the cusp of a revelation she had known would fill her with awe. *Empty promise.*

Just like her vows, though she couldn't claim she was with Harbury against her will. She was here, in this bed, in this house, in this marriage as a result of an agreement she'd initiated.

She had proposed to *Harbury* via desperate letter in the dead of night.

Of course, she'd done so only because Harbury had unthinkingly destroyed her reputation with a single, impulsive dance. And because her twin sister Eliza's attempts to restore their family to respectability had, that very night, gone horribly, irrevocably awry.

Or so Cassie had believed at the time.

Another lie.

Eliza had believed her plans had come to naught. *Cassie* had a strong feeling, even then, the Marquess of Redver had fallen as hard for Eliza as she had for him, which did turn out to be the case—so, *ha.*

But having been proven right didn't provide Cassie much comfort. Slightly more consoling was the fact that, during that brief period of uncertainty, she had taken control for the first time in her life. Taking control had felt good.

Amazingly good.

Everyone had been pleased with her choice, too. Only Eliza had tried to change her mind. Her godmother, Lady Asquith, and Harbury's sister, Lady Sarah, had each separately suggested Harbury needed *her.* Harbury needed calm-spirited, dutiful Cassie. Virtuous. Respectable. Accommodat—

Get out of my damned bed.

She covered her mouth with her free hand, as if she could hold in her fury. Because if she let him see, let him know, he might refuse to keep his end of their marital bargain. He was to do everything in his power to help her younger sisters establish themselves in the coming Season.

"Thank you, Cassandra."

Oh Heavens. Guilt, bitter as bile, poisoned her tongue. If he only knew the horrible things she'd been thinking, he'd never have said her name in such a soft, caressing tone!

"I ought to have asked before." He chuckled to himself. "*May I call you Cassandra?*"

Well, she wasn't *Miss Cassandra* to him anymore, was she? She forced a noise she hoped sounded like assent.

"There is still steam rising from the water left by your maid," he said. "Shall I help you clean—"

"No!" she interrupted, horrified. She just wanted to be alone.

His thumb stopped moving. He frowned. Something like

victory surged through her veins.

Victory followed immediately by regret.

"No, thank you," she amended. The anger within her was not appeased. "Please ring for Sally before you return to your chamber."

There. She'd done it.

She'd politely let him know she wanted him to leave. Only he didn't get out of her bed. Instead, he placed his cumbersome, very male palm against her cheek. She could smell her own scent on him. *Revolting!*

Well, a little revolting.

But, perhaps, also a *very* tiny, minuscule-morsel bit intriguing, too?

"Are you asking me to leave?" His frown deepened. "Do you truly want me to go?"

No. Tell him how you have felt about him since the moment you laid eyes on him.

Tell him you'd like to try again.

Oh, *good heavens.* She closed her eyes. Now she had *two* opposing voices competing in her head. Wasn't she vulnerable enough?

Why should she give him even more ammunition by telling him the secret feelings she harbored for him, especially since that feeling—that curious, fledgling longing—was currently making her furious?

And why had she gone from bracing herself against his onslaught, to *enjoying* the feel of him moving inside of her, to furiously ordering him out?

The distinctions between sacred, scared, and excited had blurred.

Which was she now? Scared? Excited?

Both?

Or perhaps *she* was scared, because *he* was exciting.

Carnal knowledge had certainly smeared the carefully negotiated boundaries between them.

Covertly—she hoped—she moved her gaze over his features. His color was still high from exertion. His eyes, bright. His nightshirt crumpled, askew.

Did he have to be so *distressingly* handsome?

Enchanting, he'd called her. He, heaven help her, was *spellbinding*.

He'd a wide brow, and his high cheek bones tapered down to a distinguished chin. His thick, sandy-brown hair fell over his forehead in a romantic wave. He looked, in fact, like one of the imaginary beaus she'd sketched when she'd been young.

Young and stupid enough to dream of a love match.

No. She *would not* allow his obvious good will to mute her anger.

No matter how much he'd intrigued her, no matter how much she'd wanted him, he'd stolen her dreams of love when he'd yanked her onto that dance floor. She didn't want to yield to him any more than he'd already taken. He had forced her to yield to him in public. And now...

Well, now, she'd just profoundly, intimately, *painfully* yielded to him in private.

Painfully...*at first.*

Once she'd adjusted her position, the sensation had been, not quite pleasant but—full. Friction had lit flinty sparks inside her, igniting an even deeper, hotter burn. Most confusingly, even though he'd been inside of her, still, she'd yearned for him to be closer.

She'd wanted to wrap his strange, hard body in her arms. All she'd found the courage to do was place her hands against his muscled shoulders.

And, ah, what an unexpected, overwhelming feeling...

NO! She absolutely *would not* give him the satisfaction of seeing how deeply he had—

His face blurred. No. No. *NO.*

"*Ssst,*" she said aloud, as if scolding one of her younger sisters to be quiet in church. But she couldn't stop tears from clouding her eyes and fattening enough to bubble over her lids, wetting her lashes.

"Ah," he crooned. "Ah, my dear girl."

She shrank back. She was *not* his girl. She was a married lady. She lifted her wobbly chin. A *duchess*. *His* duchess.

Oh God!

How had she ever thought marriage to Harbury would make everything easy?

With his rough man-thumb, he wiped away her tears. No man had *ever* wiped tears from her eyes. In fact, no man—save a groom—had ever been this close to her person.

Beast.

Or dream come to life? She blinked up at him.

Bad dream.

"I'm perfectly"—her voice cracked—"fine. Just tired."

A long, searching look satisfied him. His nightshirt fell around his thighs as he rose. He leaned back over the bed to kiss her forehead. She appreciated his tenderness. She also wanted to chuck a shoe at his head.

Pity her feet were bare.

"I'm not overwrought," she lied again. "Only, I could hardly sleep last night."

He smiled. "Nor I."

Because he was getting drunk with his friend Adrian, her brother-in-law!

He smoothed the troubled indentation between her brows. "I hope you will sleep well tonight. You're safe."

She wasn't. And when he cocked his head, and his stupid lock of hair fanned his forehead becomingly, her danger only increased.

"I promised to honor and keep you," he continued. "I do, you know. I honor you."

Honor. What did honor even mean?

He'd promised to love her too, but he'd given his heart to another long ago.

On the other hand, he'd been honest about his *dear Viv.*

If Cassie could not expect her husband's love, at least she could rely on his integrity. And trust was more than many couples had between them, was it not?

Even if her fury continued to billow choking plumes of smoke and ash, she must remember—she'd proposed. This marriage was not entirely his fault.

And he was...*trying.*

"Thank you," she forced. "I promised to be a good wife. And I *will*," she added with only slightly bitter resolution. "But go, Harbury. *Please.*"

An expression of concern shaded his features. Briefly, his lips parted as if he were about to speak. She didn't want him to speak.

She *couldn't* speak. Because she hadn't any words for the unwanted emotions warring inside.

All day she'd seesawed between conflicting desires.

She wanted to hold her husband. She wanted to push him away. She wanted to ask him what the future held. She wanted to tell him, in no uncertain terms, they had no future, at least no future in which they might be happy.

Thank heavens she'd her five sisters to distract her on this, the most consequential day of her life, else she might have gone mad. But they—along with Harbury's sister Sarah and Adrian's sister Emily—had already left to return to London.

She was alone with her husband. Alone on his vast, one hundred-forty-nine-thousand-acre estate. Two towns, several villages, over one hundred farmers, tradesmen, gamekeepers, and other tenants, all under the strict eye of Harbury's head steward Mr. Anderson—a man who, just this morning, had offered felicitations in a hearty tone with unwelcoming eyes, leaving her feeling unwanted, extraneous.

She did not belong here. She would never belong here.

She shivered. Harbury moved to adjust the coverlet around her person.

"Please," she repeated. "I just want to go to sleep."

He hesitated, then nodded.

She looked away as he donned his banyan. When she was certain he was fully covered, she faced her husband again.

"Good night, duchess," he said, his mouth quirking in a wry, somewhat mystified attempt at a smile.

"Good night, duke." She sniffed, offering what she hoped was a thankful expression…albeit a watery one.

Then, *finally*, he was gone.

And the new Duchess of Harbury—her heart sliced into a tripartite of silly hope she dared not indulge, sensual curiosity she feared, and furious, flowing enmity she did not know how to contain—calmly dried her tears.

For better or worse, Harbury was now her husband.

As planned, they would spend the summer here at Harbury Hall. She would come to know him, come to know his people and his land. She would be good. She would be dutiful. And then, she would reunite with Eliza and her sisters at Ravenswood, Redver's Manor home and they would all return to town for the little Season.

Her sacrifice would be her sisters' gain.

But the little Season seemed far, far away. And the duke, far, far too present. Half of her wanted to win him, the other, to ruin him.

Heaven only knew which part would prevail.

CHAPTER TWO

ASSIE HAD SLEPT—FINALLY—BUT as her consciousness dawned the following morning, her limbs felt stiff and her mind muddled. Though she'd had little true rest, with effort, she forced her eyes to open. Ripples in her bedsheets came into focus, ripples aglow with sun-kissed diamond shapes.

The hour was late. In more ways than one.

As she smoothed out the coverlet, the sparkling light patterns transferred to the back of her hand, brightening her fat, golden wedding band.

Harbury's band.

She pushed her fingers back beneath the sheets, aching with a deep, visceral longing for her twin, Eliza. Until a few weeks ago, they'd spent every night of their twenty years sharing a bed. Waking alone was still disorienting. Waking alone after having been intimately invaded…

She swallowed roughly.

Harbury's phantom touch lingered on her skin, inside and out, in visible and invisible places. In fact, a faint twinge of pain was still present in a place she'd never experienced sensation before. A *very* private place. With a mew of distress, she scooched back up against the headboard, drawing in and holding her legs with one arm while cupping her forehead with her other.

Last night, between the single, distant gong just after Harbury's departure, to the four she'd counted just before weariness won the battle with her anger, she'd existed in an unwilling wakefulness, a seemingly endless, liminal void. Since intentionally going out of her mind was not an option—at least not a viable one—she had resolved to make peace with her situation.

To aid her resolution, she'd counted the times Harbury had seen to her comfort during their courtship, even though their courtship was supposed to have been a ruse. She summoned, in detail, the memory of the cool drink he'd brought back to his dark, hot opera box during their first outing together. She relived the moment at the Harbury ball when he'd shielded Eliza from further scandal with a loud, terrible, but effectively distracting jest…a scandal Cassie had unintentionally created.

She further recalled the pained look of self-disgust he'd had as he confessed his long-standing, unrequited attachment to Vivianne, Lady Pennington. That day, he'd transformed in her eyes, from an arrogant duke into a flawed but sympathetic human.

Confiding in her had not been necessary, but he had. And so, at the very least, he deserved her trust. Finally, she came back around to the one, simple, fact she could not deny—*she'd* been the one to propose marriage. A marriage of convenience, she'd called it.

She pursed her lips.

How naive her use of the phrase seemed now.

Convenience had nothing to do with the Pandora's Box Harbury had unleashed in her last night. Skin against skin. Warm breath comingled. A private world's creation. A world known only to themselves. The experience had left her more vulnerable than she'd anticipated. And permanently altered.

Some small part of her had expected the transformation from wallflower to duchess to end in happy, settled satisfaction, like the resolution of a good novel. But she should have known better. The meat of any story was struggle. Metamorphosis can never be experienced without pain, without bafflement, confusion…and, yes, a touch of panic.

And wasn't the struggle to break free of the cocoon what

brings animation to a caterpillar's new wings? Somehow, she had to force her way through her profound distress.

She must come out stronger.

She might *feel* like her life was at stake, but no one had ever died from what was essentially embarrassment. Nor had anyone, to her knowledge, expired from anger.

So, nothing was to be done but to persevere. She was mistress of Harbury Hall, a place far removed from anything having to do with Vivianne, Lady Pennington.

With renewed determination, she rang for her new maid. Sally appeared almost immediately.

"Good morning, Your Grace." She came to stand at the foot of the bed. "His Grace suggested you might wish to take breakfast here in your room. Would you like me to go down and make you a plate?"

Already arranging her life, was he? Didn't the law give him enough power over her?

Despite her intentions, her anger sparked anew.

If he thought he could manage her day without her input, she would quickly disabuse him of the notion.

"No, thank you."

In truth, she *had* planned to request breakfast in her room.

Moreover, she'd intended to avoid her husband until she mastered schooling her features into appropriate ducal (duchessal?) composure. Her pique, however, caused an abrupt change of heart.

She tossed aside the coverlet and rose to her feet. A beam of light landed on a bright, red stain just to the right of the place she had slept. She inhaled sharply as heat flared up her neck. Sally's blush was equally dark.

They both turned their backs to the bed.

With forced dignity, Cassie managed, "My yellow morning dress, if you please."

If she couldn't feel bright and cheery, at least she could look the part.

Sally disappeared into the dressing room. By the time she returned, Cassie had discreetly covered the stain. Still, she stood frightened-rabbit still as Sally prepared her for the day.

Unlike Mary, the kind and motherly maid she had shared with Eliza and her sisters when they were all back at Willowhurst, Sally proved brisk and efficient, neither inviting confidences nor offering consolation.

On one hand, the maid's manner left Cassie even more adrift. On the other, in less than a quarter hour, Cassie's hair was arranged, her layers properly fitted, and her locket containing a miniature of her deceased mother on one side and her sisters on the other clasped around her neck.

Of her late father, she refused to carry a remembrance.

Leaning toward the mirror, Cassie pinched color into her cheeks.

There. She stood taller.

If not formidable, she was, at least, presentable, and she carried with her the love of the people she held dearest.

Keeping her posture formally erect, she made her way down the stairs. The breakfast room was easy enough to find. She, her sisters, Adrian, Harbury, Lady Sarah, and Adrian's sister Emily had met there every morning for the past fortnight.

Before, however, she'd only needed to follow the sounds of her sisters' voices.

If today had been like the prior days, Millie and Lenora would have already been exchanging witty barbs, Nettie and Emily inserting occasional dry comments, and Harbury's sister, looking from one pair to the other as if watching a game of *jeu de paume.*

Adrian and Eliza, of course, would be oblivious to all other company while sharing smoldering looks. And Harbury…

Cassie smirked.

Harbury would be lounging at the table's head, observing them all with no small amount of consternation.

Perhaps he, too, hadn't known quite the level of upheaval marriage would bring.

Girding herself with a deep inhale and a cheerful smile, Cassie stepped into the breakfast room. Her new husband, she noted, looked as sleepless as she felt. Her forced smile faltered as his troubled gaze met hers.

"Good morning." He rose from his chair. His hand hovered in the air before he changed his mind about whatever he'd been going to do and dropped his arm. "I trust you slept well."

"Well, indeed." Her gaze briefly flitted to the liveried footman next to the sidebar. "And you?"

"Capital."

They stood in uncomfortable silence, each with fixed smiles stitched to their faces, while the clock in the corner clicked as loudly and incessantly as a bad-tempered cricket.

Recalling himself, Harbury cleared his throat and then moved to the chair beside him, the same seat she'd chosen on earlier mornings because the rest of the table had been full. The legs made a rushing sound against the carpet as he pulled back the chair. With a gesture of his hand, he bid her to sit.

She inclined her head in thanks but, instead, moved to the sideboard to fill her own plate.

He remained silent while, taking her time, she served herself a bit of ham, a spoonful of berries, and a slice of toast with a slab of butter. Only when she returned to her chair did she venture a glance to see how he'd taken her rebellion.

Harbury's color was high, but, like last night, the look in his eyes suggested embarrassment rather than anger.

Gracefully, she took her seat. He aided her by adjusting her chair's position before returning to the table's head.

Cassie lifted her knife. The flatware was cold and heavy and the process of slicing her ham ridiculously labored. This was *breakfast*, for heaven's sake. A meal she took every day. So why, on this morning, was she so irritated by the sound of silver clicking against porcelain?

And why did the crunching noises Harbury made increase her annoyance?

He swallowed, patted his mouth with a napkin, then studied her with passive features.

"I've been wondering if your bedchamber is furnished to your taste."

"Yes." Cassie dropped her eyes.

Actually, she hated the profusion of pink, but she couldn't bring herself to disparage decorative choices likely made by his deceased mother. Nor had she any valid reason for complaint—the fabrics were of good quality and showed surprisingly little wear.

"If there is anything you wish to change…" He left his sentence dangling.

"Not at present."

His chair creaked and the fabric of his coat whispered. He'd shifted. Perhaps he'd taken up *the posture* and was gazing at her with the same dispassionate, but slightly perplexed expression, she'd seen him use on her sisters on prior mornings. Or maybe his eyes were burning with the same dark, hungry expression she remembered from last night…

Butter oozed over the top of her toast, slowly liquefying. She wet her lips.

"The wedding went well." His voice had gone soft.

"Yes," she answered. "Very… proper."

"I was," he paused, "well-pleased."

Good Heavens. Were they discussing the ceremony?

She feared not.

Would every discussion with him be this fraught?

Because the conversation was embarrassing, and the weight of everything they *weren't* saying was bearing hard against her chest.

If this was to be her conversational lot, she would be taking breakfast in bed for a lifetime.

Lud.

While Harbury knew he'd never been the best of conversationalists, he hadn't felt this inept in decades. He felt as if he were shrinking back into the child he'd once been.

He may be sitting at the table's head, but, if he glanced down, he half expected he'd see short pants hugging legs too small to reach the floor. Reflexively, he wiped the back of his knees, surprised when his hand met leather. He could have sworn sweat was making them stick uncomfortably to mahogany.

His mind spasmed with the same old disorientation, just as if he were a boy again and the other empty chairs contained his mother, his father and his sister Sarah. He felt the resurgent, maddening inability to enter a conversation flowing as smoothly and naturally as the stream cutting through the home wood's northwest corner.

How had the rest of his family always known just what to say to one another, just when to drop in the amusing anecdote, while he had never been able to form the proper words?

Whenever he'd tried to venture something important—birdsong he'd identified or a passage in a book he'd enjoyed—his father had scowled. In fact, he'd never had a conversational ally at the table until late adolescence, when Adrian had come to live in the household.

But Adrian was no longer here, neither in the distant past, nor as he had been just yesterday.

Harbury's own fault, too.

He'd planned everything so all their guests would leave just after the celebration. Without the Wainwright girls' incessant, mystifying chatter, he'd hoped a comfortable pattern of civility might slide into place between himself and his wife.

After all, Cassandra had been easy to talk to when they'd been "courting," even if the "courtship" had, at the time, been a pretense to satisfy her godmother's concern for her reputation.

Had her gentleness then also been pretense?

Or was her awkwardness now the anomaly?

He'd wager his last pence her gentleness had been sincere. Before, she'd had no expectations of him. But now…

Well, if she had expectations, he'd clearly failed to measure up.

He'd thought marriage would make him feel like the man he should be. Instead, his current experience was quite the opposite. And he'd no idea how to go about building a bridge between a present he hadn't expressly wanted and a future in which he might take pride. Every future he'd imagined had always contained Viv.

Vivianne's first marriage, he'd forgiven. His father had been at fault, then—no one ever defied the prior duke, least of all a penniless governess turned companion. But the man his father had forced her to wed had been of his father's generation, and he'd thought…

Well, it didn't matter what he'd thought now. Everything had changed.

Who was this lady sitting across from him?

Somewhere beneath this cold, prickly version of Cassandra, the girl with the gentle, lulling smile must still exist, unless last night had altered the terms of their "marriage in name" agreement in a way that made her impossible to reach.

Last night…

A subtle shudder sped down his spine.

Last night the pleasure—no, the *ecstasy*—had been beyond anything he could have imagined…certainly beyond those occasions when he'd been brought to release before by his own hand, or even Viv's.

The profound impact of his first complete carnal encounter had been almost enough to counterbalance the humiliation of being ordered from his wife's chamber. He couldn't bring himself to be angry. After all, he'd made her cry. But before…

Ah, before.

He closed his eyes, remembering the feel of her hands against his back, light as a swarm of summer butterflies. Her curves had been soft wonder, the tickle of her breath against his neck, sublime, and entering her welcoming heat, indescribable bliss.

He nearly groaned aloud.

He opened his eyes to find she'd stopped chewing. She pursed her lips and swallowed roughly. Her cheeks rosed.

She must have read his naked want, the residue of recollections making him both uncomfortably warm and halfway to being hard.

Good.

Despite her anger, she was not immune to him. And he wasn't going to let her forget the part she'd played in the events that had landed them here. She could have found another man to marry after his "interest" repaired her reputation, but she had proposed to him. So, some small part of her must have wanted him—even if, like himself, she hadn't anticipated the consequences of her decision.

"You remember our agreement?" Harbury asked, his voice carefully neutral.

Cassie's cup of chocolate paused halfway to her lips. He didn't think her deepening blush was the sole result of rising steam.

"Of course." She set down the drink. "The rest of the summer here in the country, a visit to Ravenswood, then back to London for the little Season."

He hadn't been referring to their schedule, as well she knew.

She wet her lips before glancing away. She'd a habit of wetting her lips when nervous, he realized. She'd no idea her actions just made her mouth more inviting. He fixed his gaze on the moisture glistening on her bottom lip—a lip still red from where she had just bitten down. Again, he imagined kissing her.

Not chastely or politely, as one would a wife one only respected, but passionately, thoroughly, soundly. Kissing was one skill he knew he'd honed. Perhaps, last night, he should have damned propriety and kissed her as he'd yearned to do. He should have taken her into his arms, claimed her mouth and left her breathless.

Right now, he was feeling a little breathless himself.

So, find a way to thaw this unexpected ice. But how?

The answer came to him like inspiration, like fire shot down directly from the gods—*apologize*. Apologize...not just for the awkward bedding and the pained conversation, but for his initial rash act, the impetus of her fall from Society's grace.

His mouth dried.

He'd never apologized for anything. *Ever.* The closest he'd ever come had been on the morning that he was supposed to ask Cassandra on their first outing. He'd promised Adrian to do better after Adrian had chastised him for surliness.

Only the weak admit they are wrong.

Another of his father's oft-repeated dictums.

Even when Harbury had been due a thrashing, his father had warned him not to admit wrongdoing, but instead, to simply accept the consequences of his actions with dignity and without any sign of pain. Only if he didn't cry out would he be forgiven.

But he couldn't exactly ask his wife to thrash him, could he?

An odd expression must have crossed his face because his wife's right eyebrow arched, and she cocked her head in impatient, unspoken inquiry. *Enough.* They needed to speak, and they needed to speak in private. He dismissed the footman.

Silently, she followed the man with her gaze until the door closed behind him.

"Is there something you wish to say?" she asked.

"I got drunk," he blurted.

She inhaled sharply and then lifted her knife and fork points-up as if the flatware were weapons. Clearly, he'd made things worse.

Why the devil had he started with drink?

"After Almack's," he clarified. "I was in no state to accept Asquith's challenge when he held that loaded flintlock to my head and ordered me to court you or face him at dawn."

"Well." She made a huffing noise. "I should think not."

She hadn't understood. He tried again. "I was drunk, so I agreed to court you in good faith."

Her head jerked back, and she blinked. "I suppose agreeing to a spurious courtship would be safer than shooting through the misty morning with an unsteady hand."

Well, hell. "No. I didn't mean—"

"What *did* you mean?" she interrupted, her tone sharper than he'd ever heard it.

"I meant that I knew I was to blame. Even if I hadn't been willing to admit as much. Adrian set me straight. When I complained to him, I told him you should have refused to dance with me—"

She inhaled in a rush.

"—and he called me an ass." Heat slowly climbed his neck. "Quite frankly, he wasn't wrong." *That's* what he had meant to say.

"How magnanimous of you to admit it."

Why yes.

He'd intended to be generous in taking culpability, though he doubted she understood his bungled words had been his best attempt at an apology. Nor did he think she understood that anyone who knew him well would find an apology from him unusual.

His gaze dropped to the tightly gripped knife in her hand.

Her use of "magnanimous" had most certainly been sarcasm. The realization of her fury's depth landed like a punch to his sternum, briefly halting his ability to respond. How could he explain his actions that night in a way that would lessen her anger?

He'd been undone with renewed grief over Viv. Knowing Viv had married another when he'd expected her to return to him had been hard; seeing her flushed and happy in her new husband's arms had been intolerable. Then, the patronesses' disproportionate response to his choice of Cassandra for the waltz in progress had left him flabbergasted.

He had just gotten around to drunkenly pondering what reparation honor would demand when he'd felt the cold barrel of Asquith's firearm against his temple. Asquith, Cassandra's guardian, who, though capable, was younger than himself and almost always quiet, reserved and serious.

But the point he'd wanted to make was, even though at the start, Asquith had forced his hand, he had enjoyed Cassandra's company. He'd found her more desirable than he'd ever anticipated. And, if he could manage to make things right between them, he thought they might become friends. And hopefully…eventually… even lovers.

He attempted to salvage the conversation. "I'm trying," he managed with difficulty, "to tell you I'm…not…" How should he say this? "…*displeased* by the turn of events."

She smacked the knife against the table so hard he thought she might have bent the tip.

"That's silver!" he exclaimed.

Her scowl suggested he was lucky said silver had not been energetically inserted into his chest. She took three deep breaths, each one further smoothing the blotches beneath her skin. When she looked up again, her face was a mask—one even more indecipherable than the one she'd worn when he began.

"Harbury—"

For the first time since his father's death, he'd the urge to ask someone to call him by his given name. In fact, his eyes burned at the mere thought of asking her to call him Edward.

"—I neither expect"—she threw down the spoon—"nor re-quire you to explain your actions to me."

"I wasn't trying to explain myself, I was—"

She waved her hand as she interrupted. "Oh, just go, would you? Right now, you appear to have lost the ability to converse."

He blinked, feeling as if the backs of his knees were again sticking to the chair.

He reminded himself she could not know how deeply he'd be wounded by such an accusation.

"Your presence could never be something I wish to escape."

His raw, honest admission surprised him but earned him nothing greater than another supercilious lift of her right brow. Perhaps he *should* retreat.

Retreat and regroup. He focused on the cutlery. Live to fight another day.

"There are, however, some estate matters I should attend."

"Estate matters?" she queried.

For the first time, she appeared genuinely interested in what he might have to say. Briefly, he imagined sharing his concerns over the anonymous letter, but *no*.

She was unhappy enough with him already. If she believed he couldn't control unrest on his own estate, her frustration with him would only increase.

Best to take care of the situation on his own. "I've, ah, letters to write."

"Then, by all means, go. I trust you will enjoy yourself." She pursed her lips, as if holding something back.

He nodded once before rising.

"Or make yourself miserable…"

He cocked his head.

"…Repeated indulgence of misery *is* a kind of joy, wouldn't you say?"

This time, there could be no mistaking her verbal dart's poison.

"Cassandra?" he asked, unsure if he could be addressing the same woman he'd courted.

"I—I beg your pardon." She dropped her gaze. "I spoke unkindly just then."

"Perpetually miserable." Absently, he rubbed his chest. "*Do* you see me as someone who is perpetually miserable?"

She glanced up, startled. A pained expression flashed in her eyes. "I don't know you. At present"—again, she wet her lips—"I'm not sure I know myself."

"I'd like for you to know me," he replied as gently as he

could. Though he clearly had not yet learned to communicate well, instinct told him if he didn't keep a steady, skilled hold of the reins during this run-away conversation, they'd both end up in a ditch. "And I'd like to know you." Even now, even hurt, this was still true.

In her eyes, the smallest hint of hope lurked behind a great haze of suspicion. A hint would have to be enough, for now. She didn't trust him at all.

Then again, why should she?

"Shall I expect you for tea, then?" she asked.

An olive branch?

"Certainly." He folded his arms behind his back to prevent himself from reaching out. "*If* you wish."

"Yes, I wish," she replied with the merest flash of a tentative smile. "Good day."

"Good day."

She rose, offered him an awkward curtsey and then turned away.

Everyone had called Cassandra the gentle one. The sweet one. The biddable one.

Everyone had been wrong.

Or, perhaps, in yoking her to him, he'd damaged her sweetness.

He'd married, in part, to distract himself from his unhappiness. Now he feared, in fateful irony, he had, instead, sentenced Cassandra to dwell with him in misery, too.

If he was going to reorient them both to a more promising future, he'd need to gather his wits and form a plan.

✦ ❧ ✦

CHAPTER THREE

ARBURY LEANED HIS shoulder against his library's arched entry, observing his wife in silence. Cassandra had shed the bright yellow morning dress she'd been wearing at breakfast for a nondescript brown one made of coarse fabric. But rather than rendering her common, the simple dress enhanced her features, contrasting her skin's soft tone and accentuating her slim figure.

Judging by the lamentations his housekeeper had subjected him to on his return from his ride, as well as by the state of his library, Cassandra's sartorial simplicity was part of a plan to turn herself into a cyclone and rampage through his books.

At this end of the library, some shelves were bare, while others were haphazardly arranged. Springing up from the floor like multifaceted stalagmites were—he counted—*fourteen* piles of books. Twenty, if he included the stacks of folios filled with paper.

What had possessed her to take on this task?

When Mrs. Pratt had accosted him, he'd steadfastly defended the havoc his wife had wrought, even going so far to imply he'd previously agreed to whatever changes she intended to make.

The duchess, he insisted without having seen the mess she had made, was not destroying the collection, but improving the organization. And she was doing so, he said, simply because the occupation pleased her.

Defense had been his duty. But when it came to his wife, he could only guess at her motivation. At least she appeared less unhappy, now.

Her upset last night, as well as her anger this morning, had weighed on him as he rode both to and from Rose Cottage. Though he had not, as hoped, found Anderson at home—in fact, no one had even answered the door—his excursion had been fruitful. He'd been able to think through their current situation without his wife's distracting presence.

Two things had become apparent: one, he and Cassandra must establish a mutual accord and two, until they had established a solid, mutual accord, they would be wise to abstain from the temptations and complications of the marriage bed.

The next time he crossed the threshold between their chambers, he wanted to be sure of his welcome.

Gazing at her now, he became ever more aware that his sacrifice was not going to be easy.

She was halfway up a ladder, piling her left arm full of books she would, no doubt, place on top of one of the many stacks. If she knew she'd sent Mrs. Pratt, a woman who prided herself on reserve, into an apoplectic frenzy, she remained unperturbed.

In fact—he leaned forward—she was *humming*.

A light feeling expanded in his heart. Very little humming had graced the spaces of Harbury Hall. At least not in the prior duke's earshot.

He cleared his throat.

Cassandra turned abruptly, setting herself and the pile of books in her arms awobble.

Harbury bounded across the room to grab hold of the rails and steady the ladder.

"Goodness!" she exclaimed, her eyes wide. "Is it already time for tea?"

"I'm a bit late, actually." He waited a breath for his heartbeat to slow. "Would you like me to help you down?"

She shook her head. "I can manage."

Nonetheless, he kept a white-knuckled grip on both siderails while she descended, willing himself not to imagine the possible consequences of a fall.

"You weren't jesting." She eyed the mantel clock. "Why it's almost three! Where did the time go?"

Into wrecking his library, apparently.

Oddly enough, he found himself amused rather than angry. Because he'd already come to her defense? Or because she looked so delighted and flushed?

"Well, clearly, you've been busy."

She deposited the last book atop a shorter stack and then faced him, a martial glint in her eye. *Oh yes.* She knew exactly how much consternation she had caused.

Sweet, docile Cassandra had a contrarian side.

And though he'd been worried her marriage to him had harmed her, at present, she was happy—a profound relief to his conscience. And, oddly enough, he liked this surprising new aspect of his wife. She identified something she wanted, and she set out to accomplish her vision.

"Tea is set out in the red salon. Can you spare the time to join me?"

Her eyes flashed with challenge. "If you recall, *I* invited *you.*"

"So, you did." He inclined his head in acknowledgement. "Would you prefer another location?" He asked even though he knew, as well as she did, she was not yet familiar enough with the rooms to judge which would be most comfortable this time of day, which was why he'd chosen the red room.

But if she insisted on moving the tea to a west-facing chamber, he decided he was willing to suffer the heat.

Her lips contracted into an enticing little pout. "The red salon will do."

He held out his arm. She hesitated for a moment then placed her hand against his sleeve. While she didn't need an escort in their own home, he hoped small civilities like this one would lead to more substantial trust.

Together, they headed toward the parlor.

Over his lifetime, he'd walked like this most frequently either with his mother or with his sister. Occasionally, in private, with Viv.

Walking with Cassandra was a different experience all together. Their intimacy last night must have increased his awareness of her femininity.

She clung to him closely. So close, in fact, her breasts occasionally brushed him. Naturally, this caused a rather uncomfortable reaction, a reaction he subdued by raising his gaze and silently counting the buttresses along the corridor. *One...two...three...*

"Were you quite behind in your correspondence?" she asked lightly.

Too lightly.

"Pardon?" he queried, glancing askance.

"You must have written a *great* many letters." She blinked rapidly, her face fixed with an expectant expression. "A letter to be sent abroad, perhaps? Translation would add difficulty, I presume."

He tilted his head, frowning.

"French, was it?" She suggested. "Italian? Finnish? Finnish, I hear, is extraordinarily challenging to master."

"I don't speak Finnish. I wouldn't know."

"Nor do I. Which is why I specifically said I'd *heard* Finnish was a difficult language."

He frowned. "Are you acquainted with someone who has attempted—"

"I know!" she interrupted. "You had to write the letter in Latin. To a scholar. One from your Oxford days."

"I beg your pardon," he said as politely as he could. "I am not following."

"No? You told me you had to take yourself off to *write letters.*"

"Ah, yes." Vaguely, he recalled having used letter writing as an excuse to depart. He held open the door and she passed by into the room.

"Well?" She folded arms in front of her chest. "Did you?"

"No. I decided to visit the steward in person. Anderson, however, was out somewhere on our estate."

She turned her head sharply at *our*. Her martial expression softened a degree.

He'd used the word accidentally, but he didn't regret the slip. Somehow, he had to convey his desire to move forward...*together*. Whatever their difficulties, they were now joined.

For better. For worse. *Until death.*

She stared at him for a moment before sitting on the settee. As she moved to spread out her skirts, he took a place by her side, a place close enough to feel the subtle jerk of her body as she tensed.

"Isn't"—her voice cracked—"sitting across from one another customary?"

"We have yet to establish what's customary for us."

Her lip-biting gesture both revealed her fluster, and, inadvertently, increased his carnal frustration. Pretending he had not noticed, he set out preparing the tea.

He didn't have to ask how she took hers. He remembered. Rich and dark with only a dollop of cream, just enough to increase the pleasure without spoiling the full-bodied taste.

She lifted the cup, her long, slender fingers wrapped around the delicate handle. When she sipped, her brief expression of closed-eyes bliss told him he'd done well.

If he weren't careful, he could lose himself in the search for other ways to inspire such a satisfied expression.

She opened her eyes only to narrow them suspiciously. "You remembered how I take my tea."

"My duty is to see to your comfort." He took a sip from his own cup before returning both cup and saucer to the tray. "My duty and my delight."

Her brows disappeared beneath the edging of her cap.

Perhaps *delight* had been layering on too strong.

Wishing he had a greater talent for conversation, he busied himself with rearranging the pot. Then, he sent her a sidelong glance before adding just a touch of cream to his own brew.

"Lessens the tartness, no?" he asked.

"To my taste, yes," she replied still staring at him as if he were an indecipherable riddle.

"Please don't take what I am about to say as criticism of your efforts," he changed the subject, "but did you consider consulting with our librarian before you took on the library reorganization?"

"I understand you—or rather, *we*—no longer have a librarian."

"We don't?" News to him.

"He left four months ago and has yet to be replaced."

"Left?" Harbury may have been in London for much of the year, but he was certain he'd seen the man's salary on Anderson's last quarterly statement.

"Yes." She hesitated. "Not to unduly criticize your staff, but—"

"Our," he interrupted.

"In this case, not 'our.' Because your librarian decamped before we married, leaving the books in no order I could discern."

"No order?"

"Mrs. Pratt suggested they might have been accidentally rearranged when the library was thoroughly dusted during the wedding preparations." She lifted one shoulder in a partial shrug. "My intention is to shelve them first by subject and then by author."

His eyes met hers over the rim of his cup. Again, the martial look.

"Are you angry?" she asked.

Were you trying to make me angry? "Whyever for? If you wish to catalog the books, by all means, catalog the books."

She exhaled, he thought, just a little deeper. One point to him.

Finally.

"Is the library at Willowhurst organized in the same fashion?"

She tensed again at his use of the name of her childhood home. Indeed, he remembered. In fact, he remembered more things his new wife had told him over the course of their courtship than he'd even realized.

"Yes, at one time. Our collection was sold at auction."

"Pity," he said sincerely. "I have considered many a books a friend."

Shadows of suspicion returned—a hint of a frown, a furrow in her brow. Clearly, she had no intention of making any overture on his part easy.

"Are you an enthusiast of the written word, too, then?" he pressed.

"I enjoy Mrs. Radcliffe's novels," she said with an edge of challenge.

"As do I…"

Her scowl deepened, but she leaned forward as if intrigued against her will.

"High in sentiment," he continued. "Excellent entertainment for those of us who enjoy…how did you put it? *Repeated indulgence of misery?*"

As he cocked his head and smiled pleasantly, waiting for her response, her teacup rattled in her saucer.

She set down the china. "I really must beg your pardon."

"You already apologized, remember? Besides, I don't want your contrition; I simply want to understand why you're angry with me." He held his breath through a long silence.

"I wish I could explain," she began tentatively, "but the truth is, I don't know why I insulted you; I only know I should not have spoken in such a wounding manner." She averted her eyes, studying her hands as she folded her lovely, long, shaking fingers into one another and then held them tightly in her lap.

Did she fear him in addition to disliking him?

Impossible. If she had feared him, she wouldn't have turned his library inside out.

"When one wishes to wound," he asked softly, "what other manner should one use?"

She raised a conflicted gaze. "I don't want to hurt you."

"Don't you?" He searched her face. "I think you do. I think you're more than angry with me. You're furious."

She stiffened. "Am I to be allowed no privacy, even in my own mind?"

"Bravo. Much better."

"Better? How?" she demanded.

"You raised your voice and lowered your tone. You were resolute. Honest."

She shook her head no. "Don't ask me to be honest." She shrank back. "As I told you this morning, I don't *know* myself right now. If I start speaking honestly, I may never be able to stop."

"Better your hatred than your indifference."

"I am not—" She stopped abruptly. She looked away. "I could *never* be indifferent to you."

Well, *not indifferent* was, at least, a place to start.

"And I don't *hate* you. I'm far from hating you."

The softness in her voice, along with her sad and reluctantly given admission made his throat thicken. He wanted friendship. Possibly even passion. But, before now, he hadn't pondered how he wanted her to feel about him.

But *not indifferent* had suddenly become insufficient.

"I'd like you to know I'm not angry about the library. However, you *have* upset someone else here at Harbury Hall. In fact, I believe you may have even inadvertently started a minor war."

"A war?"

"I've never seen poor Mrs. Pratt in such a state."

She worried her lip. "I *am* sorry."

He grinned. "No, you aren't."

She chuckled softly, as if only to herself. "You're right." She matched his smile. "I'm not."

"Did Mrs. Pratt say or do something to upset you?"

"Well"—she rearranged the angle of her cup—"when I asked about the hideous chandelier in the entry, she intimated the house must be kept exactly as your father wished."

"The tent and bag chandelier?"

She nodded. "I took her insistence as disrespectful to you—"

He leaned forward.

"—I—I reacted badly."

She'd reacted badly because she'd thought his housekeeper disrespected *him*?

After his father died, he *had* told his housekeeper he didn't expect to make many changes. At the time, however, he had anticipated he'd one day wed Viv, who'd always said she liked the Hall's old-fashioned feel. He hadn't planned on bringing home a wife who had never been here. A wife who might want to make changes of her own.

Changes, he realized, he did not oppose. Perhaps it was high time to clear out the proverbial cobwebs.

"So, you felt Mrs. Pratt had disrespected me, so you decided to tear up the library?"

"No! Not unless... Oh, *bother!*" She glanced up in consternation. "During my conversation with Mrs. Pratt, I *did* decide I would find something at Harbury Hall to change. I just didn't connect that with my later decision to reorganize the library."

He couldn't help another smile. "Have I married a secret iconoclast?"

"I can see why you might think so." Again, she laughed. "But I've only lately been inspired to rebel."

"How lately?"

She closed one eye and winced sheepishly. "Since yesterday?"

Fascinating. He feared he'd inspired misery. Instead, he'd created a reluctant radical.

She must have noticed the light of understanding in his eyes because she dropped her gaze and took a disproportionately long sip of her tea.

"Since you've started a war, you are going to need an ally." He placed his open palm between them and flashed his most charming smile. "I find myself in need of one as well."

"What do you mean?"

"I plan to visit a few of our larger tenants. You might... I mean, if you are interested..."

He'd thought making conversation difficult, but asking for help—*her* help—was *far* worse.

"Are you asking me to accompany you?"

"I thought, well... As duchess, you might want to know the estate's people. But only if you wish."

Surprise lit her features, followed by something more. Interest, he hoped. *Pleased* interest.

"I would like to join you. Very much."

He caught her gaze. And, for the first time all morning, neither of them looked away.

No. Not indifferent was definitely not going to be enough for him, especially not now. Not after he'd just experienced the rush that had accompanied her eager acceptance of his invitation.

ALLY.

For some reason, the word made all the difference in the world. Cassie didn't know Harbury, so they could not be friends. They'd made love, and yet, as she barely participated, she could not bring herself to call him her lover. Allies, however, was safe.

Allies was a start.

"Allies," she repeated.

She glanced down at his open palm and then carefully intertwined her fingers with his. He closed his other hand tightly over both of theirs.

She'd taken his hand intending to seal their agreement, but he wasn't holding hers as one would for a handshake. He was holding hers reverently as if he never wanted to let go.

He must truly desire me.

She both dreaded and yearned for his desire.

A few nights ago, Eliza had tried to tell her what to expect on her wedding night. Cassie hadn't wanted to listen.

I don't want to hear about a man's ugly hands, Eliza.

Ugly? A man's hands are fascinating, Cassie. Strong. Capable of creating experiences words could never express.

She'd thought Eliza mad. Now, she understood.

Harbury's hands were sturdy. And, yes, strong. But they could also be, as now, surprisingly gentle. Calluses along his palm pressed into the base of her fingers. Unexpected roughness, especially on a duke's hands.

Why hadn't she noticed his roughened skin last night?

Because she'd been bracing against onslaught. Shutting herself off to feeling. She wanted him and that want had made her not only angry, but terrified of giving him all of herself while receiving only crumbs in return.

She'd thought she'd resigned herself to being a convenient wife, but his touch had rekindled a desire for the very thing she'd secretly wanted from the start—the whole of Harbury's heart.

But no matter how persistent that want, she mustn't forget her husband was in love with someone else.

Just like the prior night, he was drawing small circles against her knuckles with his thumb.

Was he conscious of the movement?

How was she supposed to remember to protect herself when his skin's warmth was making her heart flutter and heat vine up her neck? How was she supposed to hold herself apart when her mind was conjuring images of other things those hands could cause her to feel?

Alarmed by the direction of her thoughts, she withdrew her hand.

"About the books," she returned to a safer subject. "I'm not even a third of the way through the shelves Even so, I—I may have attempted too much at once. What do you think?"

His gaze fixed on his now-empty hand. He flexed his fingers.

"Harbury?" she prompted.

"Pardon?"

"The library?"

He blinked, still confused.

"My project, I'm afraid, will take longer than a day. I hope you don't mind."

"Of course not," he said, looking slightly bemused. "You didn't expect to rearrange the entire Harbury collection in a single afternoon, did you?"

"I'm not sure I had a plan."

"Well…"

He smiled in the way she found equally infuriating and enticing.

"I suppose all is fair in libraries and war."

He was jesting with her. Then again, perhaps the library, the verbal sparring, even this tea, were all part of a larger negotiation. One that might, in the end, lead to something more than either of them had expected.

Dare she hope?

"While you were wreaking havoc on my books, did you discover anything interesting?"

"Our books," she braved.

"Our." His eyes glowed with approval.

Cassie grew breathless, as if the air had suddenly thinned. "Not much, yet." She forced herself to concentrate. "Did you know your father published a treatise on grasses?"

His shoulders lifted slightly, probably even involuntarily, confirming his surprise. "Impressive."

"Impractical, more like."

He chuckled.

"I was rude again." She winced. "I'm sorry."

He made a thoughtful noise. "Most people held my father in awe. Rarely have I ever heard anyone even hint at the possibility he had any shortcomings."

"Did *you?* Hold him in awe?"

His head jerked up, and his gaze fixed on a portrait of his father. "I respected him." He frowned as if he hadn't expected his lackluster answer. "Of course."

"Of course?"

In her experience, there wasn't any *of course* when it came to one's esteem for one's parents.

She'd given her own father deference but not always esteem. Her father had been a lauded Member of Parliament in public and a selfish brute in private. She'd never been able to reconcile his good qualities with his poor ones, which had far more effect on her and her sisters. As for her mother…

Unconsciously, she touched her locket.

She'd loved her mother, but she also understood things might have been very different for them all if her mother had learned to stand up for herself. Instead, whenever her father had appeared, her mama, or at least the version of *mama* the Wainwright girls had known, had simply disappeared beneath a compliant, docile façade.

She would *not* repeat her mother's marital mistakes, even if she did not quite know how to assert herself yet.

Oblivious to her thoughts, Harbury leaned forward and then rested his elbows on his knees.

"I've been duke for two years, now. Already, I've made mistakes. Mistakes"—he raised his brows—"he likely expected me to make. To be honest, I fear I will make more."

Mistakes? She unclasped and then reclasped her hands. Was he referring to their marriage?

"What mistakes?" she managed to ask, though her voice came out too strained, too needful.

"Since the war, prices have been down. I'm afraid things may have become…difficult for the tenants, our tenants." He glanced up. "As I said before, I'd like to consult with some of them. Get a better sense of what is happening on my own land than I can glean from columns of numbers."

So, he hadn't been referring to her as his *mistake.*

She spread her fingers and exhaled. She was just as relieved for herself as she was now concerned for the tenantry. "Let us plan our visits as soon as possible, then. We can decide how to proceed after we know more."

His face lit. "We?"

She smiled. "Allies, remember?"

She'd always found him attractive, but when his eyes glowed, he was irresistible.

"We can fight two wars," she added.

He frowned as if thinking. "I'm not sure I'd call indecision on how to proceed in certain aspects of estate management a separate *war* as much as another front. The important thing now is to devise battle plans—terrain assessment, logistical considerations, possible deployments, artillery locations."

"You do know how to stretch a metaphor, don't you?"

His smile turned cheeky, mischievous. "If we mean to plant our flag atop Harbury Hall, we need to proceed with stealth and intelligence."

We. Our.

They'd been bandying about those terms all afternoon. Every time he said either word a tender place inside her expanded.

"You'd welcome my advice?" she asked.

He considered. "Actually, I believe I might be very much in need of your advice."

The war for Harbury Hall appeared not to be the only one he intended to wage. He appeared to be launching a campaign, if not for her heart, at least for her friendship and affection.

Last night, when she'd ordered him from her room, she'd been protecting herself. Now, under the heat of his gaze, she understood protection was not what she truly wanted.

She wanted his attention, his desire.

He must have read something of the hope in her eyes because he drew back. Not fully apart, but enough to signal caution.

"While we figure out how to proceed, I think it best..." He looked down. His knee moved in a restless, repetitive fashion. "I'm trying to tell you I won't come to your room tonight. Or again. Until invited."

She frowned in confusion.

"You need your rest." He paused. "Strength. For battle."

She sucked in her bottom lip to keep herself from blurting out that she wanted him to come.

But though part of her did, another part of her agreed they should wait. This truce was too fragile. And whatever was happening between them, the energy felt too unpredictable.

Too dangerous.

There would be other nights. Many of them, hopefully.

"Thank you," she forced.

"No, thank *you*"—he leaned forward—"for giving me another chance."

She became aware of her lips, aware of his warm breath fanning her cheeks, aware of a full-bodied anticipation of his closeness. She closed her eyes. For one, mad moment she expected him to place his mouth against hers.

Instead of a true kiss, however, his lips simply brushed her forehead. But as he pulled back, and her eyes fluttered open, the look of longing on his face left her tingling all over.

CHAPTER FOUR

Cassie peered into the breakfast room the following morning, disappointed to find only Tull, the footman. *Poor man.* She hoped she had not kept him waiting for long. She filled her plate, sat down, adjusted her chair, and glanced uncertainly around the room.

Apart from the times when she'd been ill, she'd never taken breakfast alone.

What *was* the etiquette?

She sliced her meat and then placed a small piece against her tongue. Yesterday, Harbury's chewing had roused her ire. Today, her own felt unnaturally loud. She forced herself to swallow. Where *was* her husband?

And why did she care so much?

Ugh.

Her gaze settled on Tull's distorted figure in the bowed butler's mirror—a mirror specially fashioned so a table attendant could see everyone present and attend to their needs without being asked.

What a waste of Tull's time. So silly to keep him standing there when he was unneeded.

Harbury had dismissed him yesterday. Could she not do the same?

She glanced over her shoulder. "You may go."

He hesitated, his gaze moving uncertainly from the mirror to her own. Yesterday, he'd left immediately. Was he questioning her authority?

She felt her face heat. "I wish to dine *alone*."

Her words came out more sharply than she'd intended.

The boy blanched and then quickly left the room. She slumped as far as her half-stays would allow and then dropped her head back against the chair.

How long would it take to become comfortable in her own skin, let alone her own home?

Would Harbury Hall ever feel like home?

Sighing deeply, she finished her breakfast.

She missed the sounds of her sisters' chatter. She missed mornings at Willowhurst—at least the mornings when her father had not been present and she, her mother and sisters could prattle on about everything and nothing—neighbors, the weather, tomorrow's adventures, last night's dreams.

She set down her fork.

Even if her sisters had been present, she could never reveal the dream she'd had last night.

Not even to Eliza.

In her dream, Harbury had come to her room. Unlike their wedding night, he hadn't looked discomfited and uneasy, as if he couldn't bear to see her in the bed instead of his beloved Vivianne. Instead, he'd been decisive and intentional from the moment the door between their chambers clicked open.

Harbury, she'd whispered with sizzling anticipation as he strode across the room.

He arrived at the side of her bed and then fell to his knees, murmuring a heart-rending apology ending with *I want you so badly, I simply couldn't keep away.*

She lifted the coverlet. He climbed inside, his body radiating so much heat, the cool, slightly damp room transformed into warmth and comfort. Though his masculine presence was still as much at odds with everything she understood, in her dream, she did not fear him.

First, his lips touched her forehead, just as they had the prior afternoon—an impulsive, intimate gesture. A gesture that shifted her awareness. She no longer perceived the overwhelming contrast between them as strange and uncomfortable, but suddenly understood her softness was the perfect answer to his inordinate strength.

Next, he kissed her properly. Passionately. And then, instead of sweeping his hand over her unspeakable, private place to "check," he'd not only asked permission, but waited for her to say yes. *Yes,* to caressing her slowly, intimately until she burned.

But her dream-self felt no embarrassment, only desire. She'd welcomed his weight against her body, his flexed muscles between her limp but trembling thighs. When he entered her, instead of pain, there had been fullness…*satisfaction.*

In the present, she sighed a little and then smiled.

Surely, such pleasure must be possible beyond fantasy.

Or had her dream-mind conjured impossibilities? She wished she had a better understanding. An understanding that Harbury, like other men of his age and station, most certainly possessed.

A very-real clank abruptly jerked her out of her reverie.

Her eyes flew open, meeting Mrs. Pratt's gaze, which flitted quickly away.

"Apologies, Your Grace. The fork slipped."

Mrs. Pratt hadn't spoken in tones of disapproval, and yet her discomfort was plainly etched on her face. Cassie placed a hand against her burning cheek. Had the housekeeper been able to read Cassie's thoughts?

Taradiddle and bilgewater.

"I don't recall requesting the table be cleared." She was fairly certain the housekeeper would never have intruded on her husband in such a fashion.

"You dismissed the footman. I assumed you wished me to clear the table."

I am still seated. She held the housekeeper's gaze.

Mrs. Pratt slowly set down the cup she'd just picked up. Then, with quiet dignity she folded her hands in front of her apron. Once at her full height, she fixed her gaze on something—or nothing—just beyond Cassie's shoulder.

"I await your instruction," she said in a voice so low Cassie barely heard.

Cassie shunted aside the urge to fill the uncomfortable silence by explaining why she'd sent away the footman, or by apologizing, or by ordering the frustrating woman to take everything away. *Presently.* She wanted to shove words—any words—into the vast ravine that was her ignorance.

She'd grown up with servants on a small estate, but she'd little idea how to manage a house so large that daily life required a veritable army of people in constant motion. She'd no idea at all how to be a proper duchess.

To hide her discomfort, she lifted her napkin and tapped her mouth.

Then again, if she stopped believing there was a right way, a proper way, might she forge her own path? Perhaps Mrs. Pratt wasn't as antagonistic as she was in want of clear direction.

"I have business I wish to discuss with my husband." Her voice was calmer than before. Lower. More certain. The same tone, in fact, Harbury had praised yesterday. "Where might I find him?"

"His Grace has been in his study since before the sun rose."

In other words, estate administration had an early morning allure greater than her own.

"Of course." She inclined her head.

"He is speaking with the steward, now. He doesn't like to be disturbed when he is with the steward."

"Thank you for letting me know. I will take your concern into consideration."

Mrs. Pratt smiled faintly, as if relieved.

Cassie rose from her chair. "You may clear the table, now."

"Very good," the housekeeper replied, with a less awkward curtsey.

Believing she'd made some progress, Cassie broke into a

determined pace and headed toward Harbury's study. However, as she approached the closed door, some trepidation returned. Should she interrupt after having been expressly warned he would be displeased?

She leaned forward, straining to hear, but could not make out a single word. *Blast!* If she hovered about the study entry too long, someone was going to come along and bear witness to her shame.

She compressed her lips, exhaled roughly and scowled. She'd confront him another time.

She turned on her heel and headed toward the library.

She told herself she was taking the circuitous route to the long hall because she wanted to familiarize herself with the hall's layout and not because she didn't want to run into Mrs. Pratt yet again.

By the time she entered the library, she knew she'd been lying.

She'd reduced herself to lurking.

Worse still, as she slowly walked along the shelves, she realized her library project was neither as useful nor as necessary as she'd thought the day before. Then, she'd focused her efforts on the end of the library closest to the entry hall, assuming the whole library was equally disorganized.

On this end—she ran her gaze over the gilded print on the leather spines as she moved—the organization made sense. Atlases preceded travelogues; travelogues, History; History, Biography. Biography, philosophy. So why had the opposite end been so haphazard?

Plays, poetry, drama, agricultural instruction, etiquette guides, and dictionaries had all been jumbled together. She placed her hands on her hips and frowned.

Nothing made sense in this house, especially the house's master.

Yesterday, she'd believed they had made some sort of progress. Now, she wondered if the "progress" she'd perceived had been nothing more than a reversal. When they'd been "courting," he'd been polite, even gentlemanly, too.

Last night, he'd called them allies. This morning, he excluded her from his meeting with "their" steward. But perhaps, as before, he'd never truly meant to include her in his life.

Well.

She would insist on being included. Her first impulse had been the right impulse.

Whether or not she ruffled feathers, she was finished trying to figure out how everyone else expected her to act. Indecision and uncertainty were getting her nowhere. She had to confront the chaos at the source and on her own terms.

She headed back toward her husband's study.

She'd be disturbing the duke, whether the disturbance pleased him or not.

"...SO, YOU SEE, Your Grace, crop yields are up."

Harbury frowned, squinting down at the ledger's columns of numbers...some neat, some in a hand he hardly recognized as Anderson's. Though he struggled to discern several more recent entries, everything appeared to be in order.

He'd no reason to question his steward's assertion.

So why did Anderson's 'Your Grace' grate on his nerves?

Was he annoyed because the man had always called his father Harbury? Or had the anonymous letter planted insidious seeds of suspicion?

He placed his finger on the column, following a line, first horizontally, then vertically. "Prices, however, are down."

"Yes," Anderson replied, his voice flat. "Only to be expected. Years of war falsely inflated them. With the resumption of trade with France—"

"I understand," he interrupted testily, "the implications of trade. I may not be as well-versed in the minutiae of agricultural economics as my father was, but I assure you, I understand the relationship between supply and price."

"Just so."

Harbury glanced up. *Bad form.* Now he'd let the suspicion goad him into showing the old retainer hostility. He softened his voice. "The tenants who bring in the greatest income are Grayson, Bottlesworth, and Townsend. Correct?"

Anderson blinked. "The rents, you see, are fully documented by tract."

Not an answer.

And not the first time this morning, Anderson had hedged.

Harbury leaned back in his chair, pressing his forefinger to his bottom lip. He hadn't realized just how much trust he'd placed in Anderson before.

He'd dutifully reviewed and replied to every letter and statement his steward had sent him, but he'd left most decisions to the man's discretion.

Perhaps he ought to pay a little closer attention.

He'd like some time to go over these numbers. And he wanted to take that time without the steward hovering over his shoulder.

"You may go," he said.

Anderson reached for the ledger.

"Leave the book with me."

"Your Grace? The household accounts remain here, naturally. But the estate books have always been stored in my office." He hesitated a beat. "At Rose Cottage."

"I am aware how my father arranged things. I, however—"

"If you keep the ledger, how am I to record receipts?" Anderson interrupted, twisting his hands.

"Keep notes." Harbury sat up. "Or come here and make your entries. But I intend to take a closer look at the records, and I intend to do so at my leisure. So please leave the ledger. And have the documents mentioned in the Lady Day audit delivered to me as well."

"Is His Grace certain?"

Harbury rose from his chair.

Anderson's tone, and his mulish, annoyed, distrustful expression called to mind a different confrontation over this same desk. Only Harbury had been standing where Anderson stood now, and Harbury's father was the one occupying the seat of authority.

I asked you to come up with a hypothetical plan should prices take a precipitous fall. This drivel is what you suggest? Have you no understanding of how to lead?

His father had then made a disgusted sound.

I cannot prevent you from taking my place. God help me, I wish I could.

Harbury leaned forward, steadying himself by placing both fists on the blotter's smooth surface. In his mind, he heard clattering. He remembered his father had dropped the seal he'd been holding and transferred his grasp to his right arm. Then his father had crumpled. In seconds, he'd been dead.

Harbury glanced down.

The numbers in the book swam across the page, seeming to undulate. He might be sick again, just as he had been that day.

He *couldn't* be sick.

His father had died a long time ago. And whether his father would like it or not—whether *he* liked it or not—he was now duke. Harbury Hall, Harbury Hall's tenants *and* steward...they were all under his care.

And his command.

The responsibility was enormous. He had to be sensible. He had to be strategic. He had to shove his memories firmly back where they belonged, deep in the past. And he had to ignore the deep-seated fear of inadequacy that sprang up whenever he remembered his father's final moments.

"Harbury?" The kindly query startled him.

He couldn't place the voice until the lady stepped forward. Cassandra Wainwright. *No.* Cassandra, Duchess of Harbury.

He met her gaze. Did his eyes appear as raw as they felt? Likely, because her expression softened. For the first time since they'd wed, he recognized the woman whose proposal he'd accepted.

She touched his arm and lifted her brows, smiling a gentle smile as if encouraging him to speak. Her gaze exuded comfort. He took solace in her implied concern.

He cleared his throat. "Good morning, my dear."

If she was as startled by the endearment as he was, she didn't let the discomfiture show.

"Anderson, we are finished," he said without looking at the man. "For now. I will send for you when I have need."

Anderson neither moved nor replied.

Harbury faced him. "You may go."

Anderson stared for a moment, then frowned as if confused, shook his head and blinked. An awkward pause followed before he finally spoke.

"Very well."

Anderson acknowledged Cassandra with a nod. Then, moving as if he suffered stiffness in his joints, he left the room.

Cassandra watched the door close, then she swiveled back, a query in her eye.

Harbury imagined she wanted to know why he'd been hunched over his desk staring into nothing. How could he explain that the memory of his father's death had been so visceral, so real, he'd been seized by a sense of failure, of helplessness?

Yesterday she'd asked if he, like others, had held his father in awe. Yes, he had. His father had always seemed so large, so invincible. His death had been a shock.

That his last words had been a condemnation, less so. He knew too well he never managed to earn the man's respect.

But his father wasn't here. His lovely wife, on the other hand, was very present.

"Did you have need of me?" he asked.

"Yes. Er, rather, no." She glanced to the door and back. "It doesn't matt—" She stopped herself. "Well, yes, it does matter. I came here to say I had hoped you would include me in your meeting. And…" Her lids swept down over her eyes. "I had also hoped you would join me for breakfast."

Was he imagining things, or did she sound as if she'd missed him? When he was growing up, only Adrian wished for his company. Having someone seek him out was a strange and novel thing.

"I had intended to join you this morning, but I awoke in the middle of the night." Last night, after a perfectly polite, careful dinner they'd parted at the top of the stairs. Once in his bed chamber, he'd bolted her door on his end to keep himself from going back on his promise. There'd been a brief interlude when he'd indulged in a, ah, *pastime* he did not want to think about right now. He'd slept briefly and awoken exhausted but unable to return to sleep. So, he'd retrieved the letter, uncrumpled the paper and studied, thinking.

"When I couldn't get back to sleep, I came down here."

Something about the letter had been nagging at him. The writing was vaguely familiar, and the unplaced familiarity left him uncomfortable. He'd brought down the letter so he could compare the handwriting to letters in his father's files. He hadn't found a match.

"And when did you send for Anderson?" She asked.

"Yesterday. I'd left word at Rose Cottage that I wanted to see the account books. When Anderson arrived with the books this morning, I was still in the study."

"You could have invited me to join you. You said we were allies."

"Yes. Yes, I did."

He understood he'd hurt his wife. Oddly enough, as he looked into her eyes, her hurt became his pain, a weight against his chest.

"Allies," he repeated. He came around his desk. "You are absolutely right. In the future, I will include you."

"Of course," she hedged, "you don't need to consult me *every* time you wish to speak with your—"

"Our," he interrupted. "I did say I wanted," he paused, "no, I believe I said I *needed* your advice."

"You did." She sighed.

The room brightened. Somewhere outside, a cloud must have passed on through. With the increased light, his spirits lifted.

Cassandra looked so fresh, so young, so pretty—such a direct contrast to the vague musty scent of the old books and papers he'd been shuffling through.

A line from a book he'd once attempted to translate in school came to mind. Goethe's *Faust*, perhaps? He'd be damned if he could recall, but in the passage the protagonist declared his intention to cast aside dusty knowledge and be restored by bathing in dew.

He glanced back at the monstrously sized ledger strewn across his desk.

To the devil with numbers.

If his baffling wife wanted his company, she would have his company. All *he* wanted right now was to make her eyes soften again, this time not with concern, but with something quite different.

Something more exciting.

He flashed her his most compelling smile. "But, since I missed the pleasure of your company at breakfast, might I make up for my mistake with a ride?"

Doubtfully, she searched his face. Then, she smiled once again, sending rushing-brook bubbles of anticipation spilling through his chest.

"I would like to ride with you."

Remarkably, he liked looking at his wife. He liked when his wife looked at him. He especially liked when his wife looked at him and smiled.

How could he inspire more of those smiles? Where on the estate could he take her that would bring her pleasure?

When an answer came to him—the priory ruins—he did not think too deeply.

After all, with a distant sight of a picturesque collection of thatched cottages, but full of privacy-affording nooks, multiple published estate guides agreed the ruins were the most romantic place on the estate. And ladies liked romance, did they not?

He called for the groom to saddle their horses.

"I know just where to take you," he said, ignoring the slight discomfort that, if examined, might have served as both warning and reminder that he'd also met Viv there on many clandestine occasions.

CHAPTER FIVE

A S CASSIE'S AND Harbury's horses trotted along the bridle path, the same patch of sun that had opened over the hall expanded. As they drew up alongside a clearing in the woods, additional bands of light broke through, casting shafts across the fields. Cassie couldn't imagine what the trees hid, but from Harbury's boyish excitement, she suspected they concealed something grand.

Something special.

She took in a deep breath of country air, straining her stays. Their gallop left her feeling expansive, free, a stark contrast to her general mood over the past few weeks. With all this wide, beautiful world within reach, how could she focus only on what was wrong in her life?

Despite reservations, she did have cause to hope, didn't she?

With a sidelong glance, she took her husband's measure.

The wind had disheveled his hair, sending sandy locks into his face. His cheeks were flushed, his eyes bright, and his lips curled into a smile similar to her own. Thank heavens he no longer appeared as distressed as he had when she'd first entered his study.

She'd opened the door without knocking, fully prepared to give him a sound scolding. Instead, she'd locked gazes with the vacant-eyed steward. Then, she'd seen Harbury leaning over his desk with his head tucked into his chest.

She could have sworn he'd been about to cast up his accounts.

Concern had instantly replaced her anger.

She believed his distress had something to do with the steward. For reasons she could not quite put into words, she didn't trust Anderson. Something in the man's expression suggested he did not hold either Harbury, or herself, in esteem.

Not that she had much experience with stewards.

Her father had not employed a steward at Willowhurst; he'd made do with a secretary and used a local solicitor as bailiff. But both secretary and solicitor had treated all the Wainwrights, mother and daughters included, with respect.

They would not have failed to greet her mother if she'd entered her father's study, as Anderson had—not that her mother would ever have done so, uninvited. And they would not have needed to be asked to leave. Twice. Possibly even more, if Harbury had asked Anderson to leave before she entered.

"Shall we dismount?" Harbury suggested. "I'd like to show you something."

They had not brought a groom, so helping her dismount and remount would be her husband's office. She wasn't entirely sure Harbury was experienced enough to do so. But certainly, he would have had cause to help his sister on and off her horse more than once.

And how could she refuse him when he'd such a mischievous sparkle in his eyes?

That sparkle promised not only a treat, but a treat he'd chosen to share specifically with her.

She nodded.

He dismounted military-style, lifting his right leg over the horse's head. Then, he leapt off and smoothly landed on both feet. She could think of no reason for him having done so unless he hadn't wanted to break eye contact. *Terribly romantic.*

As he came to stand by her side, he swept his hair back into place. Then he turned up his face and held out his hand encouragingly.

First, she handed down her crop. Then, she nervously adjusted her skirts, preparing to lift her own leg over her sidesaddle's pommel. She'd done so thousands of times, but never while her husband was gazing up in expectation, arms aloft.

She resisted the urge to shoo him away. The weight of her skirts and the uneven ground could render even the most accomplished horsewoman unsteady. The last thing she needed was to ruin the moment by landing on her arse.

"There, now, Molly," he soothed the horse. "She'll be off in a thrice."

She slid gracefully onto the ground, but he placed his warm hands on either side of her waist anyway. She was now more than a little breathless and not entirely because of the way her stays pinched. The shock of contact burned even after he moved away to secure the horses to the tie weights partially concealed by shrubs.

Softly, he assured them they would not be left in discomfort for long. Then, he held out his arm. Together they navigated a small path through a thick wood.

How strange and wonderful to be on adventure with him!

Gradually, a free-standing spiral of stairs came into view, then a partial wall, then a more intact network of stone chambers. She'd read somewhere that the estate contained ruins, but the ruins spread out before her were far more impressive than she'd imagined.

"Harbury!" She exclaimed. "It is as if the abbey ruins in Wordsworth's poem have been recreated here."

"They are just as picturesque, yes. But these aren't abbey ruins. This was a priory for monks associated with the parish of St. Margaret's, where we were wed."

"Ah, yes," she glanced askance, "the *little* chapel."

He chuckled softly. "Every duke and duchess married there. I wanted to stay true to tradition. Had I given you a more accurate description, you might have cried off in fear."

No, she wouldn't have.

Then again, he didn't know just how much she'd wanted him.

Teasingly, she lifted a brow. "A more accurate description, like trading 'little church' for 'gothic behemoth?'"

"A gothic *masterpiece*, you mean. With a two-hundred-foot spire, five medieval frescos, fifteen different types of marble, and statues depicting deceased dukes and duchesses."

"So. Many. Monuments," she agreed, glancing heavenward.

"A surfeit," he acknowledged. "After my father's monument was installed as specified in his will, the rector asked me to move the lectern from the back of the chancel to the front in order for the prayerful collected to be able to see and hear his homily."

Cassie ducked under a low-hanging branch he held aloft. "Do you want to know what Millie said about the statues?"

"I'm not sure." He chuckled. "Do I?"

"She told me I must insist on pink marble when the time comes to create my monument."

"Why?"

"Because the duchesses whose likenesses were carved in gray looked too dour."

He laughed again. "The duchesses carved in gray likely *were* dour."

"As Nettie pointed out, they *are* deceased. A state unlikely to induce good humor on the present plane." She ventured a glance. "All those monuments made the *'till death do us part'* a little more daunting."

He stopped walking. She turned.

"God willing, we've a good long time before we part." He touched her cheek.

He looked sincere. Almost loving.

Between the romantic gesture of his bringing her here, and the talk of *we* and *our* and *allies*, she was coming to believe she meant something to him. But how much, she wasn't sure.

Was she always to be merely second prize, claimed only because the first had been won by another? She needed to know.

She worried her lip, and then she summoned courage. "Are you sorry we wed?"

"No." He shook his head slowly. "You're nothing like what I expected, however."

She wasn't sure how to feel about his answer.

"I'm not surprised." She knew what he'd expected. He'd expected the same, biddable young lady who had allowed him to ruin her for the sake of distraction.

For the sake of a dance.

She'd expected that lady, too.

He smiled wryly. "I should have known a lady who'd propose marriage to a gentleman must be made of stern stuff."

"Stern stuff?" She queried. "Do you mean to compliment or insult me?"

"To compliment you, of course. You've a strong will."

Did she?

She studied his face.

Millie had taken to calling herself and her sisters the Willful Wainwrights, after an offhand comment made by Cassie's godmother. Cassie, however, rarely initiated any "willful" schemes. Even the girlish games she indulged in as a child had been thought up by Eliza or Millie. And unlike her two most outspoken sisters, she had always measured her worth by approval.

But she had taken one major risk. She'd gone after what she wanted—*Harbury*.

Right now, she was glad for the approval shining in his eyes, but his approval, she realized, was no longer enough. She wanted him to want her, too.

He brushed a loose lock of hair out of her face. "Are *you* sorry we wed?"

Sorry.

To be sorry would be to regret the leap she'd taken when she'd proposed. To deny the desire of her heart—both then, and even more so now.

The secret she'd kept—even from her own consciousness—shook fully free.

She hadn't been "forced" into anything. She'd known what she was doing when she'd seized the chance and bound him in marriage. She'd wanted him ever since she'd first locked eyes with him across the room at Almack's. On her wedding night, she'd been furious, not at him, but at her own folly.

She'd wanted him badly and against her better reason.

Her anger on the first night of their marriage was because intimacy had made her see half of him would never be enough. So no, she could not be sorry she'd gone after what she wanted for the first time in her life, even if her need made her angry, and even if her desire was in vain.

"I'm not sorry," she answered him.

She walked on before he could ask her to elaborate, passing beneath the remains of an ancient arch and into what had once clearly been a chapel. Even though the space was open to the elements, a sacred feeling remained. Or, perhaps, the sense of sanctity was present because nothing stood between the chapel columns and the heavens.

She wandered through a series of half-walls and approached a spiral stair that now led only to the sky. She climbed up a few stairs to a spot in the shadow of what remained of the outer wall, then gathered her skirts and sat down.

He passed her and took a seat a step above.

She heard the rustle of fabric and craned her neck to see what he was doing. He'd loosened his cravat, letting the sides of his collar fall open. Although he'd likely done so only for relief from the afternoon's growing warmth, now he looked even more devastatingly handsome.

"Not sorry," he repeated. "Neither of us. Good to know."

And that was *all* she was going to let him know. She had no intention of revealing the extent of his hold on her heart.

She wrapped her arms around her legs. "You may not be sorry, but I feel like I am a disappointment to you."

"Are you serious?" He snorted in disbelief. "I know the pressure of high expectation too well to ever lord disappointment over anyone, let alone you. Besides, you haven't disappointed me at all."

"Not even on our wedding night?" She covered her mouth and looked away.

She had not intended for the question to slip out. She blamed those eyes of his, so solidly brown. So deceptively trustworthy.

"There's no need for shame." He stretched out his leg, placing a boot next to her skirt. "Not between us. And no, I wasn't disappointed."

"I must yield to your greater experience regarding—er— marital relations." His heat, his nearness became nearly stifling. "There is…more, isn't there?"

He looked away—back toward the chapel.

She hoped he'd answer and answer honestly. Wasn't lying in a church worse—however ruined the church appeared?

"I'm not sure what you mean by more." His Adam's apple rose before disappearing again beneath his parted collar. His eyes met hers, warmer and brighter now. "I was…pleased."

Panic bubbled up in her chest. Still, she leaned forward. "Pleased?"

"Yes, pleased." He fell silent, but his face continued to speak of longing, his posture of reluctant restraint. "And I'd very much like to please you in the same fashion. I will…provided you tell me how I can."

Kiss me. She could not be so forward. And yet, God help her, his earthy eyes were like magnets, pulling forth the truth.

"I dreamed of you," she said. "Of us." She dropped her gaze, studying the weave of the maroon thread in her linen habit…*in out, in out.* "Last night, I dreamed you came to me and then we…repeated what we'd done. Only, in the dream, you kissed me." She hesitated. "Properly. As if you couldn't get enough."

EVEN THOUGH HARBURY had loosened his cravat—generally considered a gross impropriety in front of a lady—he could still barely breathe. He'd untied the damn thing for relief from the heat…but not only just.

Part of him had wanted Cassandra to react, to blush, to give him *some* sign he could fluster her—sensually. Until now, she had not given him any verbal indication she desired him. But not only had she just acknowledged her attraction, physical signs of her arousal showed in her blush, in her damp and slightly parted lips, and in her hitched breath.

Once again, she'd upped the ante. And he was totally unprepared.

He'd brought her here simply to make her smile. Now, he wanted more.

She'd *dreamt* of him last night. He tried and failed to wrap his mind around the magnitude of her confession, while knowing he'd done more than dream of her. He'd emptied himself into a rag with a body-shaking, silent release.

Twice.

Only then had he been able to fall into a short and restless sleep.

He put his finger beneath her chin and raised her face. "Are you asking me to kiss you?"

"You must have some experience."

He'd *some* experience, if not the depth of carnal knowledge she believed.

Most of his experience had happened here, in the long, thin antechamber still completely intact, but for the roof. He'd been infinitely relieved Cassandra had headed for the stairs instead of taking refuge in what remained of the buttresses on the opposite side of the ruins.

Had he intended to seduce his wife into kissing, he would

have chosen a more private and less fraught location. Though his love of this place long preceded his clandestine meetings with Vivianne, he did not think Cassandra would appreciate knowing his history here.

An innocent mistake, but, he feared, a bad one.

Should he tell his wife the truth?

Tell her he hadn't any more true experience of carnal knowledge than she did? Tell her how what they'd done together had knitted her into his mind and shifted everything he'd believed was solid, including the very earth beneath his feet?

Even here, where memories of Viv were too close, she'd become the brighter star.

Should he confess he'd brought her here only because he'd wanted more of her smiles? Confess, too, that though she hadn't been the first person he'd wooed in these ruins, he now knew he wanted her to be the last. What better place to confess than a former Roman church?

But if he told her he'd brought Viv to this same place, this moment would end.

Confession, at present, would not be in his best interests. At least not in the best interests of the parts of him asserting increasing control.

She'd mentioned kissing.

Properly.

He stared down into his wife's trusting eyes, his swallow even rougher than before. He focused on the slight protrusion of her lower lip. The more he focused, the further his memories of Viv slipped away.

He widened his parted legs, nestling her into the space between his thighs. She went completely still as she stared up over her shoulder, eager for whatever would come next. Though when he hadn't any roadmap to follow, she appeared certain he knew exactly how to proceed.

"Tell me more," he found himself saying, "about your dream."

She tilted her head to the side, presenting the pale, tempting column of her neck.

Slowly—giving her ample time to protest—he encircled her body, and then he untied her bonnet. The silky ribbon slid softly through his fingers before he lifted it off. He set aside her hair covering, then he brought his lips to her ear.

Her sweet-scented hair was damp at her temples. The warmth of exertion and desire radiated from her skin. Still, her back remained stiff and she held herself apart. Just as well, he supposed.

He didn't want to frighten her away with his own stiffening extremities.

"Please?" he added. "Tell me what images those mischievous fairies of night delivered?"

"You kissed me," she repeated.

As she exhaled, her breasts brushed against his arm. His desire spiked, and with the spike, came an invigorating surge of confidence.

"So, you said." He brought his lips to her ear. *"Properly."* A little freckle on her jaw blurred as he drew in, ever closer. The scent of *her*, not just her hair, filled his nostrils. A heady, rich scent. "But properly how?"

"On the forehead first." She touched a place just beneath her ear. "Then here."

He pressed his lips to the place she'd indicated.

She dragged her hand across her cheek. "All along here, too."

He drew back. "Did I eventually find your mouth?"

She audibly exhaled. "Yes."

"And then?"

"And…then the dream ended."

She'd paused just long enough to let him know she was lying. *Very well.*

She was not ready to tell him more. He'd learned enough. For now. Of true intimacy, they were both ignorant. But surely, together they could find their way.

He moved a little to the side so she could turn more comfortably in his arms. He suppressed a shudder as his cock jerked…a protest, he guessed, of the increased space between them. But what he was about to do didn't concern the satisfaction of his member, at least not yet.

His aim was the seduction of her mind.

He placed his hands on her shoulders, urging her to shift her position. As she did, he briefly held her gaze. Then, he kissed her forehead, just as she'd described.

Her warm sigh tickled his neck and seeped into his collar.

Holding back a deep-throated groan cost an inordinate amount of will.

His forehead brushed along her temple as he lowered his lips back to the side of her ear. There, he improvised. A light nip on her tender lobe caused her full body to quiver in abandon.

Potential unmoored him, as if he were a dinghy ripped free of an anchor by a building storm. The other night, when she lay accommodatingly, but unresponsively, beneath him, he hadn't imagined she possessed such an arousable nature.

Blindly, he followed the line of her jaw and then…

And then, he found her lips.

The first touch was delicate, the tenderest of tests. He drew back slightly, surprised. Fleetingly, he thought of Viv, but Cassandra's scent kept him tethered to the present, aroused, curious, and attuned to her every breath.

Either he'd forgotten the shocking, enlivening sensations roused by a simple kiss, or he and Cassandra were uniquely suited. He set his lips back into the seam to better judge. *Yes.* Just a slight stimulation of the fragile skin set his blood boiling. Though he didn't need any encouragement, her lips parted in further invitation, and he tasted her deeply.

Finally, she fully relinquished caution. She yielded, bringing her neck to rest pliantly against his arm. She was his to explore.

His to devour.

He brought his free hand to her cheek, holding her still, making sure she could feel each bold stroke of his tongue. The sun beat down against his head, his neck. He welcomed the heat, heat as quickening and vital as the fire building in his body.

The sounds she made—guttural, whimpery—only whetted his appetite for more.

His own sound of satisfaction came from deep within. She didn't seem to mind. In fact, he'd just enough awareness to track her hands as they crept up his shirt, over his collar's edge and—yes, *please*—into his hair.

Did she know the light, recurring, patter of her fingers nearly matched the beat of his heart?

Whether she knew or not, her ardent response was stirring. She'd serendipitously found the very lever which, when pressed, would leave him forever vanquished.

Good God.

If he allowed the kissing to continue, he would end up taking his duchess against crumbling steps leading to nowhere, the remnants of an empire his ancestors had unjustly slashed to pieces in the pursuit of greed.

Worse still, he'd be claiming her on the site where he'd often wooed another.

Shame blossomed, an ugly, thorned weed in his mind. A rush of cold awareness shocked him, and he broke contact.

And he'd thought kissing her on their wedding night a sign of disrespect!

Bringing her to his special place with Viv, wooing her in the same fashion in the same haunting ruin, had been much worse.

She continued to clutch his neck as she made a sound of protest. Her eyes were dazed, her head heavy against his arm.

Ah, Cassandra.

She deserved so much better.

To cover his unease, he flashed an uncertain smile. "Was that comparable to your dream?"

"That"—she sighed—"was a little better than my dream."

"Proper?"

She nodded.

"Good." His voice could be a little less hoarse, but what could he do? "We've a lifetime to practice, but the horses…"

"The horses!" She pulled away. "Oh, my goodness, I'd forgotten all about the horses. They'll be uncomfortable by now, poor things."

"You're so very good." He tucked a lock of hair back into her coiffure. He wanted to apologize, but then she would want to know why, and he just couldn't bring himself to ruin what had been such a revelatory kiss.

For her, too, he suspected. When he moved to tie the ribbons beneath her chin, he saw that her fingers were shaking.

"Allow me," he said.

She stilled. Hesitantly, she raised her chin. He tied a gentle knot. Not as pretty, of course, as she might have done, but solid enough to keep the bonnet secure.

Then, he braced himself against the wall and stood, carefully stepping to the center, so when she rose, she would be on the wider part of the stair. Once she was fully on her feet, he stepped down and offered her his hand. She curled her fingers around his and did not let go as they made their way back through the wood.

A simple gesture, but one of nascent trust.

Trust he did not yet deserve but was determined to earn.

As they came into the clearing, his horse snorted his displeasure. If the horse only knew the high price his owner had paid in order to return to his mount, he'd think twice before tossing his mane!

Harbury checked the girths and straps, then turned back.

"Ready?"

She nodded.

He made a footstep by joining his hands and bending his knees.

She gazed at him skeptically, as if judging whether he'd lift her so energetically, he'd end up casting her straight over the horse.

"Don't worry. I've had plenty of practice helping—" He caught himself just before saying *Viv*. "…My, ah, sister Sarah." He forced himself to maintain his smile. "I won't throw you, I promise."

"Oh, no?" She smirked. "I'd have thought you would be keen to show off your strength."

He was glad she'd missed his slip.

"You're safe with me." He swore to himself she would be.

She placed a hand on his shoulder and stepped into his threaded palms. He lifted her up with surprising ease, still he was glad for the exertion.

"I won't expect more." He looked up into her eyes. "Tonight, I mean. We have time."

She studied him thoughtfully. "I appreciate your consideration. I, on the other hand, do have expectations. We're married now. Your problems are mine. I expect you to include me in your concerns."

Not an invitation to reopen the door between their chambers, but, perhaps, to something even more lasting. He'd believed himself in love with Viv, but Viv had never made a similar demand. In fact, she'd expected him to solve every problem they faced on his own.

Cassandra could become something he'd not known enough of the world to long for—a true ally. A lover, a friend, a companion and witness to his daily life. Someone, perhaps for the first time, on which he could fully rely.

Surprisingly, he found those possibilities infinitely better than a simple invitation to her bed.

CHAPTER SIX

THE NEXT MORNING, Cassie awoke half afraid Harbury would hide himself away again out of embarrassment for having kissed her so wantonly and openly in the light of day. So, as she caught sight of her husband in his usual chair in the breakfast room, she breathed a sigh of profound relief. Then, she took a moment to appreciate the sight.

Sunlight from the window behind him dappled his brushed-to-a-sheen coat. Fingers of light accented his high cheekbones and cleft chin, while his nose shadowed his slightly puckered lips. She stared at his mouth, remembering how those lips had conjured sensations she hadn't thought possible during the idyll they'd spent in the shelter of a crumbling spire.

She was almost certain he'd had amorous intentions when he'd taken her to such a charming, evocative place. She'd brought up the dream, but he'd initiated the kiss. He must have planned to do so, but she could be wrong.

He could have kissed her impetuously. Certainly, he'd shown a tendency to be rash before.

Almack's, for instance.

But she'd also seen glimpses of a different side of him, of a character more deliberate than his earlier actions had suggested.

She hoped he'd intended romance, because, yesterday, he'd made her feel desired—cherished, even. Unlike on their wedding night, he'd romanced her for reasons beyond duty. And, for another mark in his favor, he had not spoiled the whole thing by immediately demanding marital rights. Best of all, his presence here this morning suggested their tentative connection had not broken in the hours they'd spent apart.

Perhaps they'd finally reached solid ground and could begin to build something lasting.

She lingered in the entryway, watching him read something he held just out of her view. Then, his posture went taut. His brows bunched as if he were concentrating, or maybe even straining. Taken together, his comportment suggested a sudden, interior apprehension. In fact, his concern became so apparent, so readable, he might have been a portrait by a Dutch artist of the golden age—Rembrandt or Vermeer—if not for his modern clothing and the brightly lit room.

He lifted his troubled gaze, and his expression transformed yet again, as if the mere sight of her had caused a rush of unanticipated pleasure.

Her own lips curled in a natural, reflexive response as her heart thumped low and slow in her chest. *Ah, his smile.* She could never blunt her ardent response. And when his eyes sparkled, as they were sparkling now, she was completely doomed.

Gathering her shawl more tightly about her shoulders, she advanced into the room.

"Good morning," she said, in a voice made tender by his obvious delight.

"Good morning." He rose from his seat. "I trust you slept and"—his voice deepened—"*dreamt* well."

The indentation in his right cheek left no doubt he was teasing.

Though her face heated, she couldn't help but indulge him with a brow lift of her own. A comfortable silent moment passed. She'd rarely experienced unspoken conversation with anyone but her twin Eliza, and never with anyone outside of her family circle, especially not with a man...

But he was not just any man; he was now her family, too, was he not?

Her own children might have his features. His chin, for instance. Or his smile. Her heart skipped a beat as he rounded the table and then pulled out her seat.

"I *am* capable of adjusting my own chair," she said, again amused.

"Of course you are," he replied indulgently. "But a man is never made happier than when he can be of service."

Was he still teasing, or was he being sincere?

Perhaps service did make him happy.

That would be consistent with some of the things she'd recently observed about him. If so, how wrong her initial impression had been! Since then, she had plenty of proof that Harbury—a man she and Eliza had deemed hopelessly arrogant and self-indulgent on the night he'd swept her into a waltz without permission—could also be sensitive and thoughtful.

"May I make you a plate?" he asked, demonstrating her point.

"Please do," she replied, interested to see how he'd accomplish his mission. She seated herself to quell any temptation to supervise. "When you said man is made happier by service, were you referring to humankind in general, or males as a category?"

Or yourself in particular?

She tried to add the latter, but *no*. She wasn't brave enough. Not yet...

She still wasn't sure if he had an unusual sensitivity, an awareness of the feelings of those around him. Or perhaps, like her, he simply attempted to please everyone around him.

One thing she could say of the duke...he was observant. He returned with the same assortment she'd arranged for herself the first time they'd breakfasted together.

He laid down the plate. "I would not presume to speak for all mankind," he answered her question, though his continued twinkle suggested he presumed much. And often.

She held his gaze as she thanked him.

Briefly, he touched her cheek before returning to his seat. The gesture had been spontaneous. But his touch had made her feel cared for and comforted, and the warm sensation that followed left her a little shy.

"What is your opinion?" he asked, looking as if he honestly wanted to know what she thought.

She paused, giving the question serious consideration. First as a universal—was mankind made happier by service? *Yes.* But she didn't think his question was of a philosophical bent. He wanted to know her motivation. He wanted to know *her.*

"I enjoy being of service," she replied carefully. "Eliza tells me I am never happier than when I am needed."

In fact, when she'd told Eliza she'd proposed to Harbury, Eliza had accused her of proposing not just because she wanted to save their reputations, but because their godmother, Lady Asquith, and Harbury's sister, Lady Sarah, had both separately suggested marriage—and not *just* marriage, but marriage *to her—* would do Harbury a world of good.

Eliza had been right, but only in part.

Cassie *had* taken what they'd said to heart. But yesterday she'd realized she'd used his perceived need as an excuse to claim him, when the real reason had been as simple as it had been selfish. She'd desired Harbury. And she'd set out to have him.

Her eyes dropped to her plate.

"Oh?" He hummed thoughtfully. "You may be physically identical, but something tells me your twin does not share your giving nature."

She glanced up, smiling half-heartedly. "No," she acknowledged. "Eliza is not as…accommodating as I am."

Her sister would never deliver criticism in soft words and phrases to make a confrontation less fraught. She would never affirm an agitated person's opinion simply because she wanted to soothe their soul. And, if Eliza had been the one to propose to her husband she would have been truthful with herself—and with him—about her motivations.

Cassie, on the other hand, had deceived everyone, including herself.

What would he think of her if he knew?

Since she and Harbury had agreed to wed, they had never directly discussed the circumstances surrounding her marriage proposal. Not unless one counted Harbury revealing he'd been drunk when he'd agreed to court her.

As far as Harbury knew, she'd proposed only because she'd been concerned about her sisters' prospects. And as far as she knew, he accepted for the same reason he'd swept her onto the dance floor—Vivianne was not available. In the case of their marriage, not only was Vivianne not available, but Harbury had a ducal duty to produce an heir, and he found Cassie pretty enough.

Plus, Cassie had told him she'd understood he would always love another.

She'd lied.

As she pondered the implications of her lie, the meat she'd eaten sat uncomfortably in her stomach.

Oblivious, Harbury chuckled to himself. "Eliza might not be as naturally helpful as you are, but I believe Adrian has found in her everything he wished for in a wife. I've never seen him so undone as he was at the Harbury ball, when he called your sister by a name clearly known only to the two of them, demonstrating they'd had a scandalous connection."

She tilted her head and sighed. "My family has been embroiled in a series of dramatic events of late."

"You're as kind as you are helpful."

"Pardon?"

"Not *your family's* drama at all, was it?" He leaned back in his chair. "*I* caused the worst of the scandals, and yet I left the task of coming up with suitable reparation first to your guardian and then to you. I should not have been surprised when Asquith demanded, on pain of death, I court you. *I* should have been the one to approach you with a courtship. I should have been the one to propose…not after a false courtship, but the very moment your voucher was revoked."

Not an apology. Not exactly.

But she appreciated his effort, nonetheless. He'd told her *why* he'd swept her into a dance without asking permission when he'd confessed to an attachment to Lady Pennington, but he had never taken full responsibility. She hadn't realized just how much she'd needed him to take responsibility for what he'd done. "I'm not sure you should have proposed," she replied.

"Why not? The crowd's macabre interest would have instantly turned to jubilation. You and Eliza would have been spared mortification."

She smiled. "I'm glad you told me you feel you could have done something that night to mitigate the damage."

He nodded.

"But," she continued, "I am equally glad you did not immediately ask for my hand."

"Why?"

"Because if you had offered for me in front of all those people, I would have been compelled to accept. Instead, I offered for you in private, and, as a result, we were both able to make a choice."

His gaze moved across her face. She lowered her eyes.

Yes, she had held back a crucial truth.

Nothing, however, she was currently willing to share. She could not tell him she'd wanted him then any more than she could tell him she feared how quickly she was growing to truly care for him now. Not, at least, until she was sure he felt the same.

She was vulnerable enough.

She was vulnerable to his smiles, which made her feel warm and light and trustful inside.

And she was vulnerable to her desire, which made her hot and needy and willing to invite him back to her bed before he'd made any declaration.

But she wanted not only him, but *all* of him, body, mind, and soul.

Every time she'd been on the cusp of demanding more, an apparition of the reason he'd never publicly courted anyone else, the reason he'd been available for her to propose, appeared in her mind as a warning.

The very-much-alive Lady Pennington.

Her only consolation was that Lady Pennington was far away…out of sight and—hopefully—out of mind. She jabbed a fork into her meat, shoveled a morsel into her mouth, and forced herself to chew. The sausage was flavorful, but bitterness lingered on her tongue.

Vivianne, as he'd called her.

Viv.

"Is the meat overcooked?" he asked.

She forced herself to swallow.

"No." Her expression, she supposed, must be as readable as his. She brightened with forced cheer and recentered the conversation on an ever-shrinking parcel of safe ground. "Quite good, actually. I should like to compliment the cook."

THOUGH HIS WIFE was still present at the breakfast table, the suddenness of Cassandra's emotional retreat left Harbury reeling. They'd come close, so close, to an understanding.

This time, she pulled away.

He wanted to ask her what had caused her open expression to shutter with a clap, but some battles, like the one for her genuine esteem, had to be won by the inch. Cassandra, he was coming to understand, was not someone who responded to stark demands. She could be silenced but never coerced. She would only engage when made to feel welcome and at ease.

He shifted in his chair. He could, and would, encourage her to keep talking. He wasn't that small boy who couldn't converse any longer.

What had she just expressed?

Ah, yes—a desire to compliment the cook. "Cook, I'm sure, would appreciate any compliment, especially if delivered directly by the duchess."

A strange expression passed over her features.

What could it mean?

His mind wandered back over his internal catalog of their interactions. Every time he had called her by her station, she'd gotten the same, wary look, like a rabbit sensing a predator. If just the word "duchess" set her on uneven mental terrain, what was being the duchess causing her to feel? And if the experience was as painful as he feared, perhaps he could do something to help?

"Have you been getting on with the servants?" he asked.

"Yes," she answered far too quickly, then glanced warily at the footman. "...for the most part."

Of course. She would not want to speak in front of Tull.

He'd entirely forgotten the footman's presence. Strange, too, given the earlier admission he'd made concerning his failure to propose.

His father never would have been so indiscreet. Nor would he ever have been so wrapped up in his duchess, he forgot his surrounds.

Thoughtless.

By afternoon, the whole staff, half the estate, and likely beyond would know Cassandra had taken the unusual step of proposing to him. He didn't care about his own reputation, but he did not wish to tarnish hers. Ridicule, brought on by his actions, had hurt her before.

He'd be damned if he'd make the same mistake again.

He set down his napkin. "Tull?"

The footman turned toward Harbury.

"Needless to say," Harbury instructed, "anything you may have heard will not leave this room."

"Your Grace?" Tull blinked as if to imply he hadn't heard anything at all.

Harbury leveled his gaze. "Should I hear any gossip concerning myself and the duchess, there will be consequences. Serious consequences."

"Yes, Your Grace," the young man replied.

"You may go."

He glanced at his wife. Instead of looking alarmed, as she had when he'd dismissed the servant on their first breakfast alone together, she sighed as if relieved.

Yesterday she'd said, *we are married now, your problems are mine.*

He'd been touched.

But wasn't the same true in reverse?

He should have been more attentive to the burdens on her shoulders. Mrs. Pratt, for instance, could still be holding Cassandra's library project against her even though he'd made it clear his wife could make whatever changes she wished.

He hoped that was not the case.

He'd hate to lose a retainer, but there was no question whose well-being should be his chief concern. Cassandra should be comfortable giving instructions in her own home. He leaned forward, reaching out across the table to rest his hand close to her plate.

"Do you have any concerns you haven't shared? Something about the staff, perhaps?"

"I've had a few…ah, difficult interactions with Mrs. Pratt."

"Michaelmas is coming up," he began. "A time when many servants seek new positions, housekeepers likely among them."

"You wouldn't dismiss your housekeeper for my sake, would you?" Her eyes went wide.

"*Our* housekeeper," he corrected. "And yes, if her performance is not to your liking, I would not hesitate to ask for her resignation."

Cassie shook her head, horrified. "I don't want you to send her off."

How like her to be concerned for someone else's welfare. "I

would offer a retainer until she found another position. And I would provide references, of course."

"I don't wish to upend the household."

He suppressed a smile. She hadn't hesitated to upend his library, or his life.

"And," she continued, "I wouldn't presume—"

"You're the duchess," he interrupted her, "making such decisions is your right."

"Well, then." She paused. "I will take the possibility into consideration. But I've made a point to be clearer about my preferences. Things have been better. Truly."

"Good." He settled back in his chair. "Is there anything else not to your satisfaction?"

"Well…" She sent him a measured glance. "Would you have any objection if I changed out the carpet in my bedchamber?"

"The carpet is new." In fact, he'd had the room decorated to what he thought was her taste.

"New?" she asked. "Never you mind, then. I—I could use one from another chamber."

"You mistake me. I wasn't concerned about the expense, just surprised."

"I am not particularly enamored with pink." She wrinkled her nose apologetically.

Apologetically and adorably.

"Not enamored?"

"To be honest"—she flashed a smile—"I hate the color."

Which meant she hated the drapes and the coverlet as well as the damn rug. "I shouldn't want you to be uncomfortable in your own chamber." He drummed his fingers against his knee. "The fault, I'm afraid, is mine. I specifically chose the color because—"

"*You* redecorated the room?"

"The duchess's chamber had not been updated since the time of my grandmother. I could hardly bring you home to musty linens and a drafty room. The drapes, coverlet, and rug were of trivial expense compared to the repairs to the hearth and the replacement of the windows."

Her face went soft with the same expression she made every time he showed her even the least consideration. *Really.* Had she thought him a complete cad?

He'd told her his heart was engaged elsewhere, but he'd always intended to treat her with respect and consideration. Now—he cocked his head—he was coming to wonder if she hadn't been the better choice for him after all.

She certainly appreciated him. And he appreciated her.

"What made you think I liked pink?" she asked, completely unaware of his profound reflections.

"You favored a hat in London—one with a profusion of pink flowers and ribbons."

"Oh!" She giggled. "*Ohhh.*"

The sound of her laughter was unexpected and considerably lightened his mood.

Rare were these moments when she seemed to feel completely at ease in his presence; he not only liked them, but he was also growing greedy for them.

"Nettie made me the pink-flowered atrocity," she explained. "I felt obligated to wear it…at least to the Season's end. Now, the hat's been relegated to a box at the very back of my dressing room."

"Your sister Annette favors pink?"

She rolled her eyes. "You don't know the half."

"Then I suggest you bundle up the linens and give them to her as a gift."

"Really?" She brightened. Then, her face fell. "Millie and Lenora would never consent to sleep in a room draped in pink."

"I know they are planning on staying in a shared room in D'Acre House next Season, but they *could* come live with us, if they would prefer to have their own rooms. D'Acre House is big." He flashed a smile. "My London home is bigger."

She cocked her head. "You'd grant each of my sisters their own chamber?"

"Of course." He shrugged. "Unless they preferred otherwise."

"Thank you for the thought." Genuine gratitude sparkled in her eyes. "But I am certain they will prefer to stay with Adrian and Eliza. Nettie and Lady Emily have become fast friends."

"If that's the case, simply make the whole lot a present for Nettie's trousseau chest."

"Her trousseau chest?"

Belatedly, he remembered Cassandra hadn't had a piece of furniture where she collected items for her marriage. He didn't know how common they were, but Sarah had been gifted one from a maternal aunt when she was born, along with a stunning set of silver his sister hadn't yet had the opportunity to use.

"If she doesn't have one, we'll get one." Belatedly, he remembered Millicent and Lenora. "Three, I mean."

"Thank you," she offered quietly.

"Trifling." He waved his hand.

"You cannot know how great a relief I feel now that my sisters have powerful connections beyond Lord and Lady Asquith."

He inclined his head in acknowledgement, but he didn't want her gratitude. Well, not only her gratitude, at least.

What did he want, then?

An ally…but they'd already established a mutual desire to work cooperatively. A lover…but marital congress had always been part of their bargain. Now, however, neither of those things were enough.

He wanted to hear her little giggle more often.

He wanted to see the sudden light in her eyes. He wanted her excitement—the same excitement she'd shown when she'd first seen the priory ruins. He wanted her look of trust, like the one she'd given him when she'd stepped into the make-shift stirrup of his hands. He wanted her dreamy, breathless just-been-thoroughly-kissed expression.

He wanted them all.

Viv had been glittery, lively, and ambitious—something he'd

reached for but had never truly held. Cassandra was breathtaking in a different way. She was lovely, bright, and though willing to speak her mind, invariably considerate and kind.

And she was his.

Like a traveler who'd carefully uncovered a prize from an ancient civilization no one else had been able to see, he wanted to flaunt his new bride to all his neighbors.

…which recalled to mind something they hadn't yet discussed.

"Yesterday, when we were out, I missed a call from an old friend of my father's."

"You did?" she asked. "I'm sorry."

"Don't be," He grinned. "I would not trade the afternoon we had for a visit from the king *and* his most important dignitaries."

She blushed prettily.

"Lord Wexford left his card, of course, and an invitation to visit this afternoon."

"Didn't Mr. Townsend say he'd be available to meet with you on his farm this afternoon?"

"We can visit both. Townsend's farm is on the way."

She hesitated. "I don't think that's wise."

"Whyever not?"

"Well, I imagine the Wexfords would expect slightly more formal attire than would make a tenant farmer, even one so large and established as Mr. Townsend, comfortable."

Huh.

He hadn't considered how they'd be dressed. "You're correct, of course. I will pen a note to Lord Wexford and ask him to propose some other convenient time." He smiled. "Whatever did I do without you?"

The question may have been rhetorical, but the sentiment was sincere.

He was coming to appreciate how much a smart, witty, and thoughtful lady could add to a man's life, and he didn't want to return to the less interesting, less fulfilling drudgery he'd known before he'd married.

CHAPTER SEVEN

L ATER THAT AFTERNOON, Harbury spent time reviewing the estate records in his study while Cassandra finished dressing for their visit to Townsend farm. Since returning to Harbury Hall to be wed, he'd developed a better understanding of the way his staff worked in seamless cooperation. Sally, for instance, was far more aware of her mistress's needs and schedule than himself, as Marsden was his.

Even now, when his wife was ready, she would tell Sally, Sally would tell Marsden, and then Marsden would tell him.

Although Harbury had never pondered the details, he supposed the staff had always functioned this way. On more than one occasion, he and Adrian had tipped his father's valet to forewarn them when his parents would both be occupied. Far easier to execute covert and often reckless adventures when his father's wary eye would not be turned in his direction.

But shouldn't a man be able to speak directly to his wife? Shouldn't he have a sense of the cadence and flow of Cassandra's day?

And she, his?

She'd made clear she expected him at breakfast, and he enjoyed beginning the day together. He only wished they could end the day together, too.

Though he'd been the one to suggest delaying further intimacies, the etiquette involving the doorway separating their chambers had become an increasingly difficult conundrum.

That first night, Marsden had told him Cassandra was ready for him to enter her chamber. For the sake of his future heirs, his marriage had to be unassailable, and, for that, he'd needed proof of consummation.

But surely, the *whole* household needn't know every time he and Cassandra wished to be intimate.

Harbury shifted in his seat, all too aware of his ever-present, frustrated desire.

He shook his head and refocused on the task he'd set himself—going over the income and rents generated specifically by the Townsend farm.

So far, he'd discovered Towsend was the second largest tenant, and his family had been working the land for several generations. On paper, things appeared balanced. The farm's income, though down considerably from prior years, more than covered the recorded expenses. Still, he hoped his visit would shade in areas of understanding that mere numbers left devoid of life and breath.

Did Townsend consider his treatment fair and reasonable? Had there been any recent issues left unattended? Had unkept promises been made? In other words, did Anderson continue to be a reliable intermediary?

Harbury would have to find some way to answer the latter question without directly asking.

Although he'd received a second anonymous letter this morning, he still felt duty-bound to give Anderson the benefit of the doubt. Not only had an Anderson family member been stewarding the estate since his great-grandfather's time, but the man himself had always treated Harbury with civility, even when Harbury had given Anderson very good reason to be angry.

But cracks had appeared in Harbury's trust. The other morning, Anderson had seemed reluctant to leave the books with him. Not a major slight, but an odd one. How much concern the slight should cause wasn't clear. That morning, Harbury had been tired and vexed, both by the letter's allegations as well as the vivid memory of his father's censure.

Harbury wanted to believe his father had been wrong.

He wanted to believe he'd a good head for business and a solid understanding of human nature. He'd need both to successfully navigate these harder times, and to resolve the questions precipitated by the letters without increasing discontent or creating loyalty factions.

Marsden entered the room through a servants' door. "The duchess is ready to depart."

"Please let her know I will meet her at the bottom of the stairs in the hall."

"Shall I call for the carriage?"

Harbury considered. "I think not. I think it best to avoid ostentation."

"Very good." Marsden nodded.

"Have a stable hand ready Trusty and…" After mentioning the horse, his voice trailed as a sudden awareness prickled beneath his skin.

"The cart?" Marsden supplied, sending him a significant glance.

Harbury nodded grimly. "The cart."

Yes, he'd been about to call the damned thing *Viv's* cart.

Not because of any fondness, but because his father had the conveyance built so that Vivianne and Sarah could travel around the grounds on their own. At present, the cart was mostly used by servants for errands, but the name had stuck.

Memory snares of Vivianne littered Harbury Hall…more than he'd ever consciously noticed before Cassandra had arrived. Something of Viv lurked in every room, every outbuilding, every oft-visited site.

Had those memories influenced how long he'd held onto the hope she would eventually return to him?

Looking back, he'd had no rational reason for staying true to Vivianne other than longstanding infatuation—one that predated his ability to reason.

His stubborn infatuation had begun when he'd first became aware of the fairer sex.

Ten years his senior, Viv had never noticed him as a man until he'd become one in her eyes the summer before he'd entered Cambridge. However, as Sarah's governess, she had been present—and fascinating to him—for as long as he could remember.

Slowly, he made his way to the hall to await his wife.

Viv was his past, but Cassandra was his present and future. She was unlinked to an untested version of himself he was coming to despise.

Before his marriage, he'd been occasionally reckless and well on his way to becoming permanently morose. Now, he was a husband, a responsible landowner, and God willing, a future father. The more time he spent with Cassandra, the more rooted in those values he became.

Moreover, he liked that she'd reoriented him.

He liked the man he was becoming.

Cassandra appeared at the top of the stairs. Again, she took his breath away. The sight of his wife was as cleansing as a breeze on a spring morning.

She studied his clothing as she descended. Breeches, not trousers, serviceable boots, not buffed hessians, and a simple knotted neckcloth, rather than an elaborately fashioned cravat. Her shyly flashed smile suggested she approved.

She had chosen well, too.

She wore a dress of muslin...good quality, but simple. Around her neck she'd tied an unembellished, but pristine white neckcloth. The cap beneath her sparsely decorated hat was gathered but not edged with expensive lace. On the whole, she appeared elegant and stylish but not condescending—

As she reached the bottom, he peeked into the basket she had hanging from her arm.

"What's this?"

"Oranges from the Orangery." She laid a hand protectively

over the contents. "Calling without a gift didn't seem the thing. So, I consulted Cook, who suggested these would be welcome. Mrs. Townsend, apparently, loves them."

Though he appreciated her thoughtfulness, he frowned. "Why would our cook be aware of Mrs. Townsend's preferences?"

Cassie gave him a look he'd seen often enough on his older sister—longsuffering, but indulgent. "Because she trades what she cannot use from our kitchen gardens. In Mrs. Townsend's case, oranges for—" She stopped abruptly. "…for a certain tincture. One favored by the undermaids."

Female concerns, he decided from her blush. "I didn't know."

Cassandra shrugged. "Why should you?"

Why should he, indeed. Shouldn't he be familiar with the ways in which his household staff interacted with other parts of the estate?

Minor bartering might not make the record books, but the relationship between his cook and his tenant's spouse struck him as essential. Longstanding, trustful exchange formed an excellent foundation for lasting relationships. He should be aware of these kinds of connections.

In fact, he should be encouraging them.

He wondered if his father had.

Unlikely.

His father had been of a strict hierarchical mind. Since bartering circumvented wages, his father would have been wary. Anything that threatened the servants' dependence would have been treated with great misgiving.

Perhaps he had never won his father's approbation not because he was inherently unworthy, but because he had more reformist inclinations.

And who was to say his ideas, once implemented, would be less effective?

"I am sure your gift will delight Mrs. Townsend."

Feeling hopeful, he waved away the porter and held open the

door for her himself.

As requested, Trusty—the most steady and docile stepper in the stable—had been harnessed to the Hall's lightest and smallest gig. Though gig, truthfully, was a generous description. The conveyance was a little more than a well-crafted pony cart, low slung and stable, specifically designed for light, safe transportation about the estate.

"Your chariot awaits," he said teasingly.

"What's this?" she exclaimed.

"A pony cart." He laid a hand on the seat. "I learned to drive on this cart."

Soon after, he'd used his newly acquired skill to steal the cart from Vivianne when she'd been inside a shop, though revealing that attention-seeking prank to his wife didn't seem wise.

In fact, had he ever expressly *told* Cassandra Lady Pennington had once lived on the estate? He'd told her he'd been in love with her. He'd told her they had planned to marry. But he wasn't sure if he'd told her about Vivianne's connection to Sarah and to his home.

And he couldn't simply ask.

Bringing up his former love felt dangerous now.

Hold on a moment! *Former?*

"Harbury, did you hear me?"

He blinked.

"I asked who uses the cart now."

He brought his wife into focus. "The gig's been primarily used by staff for errands."

Cassandra continued to gaze at him in expectation, as if he should say more. He cleared his throat. "After you suggested we take care with how we dress, I thought arriving on the farm in a glossy, ducal carriage replete with crest would also be at odds with our purpose."

Again, her eyes lit with gratitude.

Yes, he'd heard. Yes, he'd listened. He wished she would stop displaying so much thankfulness when he showed her any simple consideration.

As his duchess, his consideration was her due. "Has no one ever taken your preferences to heart?"

Her face fell. Immediately, he regretted his question. He had his answer, however. *Clearly not.*

"You do," she acknowledged softly.

"And I always will."

His mood instantly shifted from fury to tenderness. He would protect her, even if he must protect her from himself, from his memories.

He placed his hand on the small of her back. "Come. Meet Trusty."

She exchanged a few soothing words with the docile white pony.

"Would you like to drive?" he asked.

She lifted her shoulders. "I do not know how."

She didn't know how to drive? He frowned. "Unusual for a lady of your station."

"I suppose my father didn't want us running away."

He wished he could take away some of that pain. "Do you wish to learn?"

She glanced doubtfully at the cart. "Is it safe?"

He examined the conveyance through her eyes. The simple bench's modest upholstery made travel over rutted roads only marginally comfortable. The two wheels were perfectly secure but still large enough to appear unstable.

"Not, perhaps, with an untrained horse. But Trusty here is as reliable as they come." He flashed a grin. "Right in his name, in fact."

"Do you think I'm tall enough to be able to brace my feet?"

"Certainly." Although she was not as tall as Vivianne. He suppressed a wince. "Being on the same level as the horse makes learning less fraught."

She nodded, but her frown suggested she didn't believe him.

"You learned on this cart?" she asked skeptically.

"Sarah, too. And I'm certain I can teach you."

She shaded her eyes to study him. Then, she smiled. "Perhaps I will give driving a try on the way back."

"There's a fighting spirit."

She pinked, he hoped, with pleasure. He handed her up into the box and then heaved himself up to slide in by her side.

"Ahem." He wiggled his brows. "I look forward to the challenge."

"Challenge?" She gave his arm a playful swat. "Hopefully not *too* much of a challenge."

"Don't worry. I'll have you ready to join the Four-in-Hand Club in no time."

She chuckled as the groom handed him the reins and stick.

"Walk on," he called to Trusty, and they were off.

He hadn't intended to offer Cassandra lessons, but it felt wrong that his wife lacked the skills to take charge of a vehicle Vivianne had used.

As evidenced by his recent recollection of Viv as his "former" love, she had been shifting from the column "forever present in his heart" to "a wound from some time past" but she still frequently intruded on his thoughts.

Too frequently.

He glanced in Cassandra's direction.

He'd a pretty, helpful, *hopeful* wife. He shouldn't be thinking of Vivianne at all.

And, when she did inadvertently cross his mind, he rather thought he should start referring to her as Lady Pennington even though, at the age he was remembering her, she'd been a long way from *Pennington*.

"See?" He forced his mind back to the present. "Quite safe."

"Does Trusty respond primarily to verbal commands?"

"He will stop and go on verbal command alone, but you'll need to use the ribbons to steer."

She looked doubtfully at the straps in his hand. "How can you steer if you're holding both in one hand?"

"You can hold one in each hand if that makes you more comfortable. But as you grow more accomplished, you'll find them easier to hold in your left hand while indicating the direction you want to go by pulling up on the proper strap with your right. I'll demonstrate."

At the drive's end, he used his forefinger to pull up, ever so gently, on the strap.

"You only have to lift lightly."

Again, she studied him closely, probably committing his movements to memory. Still, he was all too conscious of her gaze.

"I'm surprised Trusty could feel so gentle a tug."

He wasn't. He suspected even Cassandra's lightest touch could make him turn.

"He's well-trained," he explained, reminding himself he must be equally well-disciplined.

⇥⟫⟩✕⟨⟪⇤

CASSIE NOTED HARBURY'S subtle movements, but, truthfully, she was less interested in his technique than his hands. Eliza had been right, Cassie reluctantly admitted—a man's hands could be fascinating…even when gloved.

He held the reins with such a relaxed grip, he appeared carelessly indifferent, and yet, with the subtlest tug, Trusty responded. Without any apparent effort, he proved his mastery over both horse and vehicle.

Which made her think of other ways he could put those hands to good use.

Indecent ways.

To bring her wayward mind to heel, she turned her gaze to the countryside. First, they traveled past several fallow fields and then by planted rows containing multiple laborers. As they passed, the men removed their hats and stood.

Once, that is, they'd realized the duke himself was driving.

Apparently, a duke in a pony cart was quite the curiosity.

Some reactions went beyond amusement or even startled surprise. Some of the men looked downright shocked. Shocked as if every notion they held of the Duke of Harbury had come into question.

But surely, they must have all seen him—and, before him, his father—on numerous occasions. And some might even have been working the land long enough to remember Lady Sarah, and her governess, as Harbury's history of the cart indicated, gadding about the grounds.

Despite the slight discomfort of being on display, she couldn't regret Harbury's choice of conveyance. Having her husband drive her himself was…pleasant.

Natural, almost.

Of course, they were not navigating Rotten Row atop a high-sprung curricle with a pair of prime steppers during the fashionable hour. But wouldn't she feel proud if they were? For the first time, she rather regretted their departure from London.

Not that many fashionable *ton* could be found on Rotten Row this time of year.

Even Eliza, Redver, and her sisters had decamped for Ravenswood—after, according to Eliza's last letter, Eliza had returned triumphantly to Almack's final assembly of the Season and brazenly waltzed with her own husband.

Her gaze back slid toward her husband. While the Almack's incident had been the catalyst for their false courtship, the "courtship" had not officially begun until the next day.

On Rotten Row.

Hard to see him now as the same man.

On that day, at Lady Asquith's urging, she and Eliza had both worn hats with brims so wide as to be ridiculous. She'd had to tilt her head to a stargazing angle just to get a good look.

He'd worn mirror-buffed, tasseled Hessians, a coat with too many capes to count, and a hat that sat raffishly askew. As he'd drawn his horse alongside Lady Asquith's carriage, he'd lifted his chin and kept a neutral, haughty expression, but his skin had taken on a grayish hue, as if he were facing execution rather than meeting a young lady he genuinely admired.

Of course, Eliza had just given him a pointed cut…which, thankfully, he'd been gracious enough to ignore.

But when her eyes met his, his haunted look had transformed into profound consternation. She'd been devastated when she'd realized he would have swept any woman into that waltz, but his reaction to meeting her on Rotten Row had made her heart flutter with renewed hope. In that moment, she thought he was seeing her—*truly* seeing her—in a deeper way than he had at Almack's.

And she'd believed he'd liked something he saw in her, possibly even reluctantly.

But she still wasn't sure if she'd deceived herself.

Just as she was now uncertain whether his kisses, his familiar conversation, and his teasing were overtures indicating his growing attachment. She wished she could be sure they were.

Perhaps then, she could be bold enough to invite him back into her bed.

As Trusty trotted around the side of a rather large barn, the Townsend farmhouse came into view, bringing Cassie's reflections to an abrupt halt. She hadn't known exactly what to expect, but she'd a vague sense they'd be visiting a small home, possibly even a thatched-roof cottage.

Instead, the building did not fit what she considered "a cottage" at all, flexible as she knew the term to be. The Townsend dwelling was a proper house. Not nearly as large as Willowhurst, of course, but of a size rivaling the most comfortable inns along the North Road.

The Townsends had done well indeed, which became even more apparent when Harbury gave Trusty the vocal cue to stop. Both Mr. and Mrs. Townsend waited for them on recently whitewashed steps. And a well-dressed groom was ready to assist them down and then to tend to Trusty while they made their visit.

Harbury made introductions.

While Mrs. Townsend gave them both an effusive welcome, even more effusive after Cassie had revealed the contents of her basket, Mr. Townsend remained unsmiling. His manners were otherwise polite, but Cassie sensed tension in the man's stance. And she sensed anxiousness in Mrs. Townsend's manner, too.

They settled in a comfortably, if not grandly, appointed parlor, but the conversation remained stilted. Either Mr. Townsend had no intention of speaking his mind, or her presence, and his wife's, held him in check.

Cassie made a quick calculation. She knew the purpose of this visit was Harbury's desire to forge a genuine connection with this tenant, and she wanted to help. So, she contrived a reason to separate the spouses.

"Tea would be most welcome, of course," she said in response to Mrs. Townsend's offer of a hot beverage. "But might I see your kitchen garden first?" She glanced meaningfully toward the window. "On the way over, I noticed a few ominous looking clouds on the horizon, and I would not want to lose the chance."

"Surely," Mr. Townsend interjected, "a duchess has little interest in a farmer's kitchen garden."

"On the contrary, I particularly wanted to see Mrs. Townsend's fenugreek." She turned back to the woman. "I've been told your tinctures are the very best to be had."

Mrs. Townsend beamed. Then, however, she darted a nervous glance at her husband. "Well, I don't know—"

"Please, Mrs. Townsend." Harbury flashed his most charming smile. "My wife could talk of nothing else on the way here."

Cassie hadn't mentioned the plant on the drive, as Harbury well knew. But she and her husband shared another moment of unspoken communication. As far as she was concerned, he'd just given her carte blanche to make her own alliance.

"Well, then," Mrs. Townsend finally agreed. "Come this way,

Your Grace."

Cassie glanced back at her husband with an encouraging expression. "We'll return shortly."

As they passed through the kitchen to the rear door, the Townsend's maid-of-all-work stopped what she was doing and curtsied deeply. Cassie wished they hadn't encountered any staff. Her intent was not to win notice, but to establish a mutual regard with Mrs. Townsend.

So, she listened attentively as they wandered through the tidy plots, inserting a question or two when they came upon a bed with a plant she did not immediately recognize.

While Cassie had more knowledge of the topic than some, Mrs. Townsend was, indeed, quite the accomplished herbalist. A Townsend treatise would be much more useful than Harbury's father's pedantic description of ornamental grasses.

"If I were to put together a journal of sorts, would you be interested in contributing a description of your methods?"

Mrs. Townsend blushed, stammered and demurred.

"You have valuable knowledge to share," Cassie insisted.

"I will consider a contribution to the scheme if my husband agrees," Mrs. Townsend replied carefully, referring to the same husband whose raised voice interrupted their conversation at just that moment.

Both ladies pretended not to hear. Instead, they examined plant leaves until Mr. Townsend again fell silent. Cassie strained to hear her husband's response, but his conversational tone was so low and quiet, she couldn't make out any words.

Well done.

She was proud of Harbury's calm appeal to reason. Gentle ponies weren't the only thing he didn't feel the need to dominate. Unlike Mr. Townsend's apparent need to dictate his wife's actions.

"Surely," she said, looping her arm through Mrs. Townsend's, "your husband could have no objection."

Mrs. Townsend chuckled. "You haven't been married long,

have you, Your Grace?" Her face softened with a smile. "My husband is no tyrant, mind you. He's happy enough for the gifts we receive in exchange for my tinctures. But neither would he relish the idea of his wife's name on a journal in the big house."

"I'm sure your husband would have unique knowledge to share as well. For instance, we could ask him to contribute favored methods of, say, animal husbandry."

"Showing us favor might cause an uproar among the other tenants."

"I see," Cassie murmured.

"And here we are." Mrs. Townsend came to a stop in front of the largest bed in the garden and beamed proudly. "My fenu-greek."

The spindly plants were full of long, thin, pea-like pods. Though the plants looked healthy, many pods were already browning. Mrs. Townsend pinched one off and then carefully peeled back the stem. Small yellow seeds fell into her palm.

"The seeds," Mrs. Townsend explained, "not the leaves, are used to make the tincture. The pods must be carefully collected, the seeds removed just so, then left to thoroughly dry. Then, the seeds are lightly crushed with a mortar before being added to a strong spirit."

"Sounds like a good deal of work."

"Oh, it is. The seeds ripen during the summer months, and, as you can see, are near ready to be harvested."

Cassie cast a critical gaze over the bed. She couldn't imagine the length of time required to remove every pod without damaging the plant.

"I hired day help last season," Mrs. Townsend said. "This year…" her voice trailed. "Let's just say I hope I won't have to let any go to waste. The priority is, of course, the grain."

Cassie glanced up in surprise. So, despite the appearance of prosperity at the Townsend Farm, things were tighter this year than they had been the last.

"Perhaps I could be of service?"

"You?" Mrs. Townsend exclaimed in surprise.

"Yes. Unusual, I know. But my interest is a longstanding one. My mother was known for her salves. And, as my husband said, your tincture is considered the very best. I'd be very interested to see the process, and if I am to observe, I absolutely must insist on helping. I hate to be in the way."

"You're welcome, of course. Fair warning, the seeds won't be properly dried for a few days, longer, perhaps, this year."

"I will come twice, then," Cassie replied.

"Even after the grinding and mixing, it'll be four to six weeks until the spirit can be strained."

"Oh!" Cassie sighed. "I hope to be in London by then. Harbury has kindly offered to show my younger sisters the sights and to introduce them to some friends during the little Season. All three of them should have been out by now. But with five daughters—"

"*Five?*"

Cassie nodded, letting the rest go unspoken. By now, Mrs. Townsend should understand that she, though adequately provided for, had not come from great wealth.

"What a fine thing, then, you have the duke."

From inside the house, Mr. Townsend's voice rose again. Cassie made out the word *prices*. A moment later she heard the word *greed* and then, quite clearly, *no regard*.

"Oh dear. *Oh* dear." Mrs. Townsend's hands bunched in her apron. "I *told* Mr. Townsend to hold his peace."

Cassie hesitated, then laid a hand over the woman's. "Don't you worry yourself, Mrs. Townsend. If Harbury had taken offense, he would have summoned me to take leave. And if something has gone wrong, the duke needs to know."

"But he must know already." Mrs. Townsend's brow furrowed. "We have been given to understand there was to be no rent relief come Michaelmas on the duke's order."

Cassie could neither confirm nor deny the woman's assertion, but she doubted he would refuse to hear his tenant's concerns.

After all, he'd been the one to suggest they come today.

"Has relief been requested?" she asked.

"Oh yes! Anderson tells us the duke will not budge." She shifted her weight. "Pray forgive me for speaking plain."

"There's no need for forgiveness," she replied. "Especially if you are in distress."

"Not Mr. Townsend and me," she replied. "Things are tighter, yes. Profits are down. But our fields aren't as prone to flood as some of the others, and Mr. Townsend, well, he's a fierce one concerning economy."

"His care and attention show," Cassie offered encouragingly, hoping to learn more.

"He spends time *every day* reconciling his expenditures and his income." Mrs. Townsend held up her fingers and counted on them. "A strict quarter reserved for rent and salaries, a quarter for clothes, food and other expenses, a quarter for upkeep, the tithe to the church, and the rest kept in careful reserve." She dropped her hand. "His planning is why we have been able to keep all our employees even though prices have dipped and why we were able to send our youngest son to university. He's a London solicitor, now, and manages several small estates."

"Does he?" she asked, surprised. "How wonderful. But what of the other tenants? Has the refusal of rent relief caused unrest?"

Mrs. Townsend's eyes dropped. "There hasn't been any trouble as yet. But Mr. Townsend and I both fear the peace is temporary. There's growing anger among some of the tenantry."

"I see." Cassie cast a troubled gaze over the fenugreek, thinking. "When, exactly do you plan to harvest?"

"If I can find the help, I would harvest later this week. The seeds should be dried by Thursday next."

"I will see what help can be spared from the Hall for the harvest, the grinding, and the processing."

"Any help you choose to send would be much appreciated, Your Grace."

"Are there any other wives in the area you think would be

willing to join us?" Cassie ventured hopefully.

"Well"—Mrs. Townsend squinted as she thought—"Let's see. Mrs. Grayson and Mrs. Bottlesworth have both expressed interest in my garden."

"Would you be willing to invite them, too?"

Mrs. Townsend shrugged. "Many hands make light work. Some have wanted to know my secret for years, you know. The trick, however, is never as much in the recipe as in the care taken during preparation."

Cassie shared a conspiratorial smile. "Perhaps you could promise each a special bottle? Paid, of course, by me." She'd use her own pin money if she must. "And, I'll have Cook prepare a light luncheon."

"You're quite determined, aren't you?"

Cassie nodded. "I'd like to become acquainted with my husband's land…and the people."

"Ah, so your interest isn't just about fenugreek."

"No," she replied. "I'd like to develop trust, so that any concerns the wives may have can be shared and understood in comfortable environs. You know how men are. They must posture. And they must be in the right."

"I have to say, the other wives won't appreciate my having been free with my tongue."

"I've no intention of getting anyone into trouble," Cassie reassured. "Just the opposite, in fact."

Mrs. Townsend lifted her brows. "There *has* been a growing frustration between the tenants and Mr. Anderson."

"I suspected as much," Cassie confirmed. "Frustration leads to anger, anger to distrust. And then small problems become impossible to solve."

"Are you certain you wish to get involved?"

"But of course," Cassie replied. "This is my home now. The Hall can hardly thrive if the rest of the estate is suffering."

Mrs. Townsend studied Cassie. Finally, she nodded. "I will see what I can do. Provided Mr. Townsend agrees, mind you."

"Of course." Cassie replied, concealing her sudden fear Mr. Townsend would prevent the meeting.

Her own father had never wanted her mother to call on their neighbors without him. Since he'd only rarely visited Willowhurst, that meant her mother and sisters formed few friendships outside their family circle.

She'd never considered asking Harbury for permission before she made this plan. Would he have denied her if she had?

He didn't seem inclined to control her movements, but he had shown a propensity to be protective. Perhaps she needn't tell him yet.

If she didn't ask, she couldn't be refused.

First, she would discover whether or not her efforts were likely to produce fruit, *then* she'd let him know of her plans. She was far too excited at the prospect of being able to make a valuable contribution to be unnecessarily thwarted now.

CHAPTER EIGHT

Aᴏꜰᴛᴇʀ Cᴀssᴀɴᴅʀᴀ ᴀɴᴅ Mrs. Townsend returned from touring the kitchen garden, Mr. Townsend moderated his manner. Harbury sent up a short prayer of thanks. However, as the visit went on, both wives continued to flutter nervously. And throughout the tea, they exchanged more than one covert glance.

He'd been afraid Mr. Townsend's booming voice had seeped through the walls. Just how much had Cassandra heard? Mr. Townsend had made shocking accusations.

According to Townsend, Anderson had refused every concession requested, even those made by the most loyal and productive of tenants. Instead, Anderson had threatened every one of them with eviction in Harbury's name.

Harbury had made Townsend what assurances he could without completely defaming his steward. When times were hard, rumors proliferated, and tempers flared. Anderson had been with the estate for too long, and Harbury owed him too big a debt for him to take the part of a single tenant, no matter how upstanding.

On the other hand, he could no longer dismiss the anonymous letters. The warnings appeared to have at least some merit.

He and Cassandra took their leave, and Cassandra thanked the Townsends for their hospitality, going so far as to grasp the older woman's hand in a warm and friendly gesture.

He admired the way his wife put the people around her at ease, the way she easily facilitated conversation. She not only realized Townsend had something to say but would not speak freely with his wife present, but she had also acted to remove the obstacle.

He was grateful.

With an affectionate smile, Harbury settled his wife into one side of the cart and then climbed onto the other side. He ordered Trusty to walk, lifting on the horse's right rein as he navigated around a bend in the road.

If Anderson was, for reasons he could not fathom, intentionally undermining him, he had even greater cause to be appreciative of his wife. If Harbury hadn't come home when he had, the estate could be facing a much bigger crisis. Now, he'd a chance to find the problem's source.

He was glad he'd suggested they make the visit together, even if Cassandra had overheard some of Townsend's bile. Maybe he should also ask her opinion about the letters?

Briefly, his gaze flitted to Cassandra before returning to the road.

Revealing the letters' existence now would also make plain his initial reluctance to take the warning seriously, necessitating, in turn, an explanation he was not yet willing to give, at least not until Cassandra was more certain of her position and her role.

And after they'd reached a resolution on the matter of bedchamber doorway etiquette.

As they reached an area of fallow, but open field, he called for Trusty to stop.

"I think we should be well out of earshot of any of the farms by now." He waited for her to volunteer something…anything… of what had passed between herself and Mrs. Townsend. Instead, she fidgeted with her skirts.

"How much did you hear?" he asked.

"Mr. Townsend's voice certainly carries." She hesitated. "Yours, however, does not. But I didn't have to hear much to understand he was upset."

"Yes, well…" Harbury cupped the back of his neck and

winced. "The details are complicated." A plausible enough explanation. "I must consult the records more closely, else risk a false conclusion. I intend to look over the ledgers going back a dozen years or more."

She frowned. "Does the problem stem from your father's time?"

"I am inclined to believe the problem is mostly due to market conditions, but his notes in the margins of Anderson's reports could suggest a solution."

"Why don't you simply ask Mr. Anderson?"

"Oh," he kept his voice light. "I intend to consult him, of course."

She offered a slight smile. "I am sure you will find the root of the problem. And you're not alone, either," she added carefully. "Allies, remember?"

"Yes, allies." But not the kind of ally he'd expect to take the brunt of battle. Or the kind who needed to know *every* detail about the problem's potential source. "Did Mrs. Townsend mention any specific problems? Did she complain to you?"

"On the contrary. She…" For a puzzling moment, Cassandra just stared. Then she turned her face away before continuing, "Mrs. Townsend has invited me to come back next week and help with the preparation of her fenugreek tincture."

He frowned. "Have you any interest in the preparation of fenugreek?"

"Yes! I'm *very* eager to learn." She spoke with heightened enthusiasm. Though he'd asked for no explanation, she added, "My mother was known for her salves, but she prepared them covertly, because my father disapproved of witch-like ways."

"We've a still room at the hall," he said, somewhat absently. "I'm sure Cook would—"

"As I told you," she interrupted, "even Cook prefers Mrs. Townsend's tincture."

"Very well." He blinked. "Attend if you wish."

She worried her lip. "Some of the wives of your other large

tenants will be attending as well."

Other tenants? That couldn't be good. If discontent had taken root, a gathering was the last thing he needed. Gatherings were perfect for inflaming tensions.

He rested his gaze on the horizon.

Then again, if the group contained only ladies, what harm could be done?

"Will the husbands be meeting as well?"

"No. I made—" she stopped herself again. "What I *meant* to say was *Mrs. Townsend* assured me the group would consist strictly of wives."

"And do you think they would be comfortable with you in their presence? You *are* a duchess."

"I'm also the daughter of a country squire. I'm far more accustomed to farmers' wives than you'll ever be." She looked down at her hands and scowled. "And you needn't repeatedly remind me of my station. As if I needed to be reminded. As if I were likely to forget!"

Perfect.

Now, along with Townsend's, he'd set his wife's back up, too.

"Cassandra…" He dipped his head, attempting to catch her gaze. When he had no success, he placed his thumb beneath her chin and lifted her face.

"What do you want?"

"I just upset you. I want to tell you I'm sorry."

This time, the apology had slipped with surprising ease from his mouth. His eyes widened of their own accord, a mirrored expression of her own.

"I understand. This afternoon must have been difficult for you. And I appreciate your apology."

Her skin's warmth at the point of contact seeped through the layers on his glove. Combined with the brush of their thighs, any chill he'd been feeling melted.

"You must be exhausted," she continued in a softened voice. "Let's not talk through everything now. You promised me a driving lesson. Why not give me one?"

Ah yes, the driving lesson.

He'd been in a merry mood when he'd suggested the diversion. Seemed like ages hence.

"Are you sure you're up for the challenge?" he asked, trying to find the teasing note he'd used.

"*You* said I had a fighting spirit."

"So, I did." And she had remembered.

…Which meant his approval *meant* something to her, did it not? *Progress*. The afternoon's prospects brightened.

"If you sit to my right," he offered, "I can more easily assist if needed."

"Very well, then."

Mindful to keep the balance and not to startle the horse, they stood and carefully switched sides. She held his forearms while he steadied her by the waist as if executing a country dance move.

While he wasn't *extensively* familiar with women's undergarments, he'd seen enough sketches and paintings to realize her flesh's pliancy beneath his hands meant she had donned stays of the shorter variety. He wondered if they had serviceable ties attaching the arm straps, or if she fashioned them with pretty bows like—

"You may let me go, now."

Oops. She was staring at him as if he were an oddity.

"Yes, of course." He released her, steadied himself on the cart's spindled back, and then took his seat. He really had to find a way to open the door between their chambers.

And soon.

He lifted the reins and laid them across her open palm. "As I said before, you may keep the ribbons in separate hands as you learn, but once you develop a feel, you should be able to hold them both in your left hand while using your right to steer."

She tested each method. "One hand feels better."

"Good," he approved.

She braced her feet against the board. She appeared calm,

confident, but she was sitting too stiffly for him to be easy. He withheld criticism of her posture, hoping she'd find her way.

"Walk on," she called.

Trusty didn't move.

"Deeper," he suggested. "And louder."

Her quelling look caused him to purse his lips, suppressing his smile.

"Trusty," she said in a commanding voice, "Walk on."

Trusty pulled ahead at a slower pace than if she'd been stepping. Apparently, neither he, nor Trusty, had developed full confidence in Cassandra's skill.

He turned forward, so as not to increase her nerves by watching too closely. But he studied her technique with the occasional surreptitious, sideways glance.

She was doing well.

Better than he'd expected, in fact. Eventually, Trusty, too, let down his guard and moved from a walk to a trot. Cassandra's whole body tensed at the horse's increased pace.

"Loosely," he reminded.

"I *am* holding loosely."

"Trusty, slow," he called out.

The horse slowed.

Cassandra glanced heavenward. "If he responds so well to voice commands, why do I have to keep hold of the reins at all?"

"He would likely find his way home on his own, but what if the Hall was not your destination? He cannot read your mind. And once you learn to drive, you can take the cart anywhere you wish to go."

Cassandra wrinkled her nose at him.

She was terribly cute, even when flabbergasted.

"Besides," he added, "learning to drive is much easier when you can practice on a well-trained horse."

Despite his attempts at reassurance, she remained stiff.

"Trusty, stop," he called out.

The animal stopped. He took the reins and laid them carefully down.

"Give me your hand."

Reluctantly, she placed her palm into his and he circled his fingers around her wrist, pressing the pads of his fingers into her glove as if he were seeking signs of life. Fleetingly, he wished neither of them were wearing gloves. Because if they weren't wearing gloves, he could trace the vein up her arm and—

"Yes?"

Her prompt intruded on his thoughts. *Pity.* "Keep your wrist flexible. See?" He wiggled her wrist. "*This* is loosely."

Finally, she gave up resisting and relaxed her hand.

"Very good."

Her mouth twisted. "You just want me to be compliant."

He snorted. "*Occasional* compliance would be nice."

"May I have my hand back please?"

"Not yet." He ran his thumb over her fingers. "I've always liked your hands."

"You have?" She gazed at him, her expression part apprehensive, part intrigued.

"When we first met, you were always so still, so controlled, except for your hands. Your hands were nearly always in motion. Occasionally, I'd fancy that if I watched your hands enough, their movements would reveal all of your secrets."

"You *want* to know my secrets?"

He did.

He wanted to know her secrets. But he couldn't demand them until he was willing to reveal his own.

"*Are* you keeping secrets from me?" he countered.

She dropped her gaze. "Why would you ask?"

"Just a sense." Actually, he'd been speaking metaphorically, but she didn't seem as forthcoming as usual, did she? "You were fluttering your hands during tea. And you balled up your fingers just now."

"I was anxious about making a good impression at the Townsends."

A perfectly valid explanation. "And I suspect, equally anxious about making a good impression on your *irresistibly* handsome instructor?"

"Ah!" She groaned. "The insufferable duke returns."

"Insufferable? Me?" He touched his chest. "I'm wounded."

"You're not," she accused.

But his ruse had worked to dissipate the tension. She grinned as she took back the reins.

"Trusty," she commanded, "walk on."

The cart bounced along in relatively comfortable silence, except for the seat's repeated smacks to his bum. He'd have to plan a future lesson on how to avoid the worst of the ruts. Right now, she simply needed to build confidence.

"I'll tell you one secret," he whispered confidentially, "if you promise not to let anyone know."

"Yes?"

"The first time I attempted to drive, I held myself too rigidly, too."

She smiled. "Was your teacher equally as patient?"

"The coachman helped me develop my skills."

But the first time he'd driven someone else had been Viv.

After he'd stolen the cart, he'd accidentally driven into a ditch. She'd overtaken him just as he'd been peeling away his coat to work the wheel from the rut. Her scolds had quickly quieted. And, when he'd turned around, she'd shocked him by backing him up against a tree and then kissing him senseless.

The memory flitted through his mind, leaving only a twinge of embarrassment over the stupidity of his prank.

He hadn't felt even a hint of nostalgia!

Perhaps that was because there wasn't anywhere he'd rather be—in the present or in the past—than right here, teaching his wife to drive.

"My ambition was to become skilled in as short of time as possible," he went on. "A gentleman should understand the expertise of those he employs, else he might be fleeced, you know."

"Your father's maxim?" Cassandra queried.

"No." He shook his head. "My father couldn't be bothered with the concerns of his underlings. The maxim came from our old coachman."

"Were you close to him?"

"I was," he replied thoughtfully.

He conjured the old coachman in his mind's eye, heard the old man's brogue, his booming laugh. Unlike his fleeting memory of Viv, this recollection left a strange, achy feeling in his chest.

My God.

Could he possibly be missing the coachman?

Coachman—that's what they'd always called him, John Coachman…heaven only knew if he ever had another surname— had been gone for…

Well, since long before his father had passed.

He compared the sting he'd just felt with the heavy feeling he got whenever he summoned a specific memory of his father. He decided the heaviness he felt on those occasions was less grief than guilt for having fallen short of being the perfect son.

Which meant he missed John Coachman, and he missed him more than he missed his father.

Understandable, perhaps. While his father had been a model aristocrat, his skills in other areas had not been nearly as well developed.

Patience with wayward children, for instance.

Before Harbury had gone away to school, he'd been close to some of the staff. All of them—including Anderson—retainers left over from his grandfather's time. Seemed like every holiday, he'd come back to the hall only to be told another one of them had either been pensioned off or had passed on.

His father had found his interest in their welfare unseemly.

Was his father's insistence that he keep his distance from the staff then why he'd held himself so aloof from everything now? Moreover, had he held onto his single-minded attachment to Viv because indulging memories of her kept him from feeling the depth of his frustration with his father?

"Earlier—"

His wife startled him out of his reverie.

"—I called you insufferable."

"I took your insult in jest," he replied.

"I meant it in jest…" She hesitated. "*This* time. But Eliza and I used to call you insufferable. *The Insufferable Duke.* Unfair, I know. But there was the Almack's incident." She smiled apologetically. "I just want you to know I don't think of you as insufferable anymore."

"I'm glad I've improved in your estimation," he commented dryly.

"You have. And in my defense, you had nearly ruined me. If I had nearly ruined you, what would you have called me?"

Unfortunately, when he'd first told Adrian about her, he'd called her *the silly chit.*

Unfairly, too. They hadn't even been properly introduced. He'd just been piqued because he'd been drunk and angry with himself.

But what would he call her, now?

He tilted his head. "Now, I'd call you the best choice I ever made."

She blushed and looked away.

"You're catching on," he said.

Her glance was furtive.

"Driving, I mean," he clarified.

"Thank you."

Suddenly, she yanked up on the right rein and the cart jerked to one side.

"Trusty. Stop! Now." The horse came to an abrupt stop, but the cart did not, a violent see-saw of wheels nearly toppling them.

"What the—" but before he could finish his exclamation, she had jumped to the ground. She was already heading for the brush. "Cassandra!"

"I'll be back," she called over her shoulder.

Trusty made a noise melding both annoyance and protest. Harbury glanced between Cassandra and the horse before climbing down from the box and trudging over to soothe the animal.

"Sorry boy," he crooned. "I've absolutely no explanation."

Noise in the shrubbery alerted him his wife hadn't gone far. Still, he breathed a jagged sigh when she reappeared, leaves sticking willy-nilly from her hair. In her arms she held a squirming ball of mud and fur.

"Mercy," he breathed.

"How clever and excellent a name," she said beaming. "What do you think?" She spoke to the ball of filth. "Shall we call you Mercy?"

"What," he asked with some aspersion, "are you holding?"

She lifted a puppy. A disgusting, dirt-splattered puppy who couldn't have weighed more than a clove.

"I'd like to keep him."

He scowled and drew back. *Absolutely not.*

But she was flushed with happiness and crooning as if the abomination were something precious.

"Of course," he found himself saying aloud.

"Oh, thank you!" She twinkled up at him. "Would you drive the rest of the way? He's shaking, he's so afraid. I want to hold him close." She demonstrated her intention whispering. "We'll get you home and then you will be washed and fed."

His heart shifted in his chest.

She'd always be gentle with something in her care, wouldn't she?

Even when angered, she did not act in haste or, like many men he knew, out of a need to assert their authority. She'd been furious with him and the worst he'd gotten was a leveled, annoyed glance.

He was lucky, very lucky indeed he'd chosen Cassandra for that fateful waltz. And very lucky she'd proposed. Marrying her *had* been his best decision.

He glanced warily at the dog.

He only hoped the pup would not prove one of his worst.

CASSIE PRETENDED SHE did not notice Harbury's distaste for Mercy.

Not everyone, she knew, had a partiality for animals. Her father, for instance, had been renowned for the quality of dogs he raised for the hunt, but had never liked to handle them. Like everything else, the dogs had only been means to advance his ambition. Had he known his daughters played with those dogs when he was not in residence, he would have been mortified.

And objectively, in Mercy's case, disgust was a natural reaction.

Mercy's long hair was stringy in some places and completely matted in others. His floppy ears were dotted with things she suspected were pests. When she'd first spotted him by the roadside, she'd thought he was a dead rodent.

Then, rather heroically, he'd lifted himself and scrambled down the ditch.

How had he come to be there?

Had he been hit by a passing cart? Thrown from a carriage?

She smoothed the fur on either side of his face and looked down into his eyes. Apparently, she had a partiality for big brown eyes because she was instantly smitten.

The feeling did not appear to be mutual.

He turned his face toward Harbury and squirmed. She had to grip even tighter to keep the dog from scrambling into her husband's lap.

She understood the draw. She sighed. Who wouldn't want a man like Harbury?

"Settle," she crooned, running her hand from the pup's head

to his tail. *"Shhh."*

The little thing's heart was beating rapidly, his eyes were anxious. A well of anger bubbled up. What kind of monster had left something this precious by the side of the road?

She couldn't yet tell the breed, if indeed Mercy had one, but he didn't look like a mongrel. And he didn't look like a hunter or sheep dog, either. He was the kind of dog preferred by London ladies. A lap dog, she was almost sure.

Another Harbury Hall mystery to solve.

The abandoned puppy's origin. The unhappiness of supposedly well-managed tenants. The library's disorganization at only one end. Most disconcerting of all, the unclear desires of a reluctant husband who sometimes appeared no longer reluctant at all.

She stole a glance in Harbury's direction.

But she couldn't fault him for sometimes being guarded and careful.

She was, too. After all, she hadn't told him about her plan to rally the wives. And she'd also withheld the truth of her growing attachment.

He wanted her, that much was clear. She believed he liked her, too. Clearly, he had good intentions. So why were they both holding back?

She held the puppy close to her heart and, heedless of filth, pressed her lips lightly against the top of his head.

If only showing her affection to her spouse came as easily.

CHAPTER NINE

HARBURY SPENT THE rest of the trip back to the hall avoiding the curious wet nose at the tip of a cone-faced creature of single-minded intent. Once they arrived, he thought Cassandra would relegate Mercy to the stables, but no. She marched the animal toward the laundry room.

Metaphorically throwing up his hands, he headed toward his study. Then, a cacophony of exclamations echoed through the corridors. He pivoted, intending to put a quick stop to the madness.

Gently but firmly, he was going to insist the dog be given into the gamekeeper's care. A gamekeeper would know best how to care for wild things, would he not?

He reached the kitchens and searched the gaggle of cooing undermaids for his wife.

"The thing must go to the stables," he said.

"Thing?" Cassandra's gasp seemed to pass from maid to maid.

"That, your grace, is a spaniel," Mrs. Pratt said with a regal sweep of her hand.

"Of the King Charles variety," Cassandra added. "Or so Mrs. Pratt tells me."

"That's right." The housekeeper beamed at Cassandra as one would an excellent pupil. "Just the same breed," she furthered, "as the dog who stood loyally by Mary Queen of Scots and refused to leave her side when she was executed."

On this pronouncement the women all turned worshipfully

admiring gazes to the dog as if he had been the creature who'd shown such unwavering devotion. Mercy, in turn, propped himself up on his tiny front legs and lifted his chin, yipping and blinking as if in confirmation of his noble descent.

"You." Harbury set his fists on his hips. "Are just a scraggly little mutt."

"Harbury!" Cassandra stepped in front of the dog. "No!"

The maids fawned over his majesty, soothing the puppy's wounded pride with a flurry of towels, treats, and brushes.

"We have things well in hand here," Mrs. Pratt told him while unceremoniously shooing him from the room. "Your Grace, I believe, will be much more comfortable in his study."

Huh.

With an ease that left Harbury more than a little envious, Mercy had established his court. How one creature little bigger than a teacup could send an entire household into an uproar, he'd no idea.

He gave up trying to reason with the crowd and went back to his study. There, he set his mind to other pressing problems. Mercy clearly had the household in his thrall.

First, Harbury penned a note instructing Anderson to provide the footman with the rest of the account books from Rose Cottage. Then he went back to reading his father's filed correspondence.

Of the records he had on hand, he could find no evidence Anderson had ever acted against the prior duke's interests or intentions. In fact, one letter his father had filed away indicated the old duke had, indeed, used a prior slump to evict smaller tenants.

He sat back in his chair, rubbing his finger along his bottom lip.

He was not inclined to take as hard a line on the issue. If he delayed rent collection, the estate's finances would suffer a hit, but not an insurmountable one.

This drivel is what you suggest? Have you no understanding of how to lead? I cannot prevent you from taking my place—God help me, I wish I could.

He sighed. Perhaps he was wrong to break with tradition, but optional expenses, since his father's time, were down. Unlike his mother, Harbury was not fond of gambling, nor did he have his father's profligate spending habits. But dare he implement untested methods?

What if he failed, proving his father right?

And, if he must pension Anderson, how was he going to find a steward he trusted on such short notice?

He continued to ponder the questions while dining with his wife.

Cassie brought the beast with her, of course. "Because Mercy was still unused to his surrounds." She promised, on entering the dining hall, the pup would sit calmly in his basket.

Mercy had other ideas.

More than once, Harbury plucked the squirming thing from his lap. On the other hand, the pup had been cleaned, fed, and properly combed. Harbury had no choice but to admit Mercy's allure.

He was soft. He absolutely reveled in affection. And he had the habit of staring up at Harbury as if he'd never seen anything so fascinating. Harbury moved his hand through Mercy's fluffy fur, tracing a line from the pup's tiny head down to his tail.

Hard to ignore such devotion.

Harbury grimaced as he took his port. If only his wife held him in equal esteem.

Later in the evening, Harbury found himself, once again, in his bedchamber. He'd donned a banyan over his nightshirt, and stood, barefooted and curling his toes into the carpet, in front of Cassandra's door.

His desire for his wife had drawn him there, but a distinct scratching noise stopped him.

"For shame, Mercy!" Cassandra's voice bled through the cracks. "You shouldn't scratch good wood! You don't want to get banished to the stables, do you? Because"—she lowered her voice—"if he hears of this latest travesty, he'd send you there in a thrice."

Harbury snorted softly. Yes, *he* would.

At present, however, his reasons would have little to do with door scratching and more to do with a desire to be alone with his wife.

Alone and intimate.

"If you want to ingratiate yourself," she instructed, "and clearly, you *do*…you *must* be on your very best behavior. We *both* do."

Only one of those things was true. He wouldn't mind in the least if his wife decided to be naughty. Naughty, of course, in highly specific ways.

He smothered a groan and rested his forehead against the door.

"So sweet," she murmured. "So very sweet."

What the devil would he have to do to make her croon at him with such tenderness?

"*Must* you be contrary, too?" he heard her ask.

If Cassandra opened the door, he wouldn't be contrary at all. Like Mercy, he might do a little squirming and yipping, but he would be *very* content to simply snuggle at her breast.

"Very well, since you cannot be still, I will put you down."

Mercy resumed scratching in short order. Cassandra made a sound of frustration.

"Oh, so it's *him* you want? Ungrateful little thing. *I* was the one who extracted you from the briar patch. He doesn't like you at all."

Unfair.

When she'd found Mercy, the dog had been utterly disgusting, but his appearance had since improved. But for the ridiculous bow someone had tied around Mercy's neck which, in Harbury's opinion, proved a grave insult to the dog's dignity, the pup was quite cute.

Not nearly as compelling as Cassandra, but—

A thud against the wood reverberated against his forehead. His breath caught as he listened for the latch's click.

But no, the sound had not been a knock…or other request for entry but something softer. Something like her back hitting the door.

"I understand." Rustling sounds suggested she'd just moved to pick the dog up. "Believe me, I understand. I want him, too."

The downward rush of blood through his veins happened so fast he lost balance. That, he decided, constituted an invitation. He braced himself on the door handle, and, before he could talk himself out of his resolution, he unbolted and opened the door. Then, moving quickly, he successfully rescued both dog and lady from an inadvertent tumble.

One he'd caused, but still. Heroism was heroism.

"Harbury!" she exclaimed at the same time the puppy yelped.

"I heard a scratching noise," he said, carefully righting her.

She held the dog away from him as if he posed a threat. Meanwhile, Mercy used all seven-ish pounds of his puppy strength to repeatedly surge in Harbury's direction.

He sighed. "Give me the mutt."

"No!" she insisted. "I won't have him taken to the stables!"

"I won't take him to the stables. I'm not any danger to him, I promise." He placed his hand over his heart for good measure.

She sent him a warning glance before reluctantly transferring the squirming mass into his arms. Once safely against his chest, the puppy stilled. Mercy was a warm little thing. And he'd just brought them together. How could Harbury not be grateful?

"There now," he said with a touch of Scottish brogue. "Calm yourself, wee laddie."

Cassie put her hands on her hips. "Where did that come from?"

He glanced up from the dog's adoring gaze. "The thicket?"

Her turn, apparently, to roll her eyes. "I meant to inquire where a good English duke picked up a phrase like *wee laddie*?"

"It just slipped out." He frowned. "The coachman I was telling you about earlier, the one who taught me to drive, was Scottish. He used to let me play with the dalmatian pups he raised to ride alongside the carriages."

He'd forgotten all about those dogs.

"Oh!" She looked pleased. "So, you do like dogs?"

He wouldn't go so far as to say he *liked* them, but *this* dog was growing on him, and fast.

He scratched Mercy beneath his chin. The puppy sighed and went completely limp.

"I like this one. I suppose."

She briefly brightened. Then, her face fell. "Then I suppose you'll want to keep him with you tonight?"

He glanced down at the dog.

Mercy, indeed.

"You," he spoke to the dog in a commanding voice, "will get what you want if you do what you're told. Do you understand?"

The dog tossed his head and snorted.

Harbury considered that an agreement. He walked over to his bedside and then placed Mercy carefully into his pillow's crevice. His scent should be enough to keep the thing calm for a time. Mercy propped himself up on his front legs and glared upward accusingly.

"Those are expensive sheets," Harbury laid down the law. "You are not to muss them."

"He's just a pup," Cassandra said from the door. "Ergo, messes are not his fault."

"Did you hear her?" Harbury asked the dog. "A jury of one has preemptively declared you not guilty. I might be inclined to agree. However"—he glanced over his shoulder—"If I have to spend one more night in frustrated want of my wife, the consequences will not be my fault."

Her mouth formed an unspoken *oh*.

"Frustrated want in general?" She folded her arms over her night rail. "Or frustrated want specific to me?"

Harbury made a low, growling noise in his throat.

Visibly, she swallowed. "I'm not sure if that constitutes an answer."

Mercy yelped. Harbury turned his attention back to the bed. The pup ambled to the mattress's edge and barked hopefully.

"No." He pointed to the pillow. "Back."

Mercy ambled back, made a full circle, huffed again, and sat down.

"Oh. My. *Heavens*." Cassandra enunciated. "Does *everything* simply respond to your command?"

He ignored her. "Sleep."

The dog curled into a tiny ball of white, brown, and tan.

"You're very sure of yourself all of a sudden."

"No, I'm not."

He was unsure how to exercise his authority on the estate, and he was even more unsure how he should go about seducing his wife. He *was* sure, however, of his intention to seduce.

As he swiveled back, his banyan fanned out around him. "And, to answer your earlier question"—he stalked toward the door—"you're the one I want. Right now." He pointed to her chamber. "In that bed."

Her eyes widened. Then, she turned away. Had she just dismissed him or had she invited him in. *Invited*, he decided.

He crossed the threshold and closed the door behind him.

"DUCHESS."

Cassandra had swiveled and was heading into the sanctum of her too-pink bedchamber. But, as Harbury used Cassie's title as a low command, a claim of possession, tiny hairs on the back of Cassie's neck stood at prickly attention.

In fact, her whole body came alive in the manner of an animal gravely alert to the hushed presence of a predator. But she was not a puppy in need of training. Nor a dog to be ordered to come and go as he pleased.

She ignored him. Or, at least, ignoring him was what she'd intended to do.

Instead, some feral, excited part of her, oblivious both to the obvious danger and the need to take a stand, decided to turn and face her tormentor.

Harbury had come closer than she'd expected.

Close enough he didn't need to fully extend his arm to cup one hot, bare palm against her cheek. His gentleness sharply contrasted his tone. His calluses brushed against her cheekbones. He was an oven alive with flame, warming her with his desire.

As if she needed much encouragement.

If not for her occasional, self-protective sparks of anger, she would follow Harbury around with a persistence even Mercy would find excessive. But before she relented, she needed him to know she would not be satisfied with carelessly scattered crumbs.

Slowly, he compelled her to lift her head. His eyes glittered, his lips appeared soft and inviting. The dimple in his chin just begged to be touched. She gazed into his face, feeling not just trapped, but hopelessly lost.

One should never, she decided, attempt a marriage of convenience with a man so inconveniently compelling. In a reflexive gesture, she placed her hands lightly against his chest. She had intended to push him away. But she didn't push.

Instead, she became keenly aware of his muscles beneath her palms and the strength within those muscles. The rough protrusion of what must be his nipple scraped against the fleshy area just beneath her thumb, causing an increased heaviness in her breasts.

Her own nipples were already hard and aching.

Her forefinger twitched, and the fabric of his nightshirt bunched up between her fingers. Part of her hand landed on the exposed skin beneath his collar.

The jolt left her trembling.

She inhaled, an in vain attempt to steady her breathing that merely served to flatten her breasts against his ribs. Then, pressure warmed the small of her back—his other hand, she realized, urging her ever closer, increasing the contact between them. He gripped her waist, clasping her so tightly against him she could feel his male organ.

If she truly wished, she could break away, but her heart demanded she stay.

She arched, simultaneously raising her gaze and parting her lips. His face blurred as he tilted his head and claimed her mouth. The kiss was long and still, a brand, a deep impression, but for the way their bodies subtly rocked as they breathed.

Wanting to hold him closer, she fanned her hands away from his chest, up and over his mounded muscles. As her palms came to rest against his upper arms, his bicep flexed. She'd never been more aware of his power, and yet, she was no longer scared.

He withdrew. She wet her lips. His small, responsive smile embodied triumph.

"Why did you kiss me?" she asked, as though the pressure against her belly did not make the answer obvious.

"This time"—an amused light slowly dawned in his eyes, transforming his grin into a self-satisfied smirk—"we *both* required distraction."

Distraction. She scowled.

Why had he turned such a lovely moment into a jest? Not only a jest, but a joke calling forth the most difficult of their encounters.

"I could throttle you," she whispered.

"To throttle me"—he cocked a brow—"you'd have to put your arms around my neck."

"Hands," she corrected.

"Very well," he acceded lightly, "*hands.* Though hands are implied, I would argue, by the word *arms.*" He paused, and for a long moment, the only sound was that of their comingling breath. "Show me."

Her gaze dropped to the part of his neck completely male. His Adam's apple. His *throt-bolla,* in Old English. There, he was vulnerable, too. What would he do if she had him at her complete mercy the same way she was always at his?

She could turn away. Give him a dose of his own medicine.

Tell him, for instance, she had *letters to write.*

But the drive to claim him was too strong. So instead, she dragged her hands up his arms and onto his shoulders, staying fully connected to his heat. She rested her thumbs on either side of his throat just above his collarbone and her fingers on the back of his neck. There, she counted his heartbeats as they throbbed against her finger pads.

"Precarious," he murmured.

She felt him swallow. "I know." She raised her gaze. "If I pressed hard and long enough, just here…" Lightly, she demonstrated. "You would faint."

"Interesting tidbit of knowledge."

"A lady must know how to protect herself." Her turn for a small smile.

"From her husband?"

"Especially from her husband." And even more so when, like herself, the lady was in love with her husband's oblivious self. She ventured another upward glance. "By the way, if your intent was to distract me, your plan has failed miserably. I'm not distracted at all."

"Quite the opposite, in fact," he agreed, with inexplicable cheer. "I'm fully aware, too."

"Are you admitting another impulse of yours went awry?"

"I wouldn't say *awry*…my impulse has led us here, no?"

"What's here?"

"Whatever we make it."

Her sense of triumph wavered. Was she ready? She glanced to the bed and back. Could her bruised heart survive another intimate encounter without placing her fully, irrevocably in his power?

Then again, who was she jesting?

She was already fully his. She had been, since she'd first laid eyes on him at Almack's.

"I don't know how to do this," she admitted. "Not just *this*, but…be married. Married to someone I barely know." And hopelessly, unrequitedly loved. "But…"

"But what?" he encouraged.

"But I *want* to know you."

Her confession surprised them both.

"I want to know you, too."

Craning her neck, she raised herself onto her toes and leaned in. She'd intended, for the first time, to voluntarily kiss him, not the other way around. But, as their mouths met, again he took control. He advanced, with expert use of lips and tongue until her knees went weak. Soon, she was pressed back into the crook of his arm, soft, surrendered, and fully dependent on him to stand.

He broke the kiss to gaze down at her through low-lidded eyes.

"I must be mad," she whispered.

If she were sane, she would be daunted, or, at the very least, tense. She was so small in his arms, and he loomed so large…almost as large as he loomed in her mind and in her frequent, far too vivid dreams. But the heartbeat fluttering rapidly against her ribs was not beating in fear. Nor did she feel caged. This time, she was secure.

This time, she was desired.

And, yes, she was certain his desire was specific to her.

His taut cheeks, his dilated eyes betrayed his complete absorption, leaving no room for thoughts of anyone else. For once, she was sure he wanted her as much as she wanted him.

Yes, she was already lost. Yes, she was at his mercy.

And, if she had her way, he'd never forget this night.

✦ ❧ ✦

CHAPTER TEN

T HE CORDS IN the back of Harbury's neck ached with long-held tension, though less so now that his wife had threaded her fingers into his hair. She ruffled and teased his curls, unaware, he suspected, of the sensations she aroused and of how those sensations placed him entirely in her power. Beneath her fingers he became pliant, moldable—a drastic change from just a few moments ago, when he'd needed to summon an untold amount of willpower.

If I pressed right here hard and long enough, you would faint.

His Cassandra, his *sweet* Cassandra, had boldly, intentionally threatened to strangle him.

His mind had recognized her challenge as a test, but his body had seized on the danger. For one, mad moment, he thought she would succumb to the wrong kind of temptation, wrap her hands around his neck and squeeze the consciousness from his body.

How heavy her small hands had felt. His swallow had increased the pressure of her thumbs, and he'd become aware of his lifeblood throbbing. She could have, with the slightest pressure, readily restricted, restrained his access to air.

He suppressed a shiver.

Then, instead of hurting him, she'd done the opposite. She'd confessed her ignorance, her desire, and then—sweet angels in heaven—she'd lifted herself onto her toes to kiss him. Her kiss had been so gently and willingly offered, the merest touch of her lips had awoken in him something possessive, something animal.

She whispered about madness of her own, spurring him to reclaim her mouth with unthrottled, fierce desire. Her knees gave way, but his clasp was tight enough to prevent a fall.

Now, each subtle sign of her surrender heightened his focus. And, judging by the dreamy way she continued to caress his hair, passion had rendered her not only compliant, but eager. She clung to him in a way that made him feel as if he'd caught a gift dropped from the heavens.

He had, he realized.

If he had plucked some other lady from the Almack's crowd that fateful night—her sister Eliza, for instance—everything could have gone badly. Right now, however, he regretted nothing. Cassie felt as if she were made for him, not just physically, but in spirit.

He cradled her neck as he wrapped her even closer to his heart.

Could this be the first time he'd ever truly held his wife?

The devil.

He'd been inside Cassandra, for God's sake. He'd kissed her soundly, he'd held her hand, but they hadn't, to his recollection, simply embraced. If they had, he would have remembered the way her body fit to his—not when lying on a bed, but when standing, as they were now.

Everything between them had been backwards from the start. He intended to reverse course.

Now.

"I'm taking you to bed."

Not a stated desire, as in *you're the one I want. Right now. In that bed.* Nor a question, but a statement of unambiguous intent.

A fact.

He bent down, cupped the back of her already bended knees and then lifted her from the floor. She wasn't heavy, and yet every one of his muscles strained.

Anticipation left him taut. Taut and yet vibrating everywhere, all at once. If he were a string, he'd be emitting a low, clear, and soulful sound, much like he was humming a growl of possession.

She crossed her ankles, stroking one of her calves with the other while flexing her toes. The bedframe squeaked in protest beneath his knee. His ears pricked, praying the sound had not disturbed the pup.

All he heard was Cassandra's heartfelt sigh.

Gently, he released her onto the bed. As her head sank into the pillow, he followed her single, dark braid's line as the weave snaked around her neck and then down into the valley between her breasts. Even wretched with need, he could still derive profound pleasure from simply gazing at his wife.

He settled by her side, crooked his elbow over the pillow, and rested his cheek on his fist. Her breath was light and fast, her upper arms covered in gooseflesh. Her flushed skin betrayed her hunger for his touch.

He wondered how he could have ever thought her unresponsive. Then, he remembered.

The last time they'd lain thusly, she'd been hesitant and still, meeting his gaze either to then quickly close her eyes or to turn away. This time, she was gazing at him as if he had the answers to every possible question in the universe.

Her confidence gave him a sense of pride—false pride. He didn't have any answers.

Where bedding was concerned, he hardly knew more than she did. He'd been so inept at seduction on their wedding night, when she'd reached out to him, he'd kissed her and told her he was *honored*.

He suppressed a snort.

Excellent way to express yourself, Lothario.

This time he intended to keep the *intimate* in *intimacy*. To do so, however, he'd need to take a risk. And he'd need to keep her connected to him, verbally, physically, imaginatively.

"Touch me again," he urged. "Anywhere."

Her thickly lashed eyes closed, briefly, only to reopen, focused on his throat.

"That is," he amended, "if you'd like."

"Wouldn't my touching you be strange?" She raised her gaze. "For you?"

"Not strange." He paused. "Erotic." His groin tightened with anticipation "Exciting." *New.* "Go ahead…"

With hesitant, feather-soft fingers, she traced from his cheekbones, up his nose, over his eyebrows, then down past his ear. Finally, her hand rested against his jaw. She touched him as if she couldn't see him at all. In truth, he was revealing more to her than he'd ever expected to show anyone ever again.

He offered himself purposely, shielding nothing, leaving every emotion billowing up plain on his face. Not just his needs—carnal and those even deeper—but also raw, unbidden frailty spiking up from hidden, empty places, empty places he had once believed could only be filled by someone else.

Only Viv had seen those wounds.

The vulnerabilities he'd revealed to her, however, had been unintentional. He simply hadn't yet learned to fully hide weakness from a woman he loved. Not, at least, in the way he'd been trained to hide his furious, pained reactions to his father's thrashings.

He must have flinched because Cassandra frowned.

"You're thinking too much." Again, her fingers flitted over his brow. "I don't want you to think." Her tone deepened. "*Especially* of anyone else."

Yes, he was thinking. And someone else had been part of those thoughts, too. But not in the way she believed.

"I'm fully present." And he was. He was embodied and aware, like a sailor with eyes trained on the sea. He'd do everything he could to navigate to a safe harbor. "I'm not thinking of anyone else. I don't want anyone else but you."

He cupped her opposite arm, a physical entreaty that she believe him. Her breasts brushed against his chest as he leaned in to place a warm, lingering kiss just above the bridge of her nose. The furrow in her forehead gradually flattened beneath his lips.

Her hand crept up his back until her fingers were again threading through his hair.

She let out a shuddering sigh as she forced his head down.

"Kiss me again." Her breath teased his face. "Kiss me as you did at the ruins. Kiss me properly and put my dreams to shame."

"My pleasure," he replied, bringing his mouth down hard only to give himself completely to the heavenly softness of her lips.

CASSIE WAS, IN essence, trapped beneath her husband. And though she did not think she could escape him, her heart inexplicably soared free. With deliberate provocation, she bent her knee, making sure she slid her thigh along the hard length she now understood was his manhood.

In response, he groaned and deepened their kiss.

How could touching in one place—their mouths—leave her throbbing in another? A place, in fact, she didn't have a word to name?

But a lack of verbal identification didn't stop her body from demanding attention *there*. She was swollen and hot and greedy. She wanted to be beneath him, to take him fully into her body.

She'd always been told the point of the "marital act" was the planting of a babe, a tiny being to grow inside her—part him, part her. She wanted to carry his child, physical proof they would forever be entwined. But her true desire had always been to plant herself in his heart.

He pushed himself up without breaking their kiss, pressed down on the inside of her knee and maneuvered into the space between her thighs. Last time, her body had responded to his as if he were a threat. This time, his confidence, his ease, his sincerity, released her from those shackles.

He'd told her he was fully present. As his hands stroked her flesh, she didn't have anything left but the present. If she wanted to live—fully live—she must hold on for dear life.

She had no past. She sensed no future. Only now.

Only him.

He touched her as if each careful caress spread thick and vivid paint on her body's canvas, forever changing how she would be seen, how she would be perceived, both by herself and by others. She was no longer Cassandra, sweet and gentle. She was Cassandra, wanton and bold.

When finally, he pulled back, his eyes had a strange and thrilling glow.

"I missed this," he murmured. "I missed you."

How could he miss something he had never known?

As soon as her mind formed the question, her heart rebelled.

She understood what he'd meant. The promise of this passion had existed between them from the very start. What was happening felt less like an introduction and more like a return.

Under his gaze her breasts became even heavier, more exquisitely sensitive. Every time she took a breath, she tingled as her night rail raked over her puckered skin. The titillating sensations, too, were only a promise, a foreshadow of something to come.

On their wedding night, he'd caressed her nipple, and she'd mewed in embarrassed protest, not because the sensation hadn't been pleasurable, but because she'd felt too much pleasure.

Outrageous pleasure.

She'd neither anticipated nor prepared for the surge of desire. Now, if he did not touch her there soon, she thought she might thrash.

As she studied him shyly, a slight smile graced her lips.

"You can touch me," she repeated his earlier invitation. "If you want."

"Oh?" The sound he made was part groaning want, part laugh. "Oh, yes, I *want.*"

She heard the slight rumble beneath his breath and understood the implication. His desire laid bare. She sympathized. The same, torturous need driving him drove her. Earlier, she'd thought she'd gone mad. If she had, two were now locked in the same asylum, and she wouldn't want to be anywhere else.

She'd expected—*no*, desperately wanted—him to touch her breasts.

Instead, he loosened the already askew ribbon securing the bottom of her braid. Taking great care, he slowly unbound her hair. When he got to the nape of her neck, he bid her to sit up so he could finish. When he was done, her locks lay wildly about her shoulders.

She never had left her hair like this, not in front of anyone but her mother, sisters, or maid.

His gaze softened and he sighed deeply, as if the sight of her with her hair undone was something he'd desperately needed. Maybe, one day, she would ask him if he wanted to brush her hair before she made the braid.

"Cassandra?"

"Yes?" She couldn't imagine what he'd ask. Every possibility left her breathless.

"Would you take off your night rail?"

"It's pretty," she said stupidly. She'd embroidered the edges herself.

"So are you."

She blushed, but she held his gaze.

"Please?" He sent her his heart-tumbling smile. "For me?"

Was there a limit to what she'd give him? Right now, she wasn't sure. She only knew she was hot and achy and wanting desperately to know, well, not what came next…she remembered penetration well enough from the other night.

So, what did she want to know?

She wanted to know the answer to the secret, forbidden promise building in her blood.

He knew, she was sure.

And, if she had to be naked to find out, too, so be it.

She drew her legs in close and shimmied the garment up and over her body. She hadn't even gotten the thing over her head when he groaned again. She tossed the rail to the side and then lifted her mass of hair over one shoulder.

"Just let me look at you." He reached out and fingered a lock of her hair. "Looking at you makes me happy."

She lowered her eyes, all too conscious of the imperfections no one else had ever seen.

"Do you mind?" he asked.

Her answer would depend on what he meant by *mind*. Cold air wafted over her breasts and her thighs, but a feverish heat was flaming up the side of her neck. A blush, she supposed. A blush— she glanced at her upper arm—making her splotchy all over.

"Not really…but only because you seem pleased."

He hummed in assent. "More than pleased."

Mad man. But wasn't one supposed to humor a person showing signs of losing their mind? Gradually, she relaxed. She tucked her legs to the side, and slowly lowered herself back down, resting on an outstretched arm.

"Venus would be jealous," he murmured.

Still, she rewarded his praise with what she hoped was a tempting, alluring smile.

He shifted his position. If she reached out, she could touch the part of him about which she was most curious. The part she hadn't been able to acknowledge, even after…

Well, especially *after*.

"Would you like me to take off my nightshirt?"

Her gaze flew back to his face. She wasn't sure she did. But neither would she say no with his brows lifted in such a hopeful fashion.

Slowly, uncertainly, she nodded.

If he noticed hesitation, he didn't let her reluctance influence his speed. Before she could avert her gaze, his nightshirt was fluttering to the floor, and he was kneeling in front of her in all his Grecian-statue glory.

He was…different from her, to say the least.

"Too much?" he asked.

Her mouth quirked. "A little."

"Then"—he rose to his knees and lifted her back into his arms—"let us concentrate not on sight but on touch."

One more bone-melting, twisting kiss and she found herself back in the position they'd been. His weight, all his delicious weight, pressed her down into the mattress.

She turned her face into his shoulder, attempting to avoid another startling look at his manhood. She expected him to proceed directly to the bedding, just as he had before. Instead, his soothing strokes migrated upward to her breasts.

"May I?"

Though his gaze was fixed on her nipples, she wasn't sure why he was asking permission until he dipped his head. When his mouth closed around the peak, she stiffened in shock. Then, as his tongue swirled, she sighed.

Trusting him to be her guide, she gave up the last of her resistance.

He sucked gently, then more insistently. When she couldn't take anymore, he transferred his attention to the other nipple and began the process anew. She relaxed enough for her hands to wander. They found their way back into the soft curls just above base of his skull. Gradually, however, the need building between her legs became so acute, she stiffened.

By the time his hands drifted lower, she was near out of her mind with want. So out of her mind, she didn't protest at all when he put his hand between her thighs. She expected the contact to be brief—the same brief "check" he'd done before.

If she'd been "ready" on their wedding night, she was certainly ready now.

Instead, his hand lingered, hovering just above her folds while he moved his fingers in ways that left her legs shivering. She hovered beyond control, in a state of pure sensation, until something inside her cracked, drawing from her a guttural moan.

Behind her closed eyes, a blinding light ushered in a feeling of unfathomable closeness, complete connection.

His breath heated her neck as he positioned himself above her. She clung to him as he entered her. She felt no pain, only fullness, and she moved to meet each of his thrusts. Stars lingered beneath her lids, and then her body trembled with yet another, deeper release.

Soon, he was shuddering too. Shuddering and calling her name.

"Cassie," he said.

Not Cassandra. Not Duchess. But Cassie.

A name only used by those she loved and who loved her in return. Even as her heartbeat quieted, her emotions continued to mount.

Mindless of his damp hair and the sweat dotting his brow, she clutched him against her breast and softly kissed his crown.

Everything could work. Everything could, in fact, turn out far better than her wildest, most ardent dream. One day, he might even confess his love. One day, he might tell her Viv no longer mattered to him. One day he might confess he'd been a fool to mistake youthful love for what he had with Cassie, for what, together, they could build.

Once he did, only then would she be able to fully unburden her heart.

Only then could she tell him how much she loved him, how much she loved him now, and how much she would love him for the rest of her days.

CHAPTER ELEVEN

WHEN HARBURY AWOKE an hour later, Cassandra was gone. He smoothed his hand over the empty place where she'd lain; the sheets were already cool to the touch, but the bedside lantern still burned. He rolled onto his back, stretched out his legs, and pillowed his head with his arm.

After the lingering shudder of his *little death* had ended, Cassandra continued to hold him softly against her breasts—a heavenly, erotic sensation.

Bewildering, too.

His wife's sweet ministrations ushered him into a deep and restful sleep. He'd felt safe. Perhaps for the first time in his life.

Safe.

On their wedding night, he'd used the word safe. Thinking Cassandra had cried out of fear, he'd told her she was safe with him. He'd meant that she could trust him to do his duty by her, and that, as his wife, she would want for nothing. But what he wanted now was even more consuming.

He wanted, though impossible, to take away all her fears.

Occasionally, he caught her gazing blankly at some decades or even centuries-old flourish of plaster or object of art gracing the walls of Harbury Hall. She was, he suspected, finding the life of a duchess more daunting than she'd anticipated. But how could he ease her unease when he'd never mastered his own?

From the day he'd pinned on the ducal coronet, he'd been dangling above the world, suspended as if he were one of those great balloons he'd once seen floating above the ground in Hyde Park, a monstrosity held aloft by fire and heat. Like those balloons, he'd found his trajectory just as impossible to control.

Those fears, he knew, had grown out from an even deeper dread, fright that had taken root so early in his youth he couldn't place the time. He'd always been different from his family, emotional in ways they could not fathom.

Beholding beauty in the world inspired in him greater happiness; feeling pain, greater devastation. His father's actions implied the sensitivity that made him different also made him loathsome. And he'd accepted that as truth.

But, perhaps, his differences made him capable of a deeper devotion.

After Viv had left him, anger had vined up from his fears, two emotional aspects with the same germination. Ever since, the wild flora now firmly fixed within him had grown sharper and thicker thorns.

Tonight, Cassandra had pruned those thorns with her simple act of love. Previously obscured possibility appeared. Now, he was certain he could change...*improve.* He could set aside the past. He could create a better future. Not just for himself and Cassandra, but for everyone on the estate.

With care and attention, he could mend the rifts Anderson's odd behavior had created. Even if addressing the tenants' concerns would mean a fundamental change to the way the estate had been run during his father's time, he would make those changes. Anderson had always enjoyed the prior duke's complete confidence, but Harbury intended to stand his ground.

Obviously, the old way was no longer working.

But estate decisions were the last things he wanted to contemplate right now. He'd much rather be focusing on his wife. Where had she gone?

He leaned over the bed, and, with a groan, he retrieved his nightshirt and banyan from the floor. If Marsden knew how carelessly he'd cast away his garments, he would be horrified.

Almost as horrified—he smirked—as Cassandra had been when he'd first taken them off.

Ladies, apparently, were less captivated by the male form as most men were by the female shape.

By contrast, nearly every feminine figure fascinated him. Plump or skinny, heavy in the upper, rounded in the lower, or—saints be praised—shaped like a bloody violin. But he hadn't lied when he'd told Cassandra that his desire was specific to her.

Now that he knew his wife better, he understood her kind nature formed part of the secret to her allure. When he'd chosen her that night at Almack's, had some part of him grasped that her beauty was her heart made manifest?

Possibly.

One thing, he knew for certain: tonight, she'd given him the gift of her uninhibited release, a gift he intended to cherish. As for her tender and nurturing embrace… Well, unrest and uncertainty be damned, he would not allow anything in the wide world to come between them.

He'd tell her now, only, first, he had to find her.

He donned his nightshirt, shrugged back into his banyan, and rose from the bed to check his chamber. Cassandra wasn't the only creature missing. Mercy had disappeared from his bed as well. He pressed his hand into the indentation the puppy had left in his pillow.

Dry, thank heaven.

He hadn't exactly been thinking clearly when he'd ordered an untrained puppy to go to sleep atop his bed. He did not, however, regret his decision. Even a wet bed would have been worth his wife's surrender.

But now he had time to consider the puppy's very presence.

Where *had* Mercy come from?

If the dog was a King Charles Spaniel—and he'd no reason to doubt Mrs. Pratt's judgment on the subject—then the pup had been purposely bred. Mercy wasn't just a mongrel, a stray. He must have been purchased.

Somewhere on the estate, someone was missing a dog. A very expensive dog. At a time when, according to Townsend, income was tight, and people were suffering.

He made a mental note to ask Anderson—

Anderson, again.

He halted his thought.

The letters, the conversation with Townsend, the steward's strange behavior of late…taken together, they left him disinclined to trust the man regardless of his father's confidence and his own long and complicated history with him.

No, he would not be asking Anderson.

Somewhere outside, Mercy yipped. Harbury wandered over to his bedroom window. Sure enough, there she was. She had taken the little beast out to the back garden. Her white robe and nightcap fluttered behind her as she rushed to and fro, never more than a step behind the scampering pup.

He glanced up at the close-to-full moon—the hour was late. Dangerously late.

He scanned along the garden hedge for any signs she might not be alone. He spotted the form of a man holding a lantern standing in the doorway—Tull. *Thank God.* Strange things had been happening. Cassandra must be protected. She was important to him.

Possibly—he rested his forehead against the cool glass—even essential.

Just then, Mercy went bounding off in the garden gate's direction. Tull and Cassandra sprinted into motion at the same time. Mercy, however, interpreted their actions as a game—when either got too close, he darted in the other's direction.

Harbury's tension eased, and he chuckled softly. Wherever the dog had come from, the pup made Cassandra happy. From first sight, she'd adored the little terror.

So why had his initial response been to insist the pup be taken to the stables?

Below him, Mercy attempted to scoot between Tull's legs.

The footman scooped up the dog. Mercy's tiny legs continued to pump as if he could propel himself through the air. Harbury frowned. The sight sparked a hazy memory—spotted legs and a rapidly wafting tail dangling from the grasp of another footman. In memory, he lunged toward an ominously closing door.

What did I tell you, Edward? His father's voice.

Tears—then and now—pricked behind Harbury's eyes. *I'm not to bring filthy creatures into your house.* Next, his father's desk drawer had squeaked. Out had come the lash. Harbury's recollection vanished. Beatings themselves all bled together.

His father had drilled into him not to show any response many times. Still, he'd never considered his father a cruel man. Not as cruel as Adrian's father had been, anyway. Harbury knew his nature had alarmed the prior duke, giving rise in the man to an increasingly desperate need to instill his values, his methods, his idea of manhood into his son by whatever means necessary.

Harbury searched the garden below for the soothing sight of his wife.

Outside, Cassandra collected Mercy from Tull and then stopped to exchange a word. Together, they laughed, each of them shaking their heads in exasperation. Then Tull bowed respectfully.

An instinctive pull, a longing to safeguard what was precious to him left him feeling both vulnerable and yet thoroughly, heart-poundingly alert. The emotions surging through his blood were indescribable. The sting in his eyes, acute.

Oh, God.

He stepped back from the glass and pressed the base of his palms against his eyes. What was happening?

Pull yourself together.

He stiffened his spine and inhaled. One simply could not feel both brimming with hope and, at the same time, threatened by a yawning emptiness.

Not unless…

Had her gentleness left him undone? Had he succumbed to

everything his father repeatedly warned him would lead to his ruin?

Panic returned—this time, with sharper teeth.

Mawkish, his father had called him. Thin-skinned. Far too easily bruised.

Overstated, perhaps, but still, a gentleman's sentiments should never be out of his control, *especially* when he had something so vitally important to protect.

Through the doorway between their apartments, he saw her enter her own chamber, puppy in arms. As soon as Mercy caught sight of him, he began to squirm.

"You're awake," she observed.

"So is he."

"He was a very good boy." She admired the puppy with a small, downward smile. "Weren't you, Mercy?" She tickled Mercy beneath his chin. "Yes, you were."

Harbury took an involuntary step toward them both.

She glanced up, studied him, and frowned. "What's wrong?"

Nothing he was willing to admit.

He forced what he hoped was a teasing smile. "I see I have been supplanted in—" *your affections.* His heart and his words both stuttered. "At earliest opportunity, you fled."

"Nonsense." She grinned. "My first thought, I'll have you know, was for your pillow."

For his pillow. "But maybe, just a little, for me, too?"

Her smile softened. Her eyelids fluttered down. "Yes, for you, too."

One, gently whispered sentence razed the wall that dread had erected. She wouldn't lead him to ruin. She was his wife. His very pretty wife. And she was wearing nothing more than a night rail, wrapper and cap.

"Shall Mercy stay with me?" she asked. "Or do you wish him to remain with you for the night?"

"Are you inviting us both to spend the night?" He knew she hadn't been, but he couldn't resist asking.

"If you spend the night in my bed," she replied carefully, "you'll send Sally into a tizzy."

"Marsden will be up first," he reasoned. "He'll give Sally fair warning."

She hadn't rejected him outright, so he reentered her chamber, waited a moment, and then closed the door behind him. She placed Mercy on the floor. The puppy's ears flopped as he bounded over to Harbury's feet. Harbury scooped him up and settled him into the crook of his arm. Cassandra made a soft sound.

Harbury raised his gaze, catching an expression on her he'd never seen before. An expression that could—optimistically—be interpreted as love.

His limbs went heavy, and his throat thickened.

She adjusted her wrapper and then turned away. She sat down at her dressing table and, slowly, pulled off her cap. Lock by lock, her thick, tousled hair tumbled about her shoulders.

"Glorious," he said in a strained whisper.

"I didn't re-braid my hair before taking the dog out." She flashed a nervous smile. "I was too worried about your linens."

He swallowed roughly. "I'm disappointed you did not leave your hair down for me."

"I cannot sleep with it down. If I do, Sally will have a matted mess on her hands in the morning."

"I understand," he replied.

Cassandra picked up her brush and drew the pliant bristles down through the curly mass—dark and rich like chocolate, soft as the petals of a rose. Intimate, watching her tend her hair.

More intimate still, if she permitted him to touch.

He shrugged out of his banyan, transferring the dog to his other arm. Then, he used his robe to arrange a makeshift puppy cradle at the mattress's foot.

"This," he spoke in a tone Mercy would understand, "is for you."

He placed the pup on the bed. Mercy gave the banyan a thorough sniffing before deciding the arrangement would suit. Then, he curled up and sighed, leaving Harbury free to saunter over to his wife.

He rested his hands on her shoulders. "May I?"

"May you…?" she queried.

"Brush your hair."

Her doubtful gaze met his in the mirror.

"I know enough not to pull," he assured. "Whenever Sarah caught me—"

"*Caught* you?"

"Doing something I ought not…"

"Something?"

"With Adrian, undoubtedly." By her expression, he gathered that, this time, she had not missed his near slip. "Whatever the crime, the punishment Sarah extracted for keeping her silence was brushing. Forcing her indignant little brother to play lady's maid was, apparently, a temptation too great to resist."

Cassandra chuckled.

"But brushing your hair"—he leaned down and pressed a kiss to her crown—"would be no punishment."

Hesitantly, his wife relinquished the brush. He lifted a lock from her shoulder and began gently working the brush through to the ends.

"You *do* know what you're doing."

"Perhaps you should trust me more often."

"Perhaps." She closed her eyes. Gradually, the tension drained from her shoulders. "Why do you hesitate so often when you speak of your youth?"

The brush hit a snarl, and he concentrated on untangling her hair rather than answering her question.

"There can't be anything in your past I would not wish to know," she added.

He met her gaze in the mirror. "Are you sure?" *Even the bad parts? Even the embarrassing parts? Even the parts that might hurt you?*

"Yes." She straightened. "Of course."

"Your desire to know me means the world to me, Cassie."

Her gaze went warm and soft yet again.

How could he ever believe the overwhelming feelings she inspired would make him weak, when she looked at him with such tenderness in her eyes? His desire to keep Cassandra safe and whole didn't lessen him as a man, his desire—his *commitment*—made him strong. Strong enough to move mountains.

And wanting Cassandra had never been a betrayal of Viv.

Vivianne had been a raging torrent. In her presence, all he could do was keep from capsizing.

Cassandra, on the other hand, was a lifeline, a rope sailors used to save lives, with a subtle but consistent pull. Where the line might take him, he didn't know.

But he would risk everything to find out.

Yes, he still felt fear, but not the same kind of fear.

The danger here was real. This time, if he gave free rein to his feelings, Cassandra would not become some youthful, romantic attachment.

She would become his very heart.

AFTER THEIR FIRST night of true passion, Cassie and her husband— she could truthfully call him *husband* not just in word, but in actual deed—passed the next few weeks in idyllic pleasure. Harbury took up residence in her bed and showed no inclination to return to his own. He helped her finish the library reorganization, worked with her until she mastered driving the cart. And, best of all, their shared days bled into amorous nights…

Mercy, of course, was wreaking havoc on the household, but Mercy was a puppy. Chaos was expected. Unexpected, however, was the way Harbury was gazing at her right now—as if he'd grant her any wish she asked.

Which, at the moment, was another sausage.

A footman interrupted their breakfast to deliver a letter dispatched from the Townsend farm and addressed to her.

"You're obviously excited." Harbury smiled fondly. "Open it now if you wish."

"Very well." Cassie broke the seal.

She scanned the contents.

Mrs. Townsend had written that Mr. Townsend had, in no uncertain terms, declined to receive help from the Hall. However, she had not given up. She'd waited a few days and then asked him if she might invite Mrs. Grayson, Mrs. Bottlesworth, and Miss Clapham to afternoon tea along with the duchess. To this, he had not objected.

Mrs. Townsend had then taken it upon herself to visit Mrs. Grayson, Mrs. Bottlesworth, and Miss Clapham, inviting each confidentially and in person. All had been most eager to have a private audience with the new duchess.

Most eager had been underlined three times.

Mrs. Townsend then went on to apologize for the short notice, explaining she had only just learned that the men meant to go down to inspect damage to the bridge on the road to Upper Harfield today. Would her Grace, perhaps, be available this afternoon?

Yes. Her Grace would *make* herself available.

She set aside the letter and glanced across the breakfast table to her husband. "Mrs. Townsend has invited me to tea this afternoon."

He set aside his napkin. "And, by your expression, I'm guessing you'd rather attend than accompany me to the rector's?"

"If you don't mind," she replied carefully. "She'll be harvesting her fenugreek, and I did tell her I would like to learn more about how her tincture is made."

"But you also expressly wished to meet the rector's daughter, Miss Clapham."

"As it happens, Miss Clapham is also planning to attend Mrs. Townsend's tea."

His expression suggested he found this odd, but, after brief consideration, he replied, "I suppose that does tip the scales. A discussion with the rectory would be less entertaining than an afternoon tea in the company of Mrs. Townsend and Miss Clapham."

Mrs. Townsend, Miss Clapham, Mrs. Grayson, and Mrs. Bottlesworth.

She considered confiding in him, letting him know the real reason behind the tea, assuring him she only wished to form alliances on his behalf. But Mrs. Townsend had gone to a great deal of trouble, and she did not want to risk the possibility he'd ask her not to go.

Nor had she worked up the courage to destroy their fragile peace by demanding to know if he did indeed refuse to lower the rents, as Mrs. Townsend had suggested. But once she better understood the tenants' concerns, she would broach the subject.

After their visit to the Townsends, there'd been no more talk of battle plans or strategy. In fact, whenever she tried to turn the conversation to estate matters, he always found an artful way to answer her question and then quickly change the subject. Which, of course, made her even less inclined to share her own plans and intentions.

Whether he wanted to discuss the matter or not, they were both responsible for the estate's welfare. And distrust *had* been sown among the tenantry. Besides, allies didn't have to share *all* the information they gathered, did they?

Strategic secrecy was part of every diplomatic negotiation.

"I only hope," Harbury continued, "the rector and I can reach an agreement on a candidate for the living in Harford Chase."

"I still cannot believe the ducal hunting grounds include a village large enough to support a parish," she commented lightly, happy the conversation had moved to Harford Chase and away from her plans.

"The parish is at the edge of the hunting grounds." His gaze warmed. "We've a charming lodge not too far from the village. If you like, I can have the place aired out. Very snug," he added in a velvety voice. "Very secluded."

She lifted a brow. "An appropriate place for a lady, is it, this lodge?"

He shrugged. "If rumors are to be believed about the roguishness of my grandfather, not in his time."

"Was your grandfather...disreputable?"

"Oh yes," he said cheerfully. "*Terribly*. But *you* have no need for concern. My father lived above reproach, as if on a mission to restore the family's respectability." He looked away, frowned and then blinked, as if he'd never considered the two things—his grandfather's scandals and his father's rectitude—to be connected before. "As soon as my father became duke," he continued in a more thoughtful tone, "those kinds of parties ceased."

"Imagine," she said dryly. "A hunting lodge being used to...*hunt*."

"Yes." He sounded disappointed.

"And I suppose you learned to hunt by your father's side?"

"No." He cast his gaze out the window. "Anderson was tasked with teaching both Adrian and me."

She waited for him to elaborate. He did not.

Strange.

His disinclination to discuss the matter any further must have something to do with the steward.

In fact, Harbury had always been reluctant to talk about Anderson. He hadn't, for instance, told her about the shouting match between the steward and Dr. Wilton on Tuesday, a "discussion"—according to Mrs. Pratt—overheard by half the residents of Lower Harfield. Nor had he told her about the Friday prior, when Tull had found Anderson searching one of the bookcases in the library they'd just finished organizing.

She'd a growing suspicion of Anderson. Did her husband have the same?

If so, he had not spoken or acted against the man.

Harbury wiped his mouth on a napkin and arranged the cutlery. "I'll ride over to the rector's," he returned to an earlier topic, "so that you may have use of the carriage."

"Thank you," she said, though she had no intention of inconveniencing the coachman.

After Harbury left, she requested Trusty be harnessed to the cart. Then, she carried a basket of cheeses, bread, and all the oranges cook could spare out to the courtyard.

"Shall I attend you?" the groom asked.

"No, thank you," she replied, with a twinge of guilt.

Harbury had asked her not to go out without a groom. But such a restriction seemed unreasonable when she would be confined to the estate and driving on a road she had traveled on before.

She wasn't disobeying her husband, *per se*.

She was simply interpreting his instruction as one meant for destinations beyond the boundaries of Harbury land.

Perfectly reasonable.

And plausible.

She hoped.

Because bringing along a spy would *not* earn her the estate's women's trust.

CHAPTER TWELVE

Mrs. Townsend greeted Cassie on her steps, just as she had on Cassie's prior visit. Her salutation was warm, but as she introduced Mrs. Grayson, Mrs. Bottlesworth, and Miss Clapham, the atmosphere cooled.

Mrs. Townsend, Cassie judged from the age of her sons, appeared to be around forty. Mrs. Grayson, with her abundant white hair, must be much older. Both Mrs. Bottlesworth and Miss Clapham were nearer Harbury's age, leaving Cassie feeling very young. Very young, and even more inexperienced.

But she'd come too far to turn back now.

Mrs. Townsend suggested they collect the pods before tea. As they worked, Cassie inquired about the various attendees' family's size and health. She encouraged them to discuss their livestock and farms. While working side by side promoted disclosure, by the time they'd snipped half the plants clean, Cassie was running out of questions.

"Might you have anything to ask of me?" she ventured brightly.

The others exchanged significant glances.

Miss Clapham was the first to speak. "Mrs. Townsend tells us you have five sisters."

Not really a question.

Cassie wondered if Miss Clapham had only spoken because the silence had been painful. Cassie would have done something similar in the same position. A lady after her own heart, perhaps?

"Yes," Cassie replied. "I'm the eldest, though by only a few minutes. Elizabeth is my twin. Then there's Millicent and Lenora, a mere eleven months apart, and Annette, the youngest."

"Your poor mother." Mrs. Bottlesworth's eyes widened as if she could not believe she had allowed the exclamation to slip out. "I beg your pardon, Your Grace."

"You're quite right." Cassie smiled. "Motherhood took its toll. Later in her life, my mother did not enjoy good health."

"She has passed on, then?" Mrs. Bottlesworth asked.

"Yes, and my father, too."

"How good, then, that you have the duke on whom to rely." Though Mrs. Grayson's words had been kind, her tone had not.

"I count myself lucky," she responded with care.

"Your sister Elizabeth is, I believe, married to the Marquess of Redver." Mrs. Townsend came to the rescue.

"Master Adrian?" Mrs. Bottlesworth exclaimed.

"Do you remember him?" Cassie asked.

"Oh, of course! He and Master—" she stopped. "He and His Grace ran amok all over the estate when they were young." Her words may have been harsh, but, unlike Mrs. Grayson's cold eyes, the older woman's gaze held only fondness.

"They still do, I imagine," Mrs. Grayson replied wryly. "Run amok, that is."

"Cynthia!" Mrs. Townsend whispered.

Mrs. Grayson shrugged.

Cassie ignored the comment. "My sister and Adrian were here for the wedding, but they have gone back to Ravenswood to oversee the harvest. They took my younger sisters with them."

"On account of your being newlyweds," Mrs. Grayson said with a sidelong glance at Miss Clapham.

Mrs. Grayson's sarcasm confused Cassie.

She and Harbury *were*, after all, newly wed.

She set to extracting a particularly resistant pod. "I wonder..." She let her voice trail and kept her gaze on the pod, knowing she had all their attention.

"Yes, Your Grace?" Mrs. Bottlesworth prompted.

"I haven't heard much from my sisters of late. Lady Sarah is also from home. And I can no longer ask my mother, rest her soul…" She laid the pod carefully in her basket and closed her eyes. She summoned to mind painful recollections from her wedding night to force a blush. "Forgive my plain speaking, but I wonder if I might ask you a question." She paused. "A"—she cleared her throat—"*female* question…"

"Oh! Oh, my dear," Mrs. Bottlesworth said. "Are you—? I mean, could you be—?"

Cassie smiled. "I've been a little queasy in the mornings of late." She hadn't, but sickness on waking was the one symptom she could remember from her mother's last pregnancy. "Is that a sign I might be increasing?"

The collective gasp was a surprise.

Miss Clapham studied the contents of her basket. A spinster could not be expected to answer such a question. But Mrs. Grayson and Mrs. Bottlesworth said nothing either, only exchanged puzzled glances.

Mrs. Townsend, clearly feeling duty-bound as host finally said, "Why, yes. Perhaps if…"

"I am not sure, of course," Cassie interjected. "Please, keep this in confidence."

A cacophony of assurances followed.

"*Well.*" Mrs. Grayson folded her arms. "I wonder what else Mrs. Grant has been lying about."

"Pardon?" Cassie asked.

"Cynthia." Again, Mrs. Townsend used her friend's name as a chastisement.

"None of us mean to gossip." Miss Clapham laid a hand on Cassie's arm. "Only, we'd been told—" Miss Clapham's cheeks turned crimson. "Well, led to believe, that is…"

Cassie frowned in consternation. Had they been told her marriage to Harbury hadn't been consummated? By whom? And, more importantly, why?

"We'd been told," Miss Clapham started again, "scandal had forced the marriage. And that the marriage was only in name."

Cassie supposed this was her fault, proposing a marriage of convenience. Things always got out no matter how hard you tried to keep them private.

Mrs. Bottlesworth turned to Mrs. Grayson. "I told you not to put stock in what Anderson's housekeeper said. You should know better."

"We'll see, won't we?" Mrs. Grayson replied.

"Mrs. Grant?" Cassie asked. "Is she Mr. Anderson's housekeeper?"

Mrs. Townsend nodded, then quickly added, "We had better lay these out to dry and sit down to tea."

Cassie sensed if she pressed any harder, the tentative connections she'd just made would have devolved into silence and suspicion. So, during the rest of the tea, she turned the conversation back toward estate matters.

The more she demonstrated a sincere interest in their well-being, the more they revealed. They spoke of their husband's hardships and concerns, and even made a few, to Cassie's mind, ingenious suggestions for surviving the current slump.

After assuring them she'd keep the details to herself, Cassie made general notes in a tiny book she had brought. She'd have to work up the courage to share those general ideas with her husband, and she hoped that, when she did so, he would be open to implementing them.

But although she made good progress, the knowledge that Mrs. Grant—whom Cassie had neither heard of nor met—had been gossiping about her marriage churned in the back of her mind. Malice, she thought. Pure malice.

But why?

When the visit ended, Cassie, at Mrs. Townsend's encouragement, lingered, becoming the last guest to depart. As they waited for the pony cart to be brought round, Cassie thanked Mrs. Townsend for her efforts.

"The afternoon did go well," Mrs. Townsend agreed. "I knew they would take to you as I have."

"I'm not so sure about Mrs. Grayson," Cassie replied.

Mrs. Townsend glanced heavenward. "Cynthia can be a right stick. You mustn't mind her, she finds fault everywhere. But in times of need, she is the most generous of them all."

"I'd like to know more about this Mrs. Grant."

"Well, she's been with Mr. Anderson since his wife passed some twenty or more years ago. I doubt she meant any real harm."

"But *did* she make certain implications about His Grace and me?"

Mrs. Townsend pursed her lips.

Cassie sighed. "I cannot ask you to divulge someone else's words while simultaneously expecting you to keep mine confidential, can I?"

Mrs. Townsend gave a nod.

"Last time I visited," Cassie tried another tack, "you mentioned Anderson had refused concessions requested by tenants in the duke's name. I don't yet know for sure, but I don't believe the duke was ever made aware of any requested concessions. Now, I hear the man's housekeeper is gossiping…"

Mrs. Townsend's expression altered as she appeared to weigh various considerations. "I can tell you this…much as saying so pains me, Mr. Anderson has been—" She stopped herself. "Well, he is not the man I once knew."

"Could you give me an example?"

When Mrs. Townsend didn't answer, Cassie added, "From your own experience, of course."

"Well, he's always been very reliable. But the last time he was here, he told Mr. Townsend a very…" She searched for a word. "…inappropriate story. And in my hearing, too. Mind you, I don't know how men speak when there isn't anyone of the feminine persuasion around, but what I heard left me downright shocked."

Cassie frowned.

"Why had he come?"

"The reason he gave for visiting was odd, too. He said Mr. Townsend owed him for the use of an ox borrowed from the home farm, but Mr. Townsend had already paid. Lucky thing my husband keeps every receipt. But Mr. Anderson reacted very badly when Mr. Townsend produced proof. Then, a few minutes later, Anderson's mood completely changed again."

"I appreciate you telling me this." She reached out and covered the woman's hand with her own. "Keep watch, will you? If you notice anything else of concern, please don't hesitate to send me a message, just as you sent the invitation today. I know you won't betray a confidence, but if you find out anyone else has had a similar experience with the steward, please tell them they can come directly to me."

Mrs. Townsend nodded.

Cassie had been so absorbed in speaking with the older woman, she had not paid attention to the approach of a horse and single rider. When she looked over her shoulder, she found herself staring into the eyes of her husband.

She withdrew her hand and adjusted her shawl.

Harbury greeted Mrs. Townsend and apologized for not dismounting. "I've come to provide escort to my wife."

The edge in his voice would not, Cassie hoped, be recognizable to Mrs. Townsend.

"I should be getting back," Cassie said. "I can only imagine what kind of mischief Mercy has been getting up to while I've been gone."

"Mercy?" queried Mrs. Townsend.

"Did the duchess tell you we acquired a small spaniel on our way home the last time we were here?"

"A spaniel?" Mrs. Townsend asked, surprised.

"I found the poor thing all dirty and hiding in a thicket," Cassie said. "He's been a delight, but of course, we wouldn't want to keep him if he's simply run away from his owner. You didn't, perchance have a pup go missing?"

"No," Mrs. Townsend replied carefully. "But if I recall, Mr. Anderson's daughter…"

"Mr. Anderson has a daughter?" Cassie asked.

"I would have thought—" Mrs. Townsend stopped herself, then glanced between Harbury and Cassie. Finally, she shrugged. "A grown daughter, Your Grace. But the pup couldn't be hers. She's been married and gone for a very long time."

"I see," Cassie replied. Though she thought Mrs. Townsend's embarrassment odd.

"And here, at last, is your cart," Mrs. Townsend sounded relieved.

As the Townsend's man handed Cassie up into the box, she thanked her host another time. Settling herself on the seat, she took the reins, called for Trusty to walk on, and, with reins in one hand, steered the cart toward the road.

Her husband's eyes remained on her the whole time, even bringing his horse alongside the cart.

She forced herself to think of the morning's successes rather than his ire.

While she hadn't earned the wives' complete trust, she had made progress. She had learned Anderson's behavior had taken a turn. If the change were due to some sort of illness, that could explain why her husband was so reluctant to trace the estate worries back to the steward.

She only wished she had collected proof rather than innuendo.

She sent her husband a sidelong glance, wondering if he'd trust her concerns.

His face was grim, and he rode stiffly—if not rigidly—in his saddle. As a result, his horse moved more skittishly than usual.

Yes, he was angry that she'd disobeyed his instruction about the groom.

Loosely! She wanted to goad him with the same instruction he'd given her during her first driving lesson. She recalled how his fingers lightly encircled her wrist as he demonstrated what he'd meant, the way he'd only reluctantly let go of her hand.

Ugh.

Even when annoyed with him, she still found him attractive.

She couldn't stay angry with him for long. Not with his thigh at eye level, his body slowly, rhythmically rocking along with the movement of his horse, his tousled hair falling across his forehead. He looked so fine.

Then again, his fine looks had never been in question.

Her besotted mind began weaving excuses for why he'd felt the need to retrieve her from the Townsends. Perhaps he'd come to meet her simply because he hadn't been able to stay away. He had, after all, taken up residence in her room.

Sometimes the best defense wasn't an offense, but a diversion. So, as they approached a V in the road, she urged Trusty, not toward the Hall, but toward the bridle path.

"Cassandra!" he called after her. "Where do you think you are going?"

So, they were back to Cassandra, were they?

"The ruins." She tossed a haughty expression over her shoulder. "*Our* place."

"Our—" He paused, looking far more surprised than he should have.

Shouldn't he be pleased she thought with fondness of the place he'd chosen for their first excursion together? For their first kiss?

His gaze fixed on a spot above her head. "I don't like the look of those clouds."

She ignored him and urged Trusty on until, finally, she spotted the clearing with the tie weight they'd used to secure the horses the first time they were there. Without her directing Trusty to do so, the pony slowed.

Odd.

Then again, maybe not. Maybe Sarah's governess had brought Sarah here. Cassie nodded to herself. That made sense. Of course, she would have taught Sarah the estate's history. She climbed down out of the box and was hitching Trusty to the weight when Harbury finally drew up behind her.

"I don't like the look of those clouds either, but, at present…" She let her gaze roam up and down his person. "I very much admire the view."

He puckered his lips and curled the hand against his thigh into a fist as if struggling to hold back a retort.

He intended to be difficult, didn't he?

Well, she'd learned a thing or two in the prior weeks. She placed her hand against his calf. His heat seeped through the woolen stocking below his breeches.

"Surely," she said softly, "you can spare a moment…for me."

He closed his eyes. She studied the struggle on his features, hoping. When he opened them again, she knew she'd won.

She moved back, holding to her shawl while he dismounted and then tied his horse. She'd never taken particular note of the way a man dismounted, but *this* man was a different story. She'd good reason to appreciate the way he moved his body, all controlled confidence and skill.

"Cassie," he said wearily. "You know very well what I asked, and you deliberately—"

"Don't you *dare* say disobey," she interrupted, her voice even. "I agreed to bring a groom when I went out, but I didn't think your directive included a simple drive to see a neighbor on the estate."

"I worry about you."

She searched his face. He did, indeed appear more worried than angry. "What cause have you to worry when you knew I'd be in the company of your own longstanding tenant?"

He hesitated. "Not under normal circumstances, but the last time we visited, Mr. Townsend wasn't exactly welcoming."

"Yes, but *Mrs. Townsend* has been nothing but gracious." She laid a hand against his arm. "Please, Harbury. Trust my judgment."

Again, he closed his eyes. "I do. Only…"

"Only?"

He opened his eyes. The force of his gaze was a physical thud against her chest.

"Only I would be *devastated* if something happened to you."

Ah. The truth was raw on his features. She stepped forward. She placed her gloved hand lightly against his chest and lifted her face.

What fear. What fire. And all his passion was for her and her alone.

She lifted herself onto her toes and then brushed her lips over his own. Even though he did not respond, the voluntary contact sent a rush of heat through her body. Then, his shoulders fell, and he set his hands on her hips.

"You're trying to distract me."

She lifted the corner of her mouth. "I'm trying to turn our attention—both yours *and* mine—to other matters. Harbury"— she moved her hand to his arm—"I don't want to fight."

He stared down at her fingers. "You had your hand against Mrs. Townsend's arm, too."

"And?"

His brow furrowed. "Warmth comes easily to you."

"You, too."

"No."

"Yes," she insisted. "You're always so thoughtful."

"I'm *not* thoughtful." His frown deepened. "I'm not—" He bit down on his lower lip.

"Harbury?"

He closed his eyes, looking pained. "You merely preoccupy my thoughts."

"A pretty compliment." Her gaze dropped to his lips. "If only I were actually capable of such a thing."

His body subtly shuddered as he exhaled. "You are." He opened his eyes and then took her fully into his arms. "You know very well, you are."

She did, now. She smiled against his mouth as he kissed her

deeply.

Her efforts had gone very well.

Very well, indeed.

OUR PLACE, SHE'D said. *Our place.*

Her words had jolted him out of his pique because they weren't wholly true. The Priory could not truly be *their* special place to meet because the Priory had been his and Viv's place to meet.

He kissed her tenderly, more thoroughly aware than he'd ever been that he'd done her an injustice. Or, rather, several injustices. He couldn't make things right…

Or could he?

Suddenly, he recalled the one place on the estate Vivianne had never been. "Come back to the Hall with me," he said. "There is something I'd like to show you. Something unique, secret, and"—his voice dropped—"very exciting."

Her gaze moved between the pathway to the ruins, the restless horses, and the darkening sky.

"Secret?"

He nodded, cradling her cheek. "Secret, secluded, and, should the rain commence, much more comfortable for continuing…our current activities."

Finally, she nodded. "Very well, I'm intrigued."

He handed her back into the cart, and then mounted his horse.

As they made their way back to the Hall, he considered what had happened.

He'd felt a twinge of guilt when, last time they'd come to the ruins, when she'd assumed he'd brought her there with seduction in mind. And then, earlier at the Townend's, he had a sharp reminder that she didn't know as much as she thought she knew about Vivianne. Most egregiously, he'd promised they'd be allies, and he hadn't shared anything about the anonymous letters. Taken together, the three things left him with a creeping feeling such as a thief might feel—one who had gotten away with a crime but knows he will eventually be caught.

The hatchet would fall on him, too.

He'd seen the truth in Mrs. Townsend's face when she'd mentioned Anderson's daughter and Cassandra had reacted with surprise. Why, there wasn't a person on the estate who had not heard the rumor he'd tried to elope with Vivianne Anderson.

The wayward heir's humiliating heartbreak had been too delicious an *on dit* not to share, especially since Harbury's father provided so little fodder for gossip.

No fun for the telltales in gentry whose behavior was entirely above reproach.

This morning, Mrs. Townsend had chosen discretion above tattle. But what were the chances every person on the estate would follow her lead?

He'd have to find a way to tell his wife that Vivianne, Anderson's daughter, and Sarah's governess were all one and the same. And he'd have to brace for her consequent hurt.

But before he disappointed her so deeply, he could give one thing...he could take her to a place Vivianne had never seen, a place which, from thenceforth, would be entirely their own.

And a place, given her fascination with his books, that should distract her with pleasure.

...All kinds of pleasure.

They arrived at the hall, and he escorted her inside. Up until they reached the library, she went along with him willingly enough. But as soon as they entered the long hall, her feet began to drag.

"I'm quite familiar with the library," she said, as he led her by the hand.

"So you believe." He positioned himself in front of the correct bookcase, pushed back the correct book and turned back to his wife, his finger on the lever. "You, my dear, are about to become the first lady to ever learn Harbury Hall's best kept secret."

She leaned in and lowered her voice. "How secret?"

"So secret, even Sarah doesn't know." He squeezed the lever and a section of the bookcase swung open.

"A hidden room?"

"Not just *any* hidden room. An entire vault." He drew her into the space, then closed the panel behind them. "Not *vault* in the sense of crypt, mind you, but vault as in a place where valuables are stored."

Unlike the other walls which had been built of wood and then covered with whitewashed plaster, the walls within this chamber were bare stone. Three bookcases lined the room, one on each wall. A single chair and table stood in its center.

"Sarah knows nothing of this?"

"No. In fact, to my knowledge, no lady has ever entered the room."

"Let me guess?" She said, wandering. "The libertine grandfather?"

"Yes. Although, if even a quarter of the stories told about him are true, less than reputable women might have been welcomed here. In his bachelor days." He paused. "And I'm not sure I'd go as far as to call him a *libertine*. On the other hand, I do suspect he was a member of the Hellfire Club, so…"

"Harbury—*no!*"

He shrugged. "Even in his dotage, he was a good deal more fun than my father."

"From the way you've spoken about your father, I imagine he would have been."

He cocked his head. "*Have* I spoken poorly of my father?"

"Perhaps not poorly, but neither with a great deal of warmth."

He lifted his brows. "He wasn't a warm man."

"Unlike his son."

With that small comment, she'd given him a colossal gift.

Completely unaware, she wandered over to a set of shelves. "Are these books stored here because they are valuable?"

"Some are, some aren't." He came to stand behind her. "Most aren't books at all, only texts. Several languages are represented. French, Italian, a few notable works in English. They are all, however, very rare." He encircled her waist with his arms and pressed his cheek against her cap, leaving his mouth just above her ear. "And all *very* forbidden."

A blush spread pleasingly across her decolletage.

"This one might interest you." He reached over around her and slid out a copy of *Memoirs of a Woman of Pleasure*, better known as *Fanny Hill*.

She opened the book to a page she'd chosen at random. The passage described a young man's anatomy, "*...that storebag of nature's prime sweets, which is so pleasingly attached to its conduit pipe from which we receive them along.*"

She slammed the book shut, shoved it back on the shelf, and then clamped her hand over her mouth.

Uh-oh.

Perhaps the vault had been too much for her sensibilities. Perhaps bringing her here had been foolish. She was trembling.

"N-n-nature's p-p-prime s-s-sweets." She broke out into a fit of giggles. "Not just prime, but p-p-pleasingly attached!"

He closed his eyes and exhaled. Laughter was much better than mortification. And a welcome change from both the tension in their earlier confrontation and his rumination over his mistakes.

Then he chuckled, too. "Don't forget the pipe."

"The *conduit* pipe." She turned in his arms and placed her head against his shoulder. "Oh, Harbury. That *had* to have been written by a man."

"What's this?" He drew back in mock shock. "You don't find my sweets pleasing?"

Her giggles erupted anew, causing him to wrap her close.

"I thought," he said wryly, "only adolescent boys found exaggerated anatomical descriptions amusing."

"I apologize." She wiped beneath her eyes with the back of her hand.

"Apology accepted." He approximated a solemn expression. "That is, as long as you take the state of my pipe into serious consideration."

"Oh," she said with mock solemnity, "I promise I will."

That the same lady who had been mortified on their first night together could laugh and tease him now deepened his affection. She was open. She was brave. And, apparently, underneath her prim exterior, she had a rollicking sense of humor.

His grandfather would have loved her.

She retrieved another book. This one had pictures. She held the book at arm's length, twisted it sideways, and then upside down. "Is this…*pleasurable?*"

"I wouldn't know," he answered honestly.

"Oh." She sounded disappointed.

"We could try it, however," he added suggestively.

She put her hands on her hips "Is this why you brought me here?"

"No," he said sincerely. Not that he'd mind a little joint research. "I wanted to show you something special. Something…private."

"Private indeed." She turned the page. "Oh!" she gasped. "*Ohhh. What's this…?*"

"*Mmm,*" he hummed as he observed. "Looks interesting."

"Would you be willing to try this one, too?"

He groaned. "Most certainly."

"Now?" she suggested.

The books, the pictures, the confined space, the scent of her obvious arousal—they worked together, weaving an erotic spell that replaced his anxious thoughts.

He led her over to the chair, and she sat down. He knelt between her knees, placed a hand on her thigh, and then proceeded to do things with his mouth he'd not only never done, but never thought he'd wish to do.

Her reluctant groans were sweeter than music. The taste of her like nothing he could have imagined. Soon enough, he was drunk.

Drunk on her and near giddy with happiness. When she, at last, was shuddering, he felt almost as satisfied by her release as he would have been by his own.

Almost.

Her legs were splayed, her body, limp. He rested his head against her knee and wiped his mouth.

"My *stars*, Harbury."

Edward, he corrected in his thoughts. *She should call me Edward.*

Why had he never asked her to do so?

The answer was simple—because after his father died, he'd insisted everyone, including Adrian, call him Harbury. He'd thought, if he heard the title enough, he'd feel like he had a right to take his father's place.

He wanted something very different from Cassandra. However, the request she use his Christian name caught in his throat. He'd wait until after he told her everything there was to know about his past.

She peeked over her skirts. "Had you never done that before, either?"

He shook his head *no*.

She grinned. "Would you be willing to do it again?"

He couldn't help himself. He chuckled.

"Harbury!" She sat up. "Are you laughing at me?"

"Not in the least!" He pressed his fingertips to his brow. "My blood…it's collected elsewhere."

"I see." She nodded sympathetically. "Problems with your piping…?"

"You know, I *do* have problems"—he slid onto his back and worked the buttons of his falls—"But they aren't anything you can't attend."

"Oh, my." She giggled again. "Your sweets are *definitely* prime, now."

"Straddle me," he urged. "Check page 57, I believe…if you need instruction."

She held his gaze and her skirts as she knelt over him, one leg on either side. She leaned down over him, and he caught her tightly in his arms. Their exchange had been light, playful, but this—this joining, this special connection to her, could never be anything but sublime.

He savored every second of her expression as she sheathed him. He was so aroused, only a few, upward thrusts brought him to quivering release.

As the pounding in his ears softened, he realized her cheek was still pressed up against his still rapidly beating heart. He pulled off her cap and stroked her hair, content to feel her weight and listen to her breathe.

"I like page 57," she sighed.

"I made up the exact page," he confessed. "It's in there somewhere, though."

She propped her head on her elbow. "Are there any other books you specifically remember?"

She was teasing again but her teasing struck an unexpected chord. He craned his neck, looking for the book she had inadvertently made him recall. He rested his hand in the vacant space where the book should have been and frowned.

"What's wrong?" she asked.

"On our wedding night, I remembered a woodcut I'd seen in a book that should be right here."

"Our wedding night?"

He smiled sheepishly. "The woodcut depicting a noble couple's wedding night. Several people standing around the marriage bed."

"No!" Her eyes widened in horror. "The first time is awkward enough without witnesses! I'm exceedingly glad that custom fell out of favor."

"So am I," he replied. "The book wasn't otherwise salacious, but, after he found Adrian and me sniggering over the picture, my father had the book moved to the vault."

"Now it is missing?"

"Yes. And the manuscript was an original copy in French. Quite valuable, I think." He returned his gaze to the vacant space. "But it's gone."

"Do you think your father moved the book back to the wider collection?"

"Possibly," he replied.

"Well, then. There it must be," she said, twining her fingers into his hair and becoming suddenly very interested in his lips.

"Yes," he agreed. "A perfectly reasonable explanation."

And then he gave himself up to her kiss.

CHAPTER THIRTEEN

TWO WEEKS LATER, Harbury folded his hands behind his back as he leaned over his wife's shoulder, casting a careful eye over several gold chains with various lockets, cameos, and crosses laid across Cassandra's dressing table. Each had a strong point—one delicate, the next elegantly carved, another fit with deep red stones. None stood out.

"Any one of them will do," he said.

She craned her neck, squinting back in a pointed manner. "Clearly, you are unsuited for this occupation."

"You're right." He nodded. "You had better make the choice yourself."

Perhaps *then* they might be on their way. The journey to Lord Wexford's was over an hour by carriage. At this rate, they were running out of time to get there and back by nightfall.

At his feet, Mercy lifted himself up and stretched.

He scooped up the pup, carried him over to the bed, and settled himself on her side of the mattress, still holding the dog against his chest. Mercy gazed up at him with a purposeful, fixed study, as if he'd never seen anything more fascinating in the whole of his doggie life.

Harbury fanned his free arm behind his head then crossed his feet at the ankles. "At least someone appreciates my presence."

"Your boots had better not be on my new coverlet," she warned.

He moved his legs so that his feet were hanging just off the footboard. "They're not."

He was probably creasing his coat. No more so, however, than he would be once he they were traveling in the carriage. In any case, he rather needed a moment of respite.

This morning, he'd received a third anonymous letter.

He'd spent a fruitless hour questioning staff. The letters weren't franked. And no one remembered seeing anyone out of the ordinary. Not only were they coming from somewhere on the estate, but they could also be coming from inside the house.

The frequency of the letters combined with uncertainty—who was the malignant force behind them, did they have a greater purpose than the obvious one—created enough pressure to force his hand. He'd sent word to Rose Cottage that he wanted to meet with Anderson on Friday.

Cassandra would want to be included…

Which gave him only two days to tell her everything he'd been withholding.

Absently, he stroked Mercy's soft fur, quelling a sudden spike of fear. The weight against his chest was due to more than just the dog.

In the beginning, he had no intention of letting Cassie into his heart, into his interior world, therefore he had no reason to reveal his entire history. He'd only revealed that he'd been love with Lady Pennington and that every attempt to eradicate her from his heart had failed. He had not told her that Lady Pennington, too, had grown up on the estate.

But the significance of his omission had increased at the same pace as his growing devotion.

He no longer had a choice. He must face the insurmountable mass standing between himself and what he had only too briefly experienced—a marriage of tenderness, laughter, and carnal pleasure…

So much carnal pleasure.

Even now, he had to look away as she held up a cameo and dangled it before her chest. He did not wish to focus too closely on her lovely nape, lest desire spike again.

At the rate they'd been indulging his desire, he wouldn't be surprised if she was with child.

She was going to be furious when he told her all. How much worse would it be if she then found out she must be confined? When she'd proposed, her primary condition had been that he and Adrian present a united front, providing a shield her youngest sisters in their Seasons, a shield she had not experienced.

However, he could hardly escort the girls on his own, leaving him unable to adequately fulfill his promise—the reason she'd agreed to wed him in the first place.

On the other hand, if he did get her with child, then, no matter what unpleasant revelations came to light—the letters, Vivianne's former role in this house—she would have no choice but to remain with him.

No matter how hurt, she wouldn't be able to leave him.

"You're looking particularly fierce." In the mirror, she met his gaze.

Fierce, bleak…Machiavellian. A little of all the above. "We should leave soon."

"I'm almost ready." She went back to sorting her necklaces. "By the way, did you ever find the book you thought was missing?"

"No." Another troubling fact.

He'd checked again late last night. He'd gone back to the secret room, taken apart the entire French section, then the Italian, then the English. Still, he'd found no trace of *The Romance of Melusine*.

"Who else," she asked lightly, "knows about the vault?"

"Adrian," he replied. But there was someone else, wasn't there? "And Anderson," he added thoughtfully.

His father, though mortified by the collection, had wanted the books appraised, even though keeping the collection had been out of character for him.

Could Anderson have taken the book? *Why?*

"Anderson…" She repeated without looking up. "I've been thinking about Anderson…"

"Have you?" he asked lightly.

"We didn't employ a steward at Willowhurst."

"How, then, were rents collected?" he attempted to steer the conversation away from his own steward.

"The largest landowners paid at the house. If my father wasn't present, his solicitor updated the records. A common arrangement, I believe."

"Lord Blackwood employs a solicitor, though I seem to recall him saying the solicitor he uses works for several landowners."

"From what I understand, Lord Blackwell employs the same solicitor still keeping an eye on things at Willowhurst. The new owner, Mr. Vane, made the introduction. Willowhurst isn't nearly as complex as the Harbury estate, doesn't have a large rent roll, and most of the income comes from sheep."

"You discussed solicitors with Blackwood and Vane?"

"Lord Blackwood and Mr. Vane were discussing the matter at the wedding breakfast. I was only part of the conversation because I had been inquiring after my old neighbors." She held up a necklace with a small gold cross up to her neck. "Although I might have taken a deeper interest in estate matters, if Mr. Wainwright had allowed."

Mr. Wainwright. Not papa. Or even *father.*

Odd, when she referred to her Godmother, Lady Asquith, as *God Mama.*

"The night we agreed to be allies, you said you wanted to look through your father's notes on Anderson's records… Have you found anything pertinent?"

Her question caught him off guard, as his mind had briefly wandered. He should have asked her about her father, instead of allowing her to ask more about him.

"Not in the least," he answered.

"And, if I recall, you also said the last Lady Day audit was in order. Are you sure?"

"Of course, I'm sure." His words had come out harsher than he'd intended.

"Anderson has been with the estate…how long?"

Damnation. He hadn't the time for this conversation now. "Since before I was born. And his father before him."

"A family with deep roots in the community, then. Mrs. Townsend mentioned a daughter. Does he have a son? Anyone to carry on the tradition?"

"Ah…no. There is no one."

A tiny crease appeared between her brows. Yes, he knew his answer had been evasive.

"The Wexfords are expecting us," he reminded. This was not a time for confessions and explanations. "Are you close to choosing a necklace?"

"This one." She held out the necklace with the cross. "Will you help me with the clasp?"

Harbury rose from the bed while Mercy snorted his displeasure at having been abandoned. He caught up the necklace. The chain felt thin and fragile in his hand.

"The other day Mrs. Townsend told me prices have been down."

The necklace fell from his suddenly clumsy fingers. "Did she?" After locating the chain at her feet, he glanced up. "When?"

Her lids lowered. "Following the war."

He turned down his lips. Ten to one, her misunderstanding of his question had been deliberate.

"I've been thinking," she continued. "One way to alleviate some of the hardship would be to delay rent collection from Michaelmas to Christmas, or even Lady Day. Better still, to give further reductions based on any documented improvements made by the leaseholder over the winter months."

He stared at her in astonishment.

"Estate income would be down, of course," she continued, "but we could economize…" Her voice trailed.

She'd been doing far deeper analysis than light contemplation. She'd come up with a plan similar to the one he'd been contemplating, the one based on Townsend's information.

Coincidence?

Unlikely.

She kept an expectant gaze on him as he rose. "The tenants would then be secure in the knowledge they can count on fair treatment during challenging times," she added.

"You said your interest in attending tea with Mrs. Townsend was because of your fascination with her fenugreek."

"I *am* interested in her fenugreek." She shifted her hands in her lap, folding one atop the other and then reversing their positions. "I am also interested in her concerns. In *your* concerns. We ladies are equally aware of troubles. You men give us ladies much less credit than we deserve."

"Apparently!"

"Don't be angry." She reached out. "Allies, remember?"

"Allies share strategy," he pointed out. "They don't sneak around behind each other's backs."

"Allies"—she raised her chin—"don't dismiss each other's concerns, either."

"I *have not* dismissed your concerns."

"You are doing so right now."

"No. Your plan is extraordinarily close to one I've been contemplating."

"Really?" Her shoulders slumped as she exhaled, looking vastly relieved. "I'm glad to hear." She paused. "But what of Mr. Anderson?"

"Mr. Anderson?" he queried, with greater alarm.

"Mr. Townsend told you that Mr. Anderson's quality of work has declined. The disorganized library, the missing book, the strange encounters other tenants have had with him. Not to mention that he doesn't treat you as he should. I can't understand why you haven't relieved him of his position."

Her breath had deepened. Her eyes had widened. She knew he was withholding something, didn't she? "Allow me to deal with him in my own way, and in my own time. *Please*. Finding a replacement will take time."

"Mrs. Townsend's son is a London solicitor, and she recently suggested he might be interested in the position."

"Pardon?"

"When you—" She stopped abruptly. "I mean, *if* you find yourself in need of a new steward, he knows the estate. And his father has a vested interest."

The points of her gold cross bit into his palm. "I can handle my own concerns, Cassandra."

"*Our,*" she said derisively, looking hurt. "Our concerns."

His conscience panged. She was right to look hurt.

She'd gone behind his back, she'd discussed estate problems with tenants without his presence. But she'd done so because she wanted to help. And he *had* asked for her opinion.

In other words, his withholding of information was still the greater omission.

"I will have a talk with Mr. Townsend," he said finally. "And I will arrange for us to meet with his son."

"Before Michaelmas?"

"Before Michaelmas."

She reached out and touched his arm. "Thank you."

She turned back around and lifted the bottom of her cap. He positioned the necklace so the cross rested in the valley between her collarbones, clasped the ends, and then rested his hands against her shoulders.

"And I must beg your pardon," he said contritely. "I was too abrupt."

"No matter."

Her smile lifted only her lips—a pale specter of the sweet smile he'd come to know, love, and long for.

He wasn't angry at her for meddling. She was simply getting too close to a truth he wasn't yet ready to reveal. He had to tell her everything. And he would. Tonight.

CASSIE FLASHED YET another look of worried inquiry across the jostling carriage, but Harbury remained reluctant to meet her gaze. As they made their way to the meeting with her husband's father's friends, he angled himself toward the fields outside the carriage window, and he kept a pale-knuckled grip on the strap.

His posture made her feel as if he were deliberately separating their bodies, the same way his abrupt manner during their earlier discussion had suggested he was withholding something on his mind.

Perhaps she should have chosen a better time to bring up the issue, but she'd only just had the conversation with Mrs. Townsend about her son. She'd sensed her interference in estate matters would not be as welcome as he'd intimated in their early discussions, but she hadn't anticipated this level of upset.

True, he'd been quick to recognize his rudeness and apologize, but she didn't feel as if he'd truly addressed her concerns. In fact, she'd felt his apology had been a way to distract her from another, more complicated truth.

She'd known keeping the real reason for her attempted alliance with the wives a secret from Harbury hadn't been honest. And she hadn't been sure *why* she had decided not to be forthcoming, other than an instinct Harbury had been hiding something himself.

Her suspicion was no longer only instinct. Harbury *was* hiding something. And whatever he was hiding was slowly breaking apart the foundation they'd laid together.

"We should have brought Mercy," she said to break the silence.

"Mercy hates to be taken in the carriage."

So much for that attempted line of conversation. She tried something else. "Did I tell you I finally received another letter from Eliza, this one from Ravenswood?"

"No."

She continued, even though he hadn't sounded the least interested. "Lord Neville has come to visit and is making a nuisance of himself…"

Nothing.

"…I don't know why Neville feels he has to bother Millie. No one else ever complains about her behavior. She could be considered somewhat outspoken, I suppose. But he treats her as if she were outrageous, and—"

"*Is* he bothering Millie? Or is the problem the Wainwright ladies, who all appear to delight in creating turmoil?"

"Harbury!" She scowled. "What an unkind thing to say." She cast her own gaze out the window. "Unkind *and* unfair."

He exhaled harshly. "Just so. I must beg your pardon." He paused. "*Again.*"

She glanced askance. "Why did your 'apology' just make me feel worse?"

Finally, his troubled gaze met hers. "Truthfully? I'm dreading this visit."

At least he'd told her *something.* "I thought the Wexfords were old family friends."

"They are."

"Well, what more can you tell me about them?"

"An older couple. Longtime friends of my parents." He hesitated. "I expect they are eager to make your acquaintance."

"But you aren't eager for me to make theirs?"

He remained silent.

"Harbury…" She placed her palms against her knees. "Do I embarrass you?"

He closed his eyes. His purse lips suggested an inner battle. Then, without looking, he grasped her hand and raised her fingers to his lips.

Her heart squeezed as he held his mouth against her knuckles for far longer than a simple kiss would have warranted. When he returned his own to his lap, he kept hold of hers, apparently inordinately interested in the row of embroidered flowers decorating the edge of her glove.

"No," he said hoarsely. "Never. Have I ever given you reason to believe such a thing?"

"You must realize you've been acting strangely of late. Especially whenever we discuss the estate."

"You're right." His hand tightened over hers. "I don't wish to let Anderson go, but I'm starting to see I have little choice. Do you understand what forcing him out of not only his position, but his home will mean for him?"

"He wouldn't *have* to leave Rose Cottage."

"He's a man of deep pride. He would not stay if he were not employed, especially if he were forced from his post."

"What of his daughter?"

Warily, he held her gaze.

"Perhaps she would be willing to take him in?" She shifted. Their knees bumped. "Perhaps you can write to her."

"Perhaps," he echoed, looking exceedingly bleak.

She squeezed his hand reassuringly as the coachman called out to the horses, and the carriage rolled to a stop. Her fear the Wexfords would find fault with her was not realized, and the older couple welcomed them into their home with delight.

First, they were taken on a house tour, which turned out to be a solid affair about the size of Willowhurst. By the time they sat down for tea, Cassie felt warm and welcome.

If Harbury had not been so stiff, her happiness with the visit would have been complete.

But if the Wexfords noticed his stilted behavior, they didn't make mention of it. They settled amiably in a parlor with large-paned windows looking out over a pond. Two white swans glided peacefully over the water.

"Well, son," Lord Wexford said. "I'd say you've done well in your choice of a spouse, very well indeed. Your father would be proud."

"I'm honored you think so," Harbury cordially replied. "My

wife charms everyone she meets. Her overtures toward the tenants' wives have been received with great enthusiasm."

Cassie smiled, though she wasn't sure he meant his description as a compliment.

"Then you at The Hall will never again be ignorant of the latest *on dit*," Lady Wexford offered.

"How right you are." Harbury chuckled without mirth, as if Lady Wexford's assertion matched his greatest fear. "And how goes things here?"

Lord Wexford exchanged a glance with his wife. "Our son manages most things these days."

"Most," Lady Wexford agreed. "But not enough."

"Hard for a man to let go." Lord Wexford shrugged as he crossed his legs. "Although *you* do not have to worry about letting go for a very long while, Harbury." He cocked his head fondly. "Still odd to refer to you as Harbury. How fast the time has gone. How long has it been?"

"Nearly two years," Lady Wexford offered.

"Two years!" Lord Wexford shook his head. "Is Anderson still at his post or have you replaced him?"

"At present, he remains my steward," Harbury replied. "You say your son has been managing the place? It's been a long time since I've talked to Arthur. I'd love to see him. Is he—"

"What a mess your father had on his hands." Lord Wexford shook his head, seemingly so lost in recollection he hadn't heard Harbury. "How is that former governess, er, rather, companion of Lady Sarah's?"

Beside her, Harbury stiffened.

"Moved up in the world, last I heard," Lord Wexford mused. "Twice, I believe. Just as she always intended, but I don't have to remind you, now do I?" He chuckled as if he'd said something witty. "She would have caught you in the parson's trap, Harbury, wouldn't she? That is, if your father hadn't acted so quickly and shrewdly. A boon for you, my dear."

Unable to respond, Cassie fixed her gaze on a mole just beneath Lord Wexford's right eye. *A boon?*

"Please excuse Lord Wexford, duchess. He is such a great tease," Lady Wexford said with a laugh.

A laugh Cassie hardly heard because the thudding in her ears deadened all sound.

Parson's trap...

Unless her husband had left some other youthful attachment unrevealed, she only knew of one lady he'd ever wanted to marry. But Lord Wexford couldn't possibly be referring to Lady Pennington.

Lady Pennington lived in London.

Lady Pennington was a *countess*.

Lady Pennington, as far as she knew, had never come to the Harbury estate.

"All that was so long ago," Lady Wexford continued. "And surely of no interest, now. Why don't we—"

"She was a handsome thing, if I recall," Lord Wexford interrupted, his unfixed eyes still lost in memory. "Not as pretty as your duchess, but stately. Come now, Lydia, what was her name? You remember."

"I'm sure I don't," Lady Wexford raised her voice.

"Lady Pennington, I believe." Cassie responded quietly. "Her name is Vivianne, Lady Pennington."

"Vivianne!" Lord Wexford cheerfully exclaimed. "Yes! Her name *is* Vivianne. Only she was Vivianne Anderson then."

The bit of cake Cassie had eaten sat uneasily in her stomach.

Like the pieces of a dissected map, the puzzle came together, finally making sense. Harbury's reluctance to dismiss the steward. His evasiveness when talking about his past. His reaction when she suggested he write Anderson's daughter.

How *could* he have kept such a thing from her? *Why* hadn't he told her?

She didn't know how her heart could simultaneously be beating in her throat and broken into a million pieces.

She'd thought they were building something new.

All the while, she'd existed only in her rival's long shadow.

CHAPTER FOURTEEN

A s their visit to the Wexfords droned on, Cassie kept her responses pleasant, her interested expression fixed, but, all the while, a dirge was echoing in her mind. Lady Pennington—*Harbury's precious Viv*—had grown up with her husband on the estate.

Though she refused to face him, what she could see of his profile grew increasingly ashen—an obvious sign of guilt. Clearly, he'd known exactly how she would feel about the revelation.

She ignored him and his imploring, puppy-in-repentance looks—looks which, even out of the corner of her eye, impressively rivaled Mercy's. But she couldn't give him her attention. If she did, she was certain she would erupt. And she refused to relinquish what remained of her dignity.

Her husband had damaged her pride quite enough.

"Thank you for your hospitality," she said to Lord and Lady Wexford as they were leaving, "I do look forward to seeing you again."

She grasped the older woman's hand warmly, smiling with a false cheer that would have rivaled her mother's counterfeit gaiety, and her mother had been the best actress Cassie had ever known when it came to the dutifully polite concealment of internal distress.

The coachman helped her back into the carriage. She angled herself resolutely toward the view, very aware of—but still not acknowledging—her husband.

No sooner had he taken his place by her side than he attempted to speak. "Cassandra—"

"Don't." She crossed her arm over her chest and raised her flat hand over her shoulder…a universal signal to *stop*.

"Please—"

She shook her head. "Not now." And possibly not *ever*.

She didn't want to see him. She didn't want to hear him. And she most certainly did not want to feel his touch.

"*Cassie—*"

"Are you as hard of hearing as your father's friend? Or only equally uncaringly oblivious?"

The only response to her query was the squeak of the carriage's wheels.

After a few long minutes, she heard Harbury sigh. She'd no idea what, if anything, he was trying to communicate by his audible exhalation, but, for a time, they jostled along in blessed, *blessed* silence. Then, the coach hit a rutted bit of road, and she grasped the strap to keep herself from being jostled backwards and inadvertently landed in her husband's lap.

She couldn't bear contact and only wished the strap could also stop her battered, bruised heart from knocking around inside of her chest.

Behind her, something thudded against the bench's padding. *A fist?*

"Cassandra, I *demand* the chance to speak."

Demand? She shot him a hard, sidelong glance.

But a husband could, couldn't he?

By law, he could demand of a wife almost anything he wished.

How utterly unfair.

Slowly, she turned to face him. So much heat radiated in her face she felt as if fire were spitting from every pore, a stark contrast to his deathly pale pallor.

"If you *insist* on speaking," she schooled her tone to a calm she was far from feeling, "then you may list the reasons why you didn't tell me your *beloved Viv* was *Anderson's daughter.*"

He opened his mouth, then quickly clamped it shut again. "She's not my Viv."

"Forgive me." She puckered her brow as if confused. "But I don't think I heard you list a reason."

He clenched his teeth, dug his thumb beneath his cravat's knot, then yanked. After the tie loosened, he took a deep breath.

"Very well, then. I'll give you a reason. Because I feared you would react exactly as you are reacting right now. *Badly.* I knew you would be upset when you learned the truth."

"I'm not reacting to the truth, but to the fact you purposefully *concealed* the truth."

"At first, I didn't think her history here was relevant."

"You. Didn't. Think. Her. History. Here. Was. Relevant," she slowly and carefully parroted each of his words.

"No," he insisted. "I didn't."

"You didn't think Vivianne having been born on the estate—having *lived* in Harbury Hall—relevant?"

"No." He paused. "Not at first."

Which meant at some point, he'd become aware of how this slice of information from the past significantly shaded the present.

"I don't know what is worse," she said. "Your initial obliviousness or your continued insistence on withholding the truth even after you realized how much I would be hurt."

He jerked back as if struck. "You knew about Viv. Our marriage was to be one of convenience."

"I am well aware of the agreement we made."

"Then what would you want me to have done? I can't change the past."

"I just *told* you I'm not angry about the past." Her eyes locked on his. "I'm angry because you must have known that *anyone*, at any time, might have revealed the truth. I was only spared even greater humiliation because the Wexfords, who had no malicious intent, happened to be the ones to enlighten me and seemed to believe Vivianne was someone currently insignificant to you."

His breath deepened, but he did not attempt to give her any additional excuses. Because no proper excuse existed for withholding such crucial, painful information.

"If," she continued, "you and I had maintained a polite distance as we originally intended, I might have understood." She paused, struggling to keep her voice from cracking. "But you know we didn't."

He'd made love to her. Sweetly. Passionately. He'd laughed with her. *Held* her. Made her feel as if her feelings mattered.

When had he realized she would be harmed when she eventually discovered the truth?

Good heavens. She remembered the odd exchange that led to the revelation Anderson had a daughter in the first place. She placed her hand on her forehead. "Until Mrs. Townsend mentioned Vivianne on the day you came to escort me home, you *didn't* fully understand how the truth would affect me, did you? She was surprised I didn't know Anderson had a daughter. At the time, I couldn't grasp why *you* looked so stricken."

Cassie knew she'd guessed correctly by the way he sucked in his lips.

She recalled the inexplicable look the tenant and her husband had exchanged just before Mrs. Townsend quickly changed the subject. Mrs. Townsend, who had also been falsely informed she and Harbury did not have a real marriage.

Cassie snorted in disbelief. "She must have thought me such a goose! My heavens, Harbury, you've made me a laughingstock."

"No!"

He reached out, but she wedged herself into the carriage's corner to avoid his touch.

"Mrs. Townsend hadn't thought anything of bringing up Vivianne, not until I professed ignorance of her existence." She inhaled through her teeth. "She said Anderson's daughter had a spaniel. Harbury—could Mercy be Vivianne's dog?"

"I don't know." He winced. "Possibly."

She turned her face away.

"Before she was Lady Pennington, she did have a spaniel...I think."

"You *think*."

"Honestly, I had forgotten all about V—Lady Pennington's damn dog," he said harshly. He softened his tone. "Besides, Mercy is a puppy."

"Damn dog," she repeated. He'd not only raised his voice to her, but he'd also just *cursed* in her presence, yet another diminishing blow.

Harbury, meanwhile, seemed to be increasing in size. He filled the carriage until all she could see was him as he loomed over her in a threatening manner.

"Sit back!" she commanded, her narrowing eyes as menacing as her tone. "And don't you *ever* use such foul language in my presence again."

Her father had also delivered each of his many disappointments in a booming voice with precise, hard-consonated, brutal words.

Only in private, of course.

Just as she and Harbury were now.

And she was reacting in just the same way. She couldn't breathe. Her blood was roaring in her ears, her heart beating jaggedly in her chest. She hadn't felt this disturbing melding of fiery anger and primal fear since...

Since before her father had died.

After her father died, she'd vowed she'd never allow any man to insult her in the same fashion. She certainly wasn't going to make an exception for her husband, the person who was supposed to hold her in the highest regard.

"*No* foul language," she repeated, louder this time.

"I beg your—"

"Stop!" The last thing she needed was another empty apology. She squeezed the bridge of her nose and willed away the sting. On her wedding night, her anger had turned to tears. She'd wouldn't let Harbury humiliate her again. "Just stop!"

"But you're not letting me get in a word!"

"And yet your mouth keeps moving." She looked out the window. A gentle breeze rippled across a field of barley, giving her a moment of much-needed calm. "Earlier today, you intimated you were weary of apologizing to me. So, I release you from your obligation. Apologies can never excuse you...excuse *this*."

"Cassie, please! I was such a young man then," he said imploringly. "Younger, in fact, than my years."

"You weren't so very young last month when we visited the Royal Academy and nearly collided with Lord and Lady Pennington." She shook her head slowly, remembering. "You were so shaken, I was alarmed enough to take you aside so that you might collect yourself. Do you remember what you said?"

"I know what I said."

"You told me then your heart would always belong to her."

His gaze bored into hers. "I was wrong."

Cassie's heart tripped. But a more vulnerable part of her refused to be moved.

"She lived here. She *lived* here. She was Sarah's governess, her companion. The pony cart. Oh, my sweet heavens. You must have taken her to the Priory, too! *Ugh*." The gutturally expelled grunt wasn't strong enough to embody even half her disgust. "Did you kiss me with my back toward you because you wanted to pretend I was Vivianne?"

A look of pure horror crossed his features.

Perhaps, she thought warily, she'd crossed a line.

For a long moment, they stared at each other in silence. Small capillaries became increasingly visible at the edges of his eyes. She didn't know if he was about to scream or cry.

"I would *never* pretend you were Vivianne," he said with dangerous precision.

The force of his declaration took her aback, as did the ugly snarl accompanying his words.

She'd seen Harbury bewildered. She'd seen him hurt. She'd

seen him delighted. And she'd seen him in the very depths of passion. But she'd never seen him like this.

His pupils had expanded so much, his brown eyes appeared to be black. Her mouth dried as she focused on a vein bulging menacingly in his neck. Instinctively, she threw up her arm, turning away to shield her face.

"My God! Cassandra!"

She cringed, knowing she had responded as she would have, not to Harbury, but to her father.

"Do you know me so little?" he whispered.

She pressed the back of her wrist against her eyes. "I don't know you at all."

To her shame, a great, ugly sob racked her body. To prevent another, she gritted her teeth. *Hard.* So hard the second sound that tore from the deepest part of her ache was not a sob, but a battle cry. Then, she closed her eyes, shutting out not only him, but the world.

She gave herself over to the sorrow and wept.

"You know me," he said softly, gently.

She thrust out the arm she'd been holding aloft—not to hit him, but to stop him from coming any closer. Already, he was too close. She couldn't bear any greater proximity.

"You know me," he repeated, entreaty in his voice.

She closed her eyes and shook her head, willing her ears to deafen his words.

But he would not be silenced. He just kept repeating the phrase.

The words clanged through the carriage, unstoppable as the wheels on a runaway cart. It was as if he thought repetition would force her to listen. But reiteration had precisely the opposite effect.

His murmurings blended one into another, saturating and hissing in her mind until his individual words held no meaning. The sounds burrowed beneath her skin, forcing her to twist toward the corner, curl her neck inward, and hunch her body.

She didn't even notice when he took her into his arms, nor did she realize the rocking she did feel was no longer due to the carriage, but only to the rise and fall of his chest as he breathed. He cradled her cheek against his shoulder, his large, chilled fingers cooling her face. By degrees, she lost the will to physically fight, even as her inner walls stood firm.

"You know me." He spoke against her ear. "You know me better than she ever did."

His final phrase splintered into her mind, driving holes in the places where she was most vulnerable. Holes not big enough to break down her resistance, but big enough to let in light.

The pounding in her ears lessened, gradually replaced by the steady beat of his heart.

The carriage had stopped.

How long ago, she didn't know. Gradually, she became aware of birdsong. Of a light breeze through the copse of trees adjacent to the Hall.

She rubbed her prickly nose and then wiped beneath her eyes.

Beyond the ruffle of his collar, she could just make out the grayish stone of Harbury Hall.

Her gasping slowed as he continued to stroke her hair. At some point, she'd lost her bonnet, but what did she care if she looked a fright?

She was in love with a man who'd just devastated her. And somehow, she was going to have to pull herself together.

How could she do this?

How could she walk back into her home, knowing that woman's ghost haunted every room?

She closed her eyes, allowing herself one last sob.

At least, from the crumpled fabric beneath her cheek, she knew she'd ruined Harbury's stupid, starched collar. She concentrated on the pressure of his hand against her head, willing herself to remember his words. *You know me better than she ever did.*

If he wasn't truly sorry for hurting her, would he be holding her this close?

Perhaps he was right. Perhaps she did know him.

She knew he stirred his tea three times before taking a sip. She knew he had a special, silly voice he used only for penitent puppies. She knew he was gentle with a hairbrush and precise about slicing his morning sausage. She knew the birthmark just below his belly button.

She knew how he sighed when she stroked his hair. She knew—

Someone rapped against the door, interrupting her thoughts.

"Leave us," Harbury growled.

His tone very nearly brought a smile to her lips. He *must* care. Perhaps not as much as he'd cared for—

"I'm sorry, Edward—"

The cut-glass feminine vowels spoken from just outside the open carriage door sent a chill through Cassie's blood.

"—I can't leave."

Though Harbury continued to hold Cassie close, she felt him turn toward the window. A jolt surged through his body.

She knew who had spoken even before he said her name.

"*Viv!*" she heard him exclaim. "What the devil are you doing here?"

HARBURY WOULD HAVE kept on clinging to his wife had she not wrenched herself from his arms while he was still reeling from the shock of seeing Vivianne. Now, short of yanking her back by the crumpled red ribbons dangling from the bonnet she'd just refixed to her head, he could think of no way to keep her by his side.

Circumstance had not reduced him to the level of a primal brute. Not yet.

Emphasis on *yet*.

She reached for the carriage door.

"Cassandra," he called sharply.

She glanced back over her shoulder at him but kept hold of the door handle. Her eyes held a warning clear as day—*do not give me an order.*

He didn't need to be cautioned. Still, he could not allow his wife's honor to suffer another blow by his—or anyone else's—hand.

Especially Vivianne's.

"Give us a moment, please?" he asked Viv.

Cassandra snorted.

"Certainly." Viv folded her arms. "Settle your little row. Take all the time you require. After all, my father has only gone *missing.*"

He swore. Under his breath, this time. And then turned toward his wife with a contrite expression. Behind him, Vivianne spoke again.

"Edward—"

His name coming from Lady Pennington's mouth acted like a fingernail grinding down slate. He shivered. *Literally shivered.* Cassandra must have misinterpreted his reaction as one of longing because she slowly shook her head in disbelief.

"—this is a crisis. I need you, now."

"She needs you," Cassandra echoed, her voice sickly sweet.

His wife opened the door, then called out for the coachman. The man appeared at once to position the stepping stool and offer his hand. She took it. Holding her head high, she stepped down.

"Lady Pennington," Harbury said, "I don't know what's happened—"

"Didn't you get my letters?" she interrupted.

He jerked back. "*You* wrote the anonymous letters?"

He'd known he recognized the handwriting. But he'd burned the ones she'd sent him in a fit of pique.

"What letters?" Cassandra demanded.

"Well, I couldn't sign them, of course…"

Cassandra's brows rose, then she gave a little snort before shaking her head and turning away again. He thrust his hand into his hair.

He didn't understand any of this. Why would Vivianne write letters impugning her own father? He wanted to demand answers, but first he had to stop his wife from making a rash decision.

"Viv," he said, "I realize you are distressed—"

"I should hope you'd be able to tell."

Cassandra huffed as she continued her march toward the door.

"For heaven's sake!" he said to Lady Pennington. "This is not a good time."

"So I can see. But my father hasn't been seen since yesterday morning. Mrs. Grant is frantic with worry."

"How did *you* get here so quickly?"

"At Mrs. Grant's request, I've been staying at Rose Cottage for the past few weeks."

Ever farther behind them, Cassandra made another sound of disgust.

"Why would such a short disappearance cause such alarm? Mightn't he have gone, as he sometimes did, to one of the more remote villages on the estate? Mightn't he simply take himself off for a solitary ramble?"

"I'm afraid he is not well."

Cassandra's footfalls ceased.

Harbury inhaled through his teeth. "I will be back to discuss the matter. But not before I've had a brief—and private—talk with my wife."

"Darling," Vivianne smiled sweetly, "I don't think a talk— brief or not—will help."

He studied her face, surprised by her sarcastic tone, by the malice underlying it. She was worried for her father, yes, but she was also relishing his distress.

Cassandra's distress.

He'd fallen in love with this woman so long ago his under-standing of her had become deeply entwined with his sense of himself. So entwined, he wondered if he'd ever truly known her at all.

Had the qualities he'd loved ever been real?

Or were they simply things he'd wanted to see?

"You may wait here," he replied, curt. "You are not permitted in the house."

"Pratt, the old hag, wouldn't let me in, either." She shrugged. "Not that I have any interest in this rotting pile of stone anymore, anyway. Another few decades and the Hall will be as picturesque as the Priory."

She'd spoken loudly enough for Cassandra to hear.

"Damn you, Viv," he said in a low voice.

He ignored her snort, launched himself from the carriage, and bounded after his wife. He caught up to her at the Hall's front steps. He hardly recognized her. The Cassandra he knew had disappeared again behind a smile even more frightful than the one she'd worn at the Wexfords.

"Shall I prepare us tea?" she asked brightly. "But of course not. Vivianne *needs* you." She turned out her palms and widened her eyes. "What choice do you have but to go?"

He growled as he grasped her elbow and hustled them both into the Hall.

"Leave us," he barked at the porter.

The porter and every servant present immediately heeded his command, and the commotion in the courtyard had drawn quite a few to the front-facing windows.

"So"—Cassandra blinked innocently—"you also failed to mention receiving letters from Lady Pennington?"

"Lord, Cassie," he whispered harshly. "I didn't know who was sending the letters."

"Did you think you had *another* admirer?"

"They weren't those kinds of letters."

Her brows went up. "What kind of letters were they?"

"They suggested Anderson was not to be trusted. They warned me if I did not hire a new steward, unrest would come to the estate."

"So, let me see…" She tapped the sole of her half boot against the marble floor. "An unsigned letter warned you your steward was not to be trusted and yet you became angry with me this morning when I suggested the same?"

"I wasn't angry with you. I was uncomfortable because you were getting too close to the truth, and I hadn't yet decided how to tell you. I hoped the letters were a prank. *Anyone* could have sent them. Also, my father held Anderson in the highest esteem. I didn't want to put the wealth of historical knowledge he possesses at risk. Besides, I owed Anderson…"

She lifted her brow.

"No matter what has happened since, in my youthful folly, I nearly ruined his daughter."

"I'm so very glad you grew out of your youthful folly," she quipped, "before you could, say, nearly ruin *another lady's reputation*. Why, you might even have ended up *miserably* wed."

"Cassie," he grasped her upper arms, "marrying you was the best choice I ever made."

She closed her eyes, absenting herself in spirit even as he held tight to her person.

I love you. The words clogged his throat, stealing his breath.

But if he said them now, she wouldn't be able to feel them. She might not even be able to hear them. He let go of her arms and, instead, cradled her cheeks. As he lifted her face, her bonnet once again fell away. Her lids fluttered, leaving him to gaze down at her dampened lashes.

At least her tears indicated she was not as immune to his entreaties as she would have him believe. He touched a lingering kiss against her forehead, silently willing her to understand, to forgive.

"I am sorry, love," he apologized again. "But I need to find out why Anderson's mysterious departure would cause Vivienne and Mrs. Grant such distress. I must find out what has been going on…not for her sake, or even for his, but for my own and for the estate."

"I know." She exhaled, sounding weary. "Go, Harbury. Go and do whatever you must."

"Promise me you will be here when I return."

She lifted her lids. Blankly—mutely—she gazed into his eyes. Every second of her silence thrust another lance deep inside his heart.

Finally, she spoke.

"I will be here when you return." Her voice was spiritless, carefully even. "You may release me now."

"Yes." He dropped his hands. "Yes, of course."

She turned away.

As he watched her climb the stairs, part of his spirit snapped. He was being torn asunder. His yearning for her had taken such deep root, releasing her had felt like giving up a part of his very body. A bone. A *rib*.

Didn't Genesis describe how Eve was created from Adam's rib?

He grieved like Adam, now.

Something necessary, vitally necessary, to his being, to the physical structure of his body, had been torn from him wholly against his will, leaving tender, visceral organs unprotected. Then, the missing part had been fashioned into something entirely different, something he didn't understand. Something…some*one* who would ultimately be his downfall.

Or, Lord willing, his salvation.

CHAPTER FIFTEEN

HARBURY WATCHED AGHAST as Cassandra disappeared behind the door to her apartments. Placing his thumb and forefinger on either side of his nose, he closed his eyes and squeezed.

Hard.

Rise and fall, advance and retreat. Whenever he, or Cassandra, steadied, the other wavered. Like the opposite sides of an unbalanced scale.

The constant vacillation had been bad enough, but what if the fulcrum had just snapped?

He couldn't be left without recourse. She'd just promised to be here when he returned. He'd time to save his marriage. He had to trust his wife, had to believe she would keep her vow. If not, he would not be able to turn his mind toward the problem Anderson—and Viv—presented.

Delaying action was no longer an option.

He took one last look up the staircase and then forced himself to turn back toward the entry. Deep in thought, he made his way back across the courtyard.

Today was the first time he'd seen Lady Pennington since the end of last Season, when he and Cassandra had almost collided with her and her husband during a visit to the Royal Academy.

This time, he had not experienced the same sharp pain of unrequited love that he had felt at both the Academy and at Almack's. Instead, he'd felt shocked—a natural response to seeing anyone in a place they were not expected.

And already, his shock had dissipated.

He fixed his gaze on Lady Pennington's carriage, where she had chosen to rest while he'd been trying to reason with Cassie. Even though she was well known to all his staff, none of them had made any effort to make her feel welcome.

Apparently, their loyalty was to the duchess.

As was his.

He came to a stop, leaving ample room between them. He studied her face, a face that had once haunted him as much during his waking hours as during his sleep.

Present as ever were the echoes of a thousand conversations, as well as an equal number of silent exchanges. However, the ache of longing he'd grown accustomed to expecting was, indeed, simply gone.

If he felt anything for her at all, it was only the distant pang of sadness.

Perhaps sadness was what he'd been distracting himself from all along.

When he'd told Cassandra he would always love Vivianne, he'd honestly believed he would be forever trapped, unable to court or to marry any lady, because he would never be at liberty to give another his heart.

Now, after experiencing the joy of true connection with Cassandra, he was certain his misery, his loss, had been caused, not by unrequited love, but by the absence of love itself.

He only hoped his realization had not come too late.

He folded his hands behind his back. "Lady Pennington."

She *humphed*. "Do you intend to pretend we are merely acquaintances?"

"We *are* merely acquaintances."

She lifted one shoulder, as if his manner toward her was of no consequence. "Pratt lets in riff-raff." She waved her arm in the kitchen entrance's direction. "While I, on the other hand, am forced to wait in the hot sun."

He glanced over his shoulder. He hadn't even noticed the two ladies arriving on foot. But before he could identify them, Mrs. Pratt ushered them into the house.

He turned back to Vivianne. "You look comfortable enough."

She rolled her eyes.

Had she always been so peevish?

"Out of mutual respect and concern for your father," he said with lowered tone, "we will agree to treat one another with civility."

"Do not speak to me as if I was your vassal."

He frowned. "When have I ever treated you poorly?"

"Nearly every day I worked at the Hall." She glanced heavenward. "Getting in my way. Stealing my cart. Accosting me in out of the way places."

"I seem to remember your enthusiastic participation."

"Perhaps."

"And," he drew the word out, "I was deeply infatuated."

"Oh! I *know*. And how you exploited your advantages…"

"I wanted to marry you. I *would* have married you."

She didn't argue. She couldn't.

"You married your baron instead," he finished.

"My baron." She shivered slightly but covered the reaction with another lift of her shoulder. "How galled your father was by having to treat me with civility. Every time I met him in town, he stumbled over naming me *Lady*."

A discordant note rung in Harbury's mind.

His father had led him to believe he'd arranged Vivianne's first marriage. If so, why would he have resented her elevation?

Had the old duke resented the lengths he had to go to extract her from his son's life?

Or had he left out—or altered—pertinent details about the events surrounding the interruption of their elopement?

He tucked the question away. His main concern, at present, must be Anderson.

"Tell me about your father. When, exactly, was the last time he was seen? And do you have any idea where he might have gone?"

"He and I parted just after dinner. He took his port at the usual time in the usual fashion. When Mrs. Grant came in to collect the glass and remind him to go up to bed, the only odd thing she noticed was the book he held in his lap. She said she'd never seen the book before."

Harbury felt a rushing sensation. "What was the book's name?"

"The title was not in English."

The Romance of Melusine, he'd wager.

"What's more," Vivianne continued, "He said something odd. He said, 'The imposter found the chamber and *must* be stopped.' I assume he meant you."

"Imposter? Me? What the devil, Viv?!"

"I *told* you he's been ill."

"Are you suggesting your father is not in his right mind?"

Vivianne's gaze raked him first up, then down. She pursed her lips and then shook her head. "Did you not *read* the letters I sent?"

"But those letters merely suggested he couldn't be trusted, not that his faculties had declined."

She stared at him for a long, hard moment. Then she looked away. "Apparently, he's been acting oddly for some time, but Mrs. Grant only informed me just after Lady Day."

"March?!" he exclaimed. "Why it's nearly harvest."

"At that point, he had only just started complaining to her about 'the *other* Mrs. Grant.' Needless to say, there isn't any *other* Mrs. Grant. And when she pressed him on what, specifically, this other Mrs. Grant had done to offend him, he referred to something she remembered having done for him earlier."

Harbury thrust his hand into his hair.

"I attributed his odd lapse to strain, as did she," Lady Pennington continued. "Mrs. Grant doesn't hold you in very high esteem. Prices were down, tenants were unhappy. The *young duke,* she wrote me, seemed as disinclined as ever to attend his duties." Her eyes flashed. "You could have been more involved, you know."

There, he couldn't argue.

"But your father never wrote to me of any tenant displeasure."

"And now we know why. He wouldn't have, would he? Not if he believed you an imposter."

"And you were aware of all this since *March?*"

"No, not the latter. Until last night, nothing he said revealed any delusion pertaining to you. In fact, the problem's scale did not become apparent until recently. In April, he'd started using the wrong words. By June, he sometimes appeared not to know where he was. By late July, Mrs. Grant became alarmed enough to ask me to visit."

He paced the length of the carriage and back. He'd seen signs Anderson's acuity was slipping, hadn't he? Anderson hadn't seemed himself since Harbury had returned from London.

In this, Lady Pennington was right.

He should have paid more attention. He should have dug deeper. Inquired more widely. If disease had struck, Anderson was not to blame for his behavior.

"I couldn't leave London at that time." She swept a speck from her glove. "By letter, however, I implored him to relinquish his post and come stay with me. But he refused to, as he called it, 'shirk' his duties."

"So, you wrote to me. Anonymously."

"No. That was after I'd seen him myself. I thought he just needed cheering, so I brought him a puppy from my dog's litter. Unfortunately, when we were taking a ride the other day, he cast the poor thing out the carriage window."

Briefly, he closed his eyes. *The devil.* Cassandra's heart would break again if she had to hand Mercy over to Vivianne. "The puppy is fine."

"Is he?" She brightened. "Well, that, at least, is a *great* relief.

We searched high and low. When we couldn't find him, I delivered the first letter. The Hall was nearly empty but for that nice little stable boy who agreed to help me."

"The Hall was near empty because I was getting married."

"I'm sorry my father's health did not wait on your convenience, *Your Grace*. Would you have preferred me to show up on your doorstep? Just after you'd wed another? Believe it or not, I don't wish either of you ill." She adjusted her position. "Not truly. How do you think my sudden appearance would have made your new bride feel?"

Her words stung.

Vivianne should not have had more consideration for Cassie's feeling than he had. "If you care so much about my wife's feelings, then why did you antagonize her just now?"

She gave another annoyingly careless shrug. "I was piqued when Pratt refused me entry." She lifted a pointed gaze. "And seeing you both wrapped up in one another's arms wasn't exactly easy for me. Neither was nearly stumbling upon the two of you fondly caressing one another in *our* place."

"*Not* our place." Not any longer.

And how could she claim to be hurt when she had been the one to abandon him?

She turned her face away. Her lower lip quivered.

"Don't cry." He softened his voice. "We'll find him. I just wish you had told me directly and honestly of your concerns. What did you expect me to do in response to those letters?"

Her dropped chin and suddenly impassive features suggested the answer should have been obvious. She sniffed. "I expected you to dispatch my father in the same abrupt and thoughtless manner you dispatched me." She paused significantly. "Your bribe?"

"I don't understand." He frowned. "You mean my father's bribe?"

"Don't try to blame your father. He, at least, was all civility when he delivered your note."

"My note," he repeated.

"The letter you wrote explaining how, after realizing the shame you would bring to your name, you could not go through with our elopement."

He stared at her in consternation. He'd never written any such words.

"You may stop glaring at me in an accusing fashion," she continued. "Three generations of my family protected the wealth of yours. I had no reservations taking your money."

My God.

All this time, she thought he'd cast her off, the same way he thought she'd cast him off.

His father had lied to her, and his father had lied to him.

His fine, upstanding, morally perfect father had lied in order to separate two people who were, at the time, sincerely attached to one another. And he'd done so simply to preserve his pride.

If he'd known about his father's lie then, he would have moved heaven and earth to find Vivianne and go through with the elopement as planned.

"I suffered through one, terrible marriage"—she lifted her chin—"but I'm happy now. Happier than I ever could have been with you."

Harbury steadied himself against the carriage while casting his gaze over his shoulder toward the Hall. He'd the mad desire to either laugh, or weep.

He turned back to Viv again, with an altered, sadder gaze.

But she was happy with Pennington. And he…

Well, he knew now the pain, the sadness, the desperate longing he'd felt had been not for her, but for something he'd known in his heart was possible—the joining of two bodies, two spirits, two souls into a single, stronger entity.

A marriage, as Cassie's God Mama was fond of saying, of minds.

That kind of marriage, that kind of *love,* had quietly sidled into his life, sneaking beneath his defenses in the form of a lady with a wide-open heart and a feather-soft touch.

His father had lied to him and Viv both, ending what Harbury had then believed to be the only love he'd ever know. But in all those years that he'd protected and nurtured that flame, he had never, ever felt the pain he had earlier this morning when he'd thought Cassandra would leave him.

"We would not have suited," he said.

"Likely not." She sighed. Her gaze moved beyond his shoulder. "I did love this place, though."

This place. Not him.

How telling.

SETTLE YOUR LITTLE row.

The icy calm that had descended over Cassie when Vivianne said those snide words had not yet dissipated. Her body continued to function—she could blink her eyes, turn her head, and even, by deliberately placing one foot in the center of several succeeding risers, climb the stairs.

Her spirit, however, had become a separate being, floating somewhere behind her in murky, moon-shadow darkness, somewhere equally cold.

She'd told Harbury she would be here when he came back. She hadn't, however, let him know she intended to leave in the morning. But as she'd exited the carriage, she'd made that inalterable decision.

If her wounds were to heal, she had to know what she truly wanted. And to know what she truly wanted she needed perspective, a vantage point to view her marriage. The latter was impossible when Harbury was close.

When he was close, her body anticipated his touch, her mind remained clouded, and her heart stayed vulnerable to his persuasion.

Ergo, she must seek refuge from Harbury's influence.

Now, she'd only two questions to answer…where should she go?

And for how long should she stay away?

The answer to the first came readily enough.

Her twin, her other half, was the only one in the world who could stitch her flayed skin back to her body. However, Eliza was married to Harbury's sworn brother, possibly posing a problem.

But the problem could not be helped.

If Adrian knew what was good for him—and he'd always struck her as a perceptive and intelligent man—he would *not* come between two sisters, let alone twins.

The second question, though, she could not yet answer.

Even if she could define what she wanted from him now, she did not have the means, let alone the will, to fight. She was exhausted.

She lifted the latch and pushed open the door to her chamber.

Mercy's head popped up, suddenly alert. He threw back his head and let out a happy bark, then he ambled over to her feet with his sweet, fluffy ears flopping, punctuating his progression with a series of excited yips.

Despite herself, she smiled.

She scooped him up and buried her nose into his soft puppy fur. The dog licked her cheek and whimpered, struggling to see over her shoulder.

"He's not coming," she murmured consolingly.

Mercy whined.

"Don't you defend him! I'm *furious*. And, besides, you always take his side, don't you?"

Mercy ceased wiggling, then fixed his soulful puppy gaze on hers as if to say, *"But we love him."*

"I know." She grunted. "You're thinking whatever he's done is not his fault. You're thinking he can't help himself from falling into scrapes any more than you could resist destroying my favorite pair of slippers."

Mercy dipped his head.

She hugged the dog close. "Still, he was a very bad boy, and he must suffer *some* consequences."

Mercy let out another, mournful whine.

"Consequences," she repeated. "You understand those, right?"

She *was* going to leave.

And she was going to stay away until either she felt strong enough to fight for him or he came to his senses and decided to fight for her.

If he came to his senses at all.

He could force her back, of course. Not only was the law on his side, but underneath her searing pain, her love for him persisted.

Stubbornly.

Irrationally.

As faithful as Mercy's own adoration of the man.

"I belong in Bedlam," she confided.

Mercy looked away, as if seriously considering whether or not he agreed.

Bedlam-worthy or not, she couldn't accept either apology or explanation until she'd had time to heal. She needed to spend time with her sisters. With their love, she'd gather her wounded pieces and bind them back together.

She knew enough of wounds to expect, eventually, the bleeding would cease.

A knock sounded at the doorway to the corridor.

Mercy yowled in indignant protest.

"I know…how dare anyone interrupt our confidential tête-à-tête?" She placed him back on the bed before hesitantly opening the door.

"I do beg your pardon, Your Grace," Mrs. Pratt wrung her hands. "But the lad—"

"I will not have that woman in my house," Cassie interrupted, surprised at her own vehemence.

"Of course not." Mrs. Pratt drew back, affronted. "I already told Miss An—Lady Pennington, I mean—that if she insisted on waiting for you to return, she was welcome to wait outside in the comfort of her own carriage. Imagine!" She huffed. "Her coming right to the door, demanding to see His Grace."

Cassie hadn't expected Mrs. Pratt to express her loyalty with such fervor. She couldn't help a deep exhale.

"Mind you," Mrs. Pratt went on. "I understand she is worried. If I hadn't been certain Your Graces would share her concern for Mr. Anderson, I would have told her to turn her carriage right around." She pulled herself up to her full height. "I would not take the part of anyone with the effrontery to disturb you just weeks after you were wed."

Well, well. She had made at least one true ally. "Thank you, Mrs. Pratt."

"Only right," the housekeeper quipped. "But I came to tell you about the *other* ladies at the door. Miss Clapham and Mrs. Townsend have requested an audience with you, and only you. I would have turned them away, too, but Mrs. Townsend said their visit has to do with Mr. Anderson."

"Take me down." She would hear the ladies first before deciding if she should interrupt Harbury. "But inform Mr. Marsden I'd like him to keep an eye on the duke. I don't want Harbury running off in a mad search if one is not necessary. And stay close, if you will. I may need you."

"I will," Mrs. Pratt said. "I knew you'd know just how to handle things."

She felt a sweeping sense of gratitude for her staff as Mrs. Pratt led her down the stairs. Mrs. Pratt's loyalty touched Cassie more than she could say.

The housekeeper announced her entry.

"Mrs. Townsend," she greeted. "Miss Clapham. So good of you to visit. Please have a seat."

The ladies did as she bid, though they exchanged a nervous glance.

"You asked me to contact you," Mrs. Townsend began. "If I noticed anything unusual, that is."

"What's happened?" Cassie inquired.

"This morning, Mr. Townsend and I were on our way to town when we spotted Mr. Anderson on the roadside. He was unshaven. Almost frantic. When my husband asked where he was going, he refused to answer. And when he tried to question him further, he ran away."

"Oh!" Cassie exclaimed. "Oh, my."

"We thought Anderson's behavior strange, of course, but Mr. Townsend did not wish to become involved with something he did not consider to be his concern. 'Like as not,' he said, 'he's been at the punch.'"

She and Miss Clapham exchanged another glance.

"I held my peace, though *I* didn't think him in his cups, if you'll forgive the parlance. Taking a page from the old duke, Mr. Anderson rarely overindulges in spirits."

"Then later this morning," Miss Clapham continued the story, "when my father visited Rose Cottage, he found Mrs. Grant frantic. She said she hadn't seen Mr. Anderson since yesterday, when he'd told her 'the impostor must be stopped.' This morning, she discovered the tinder box missing. She claimed not to understand what Mr. Anderson had meant."

"Miss Clapham and I think we might, though," Mrs. Townsend ventured.

"He thinks my husband is an imposter," Cassie breathed, equal parts concerned and sad.

The two ladies nodded in unison.

"Toward the end of my aunt's life," Miss Clapham ventured, "she was absolutely convinced I was not myself. In fact, each time I visited, she told her maid to send me away thinking I was a stranger. I'm afraid Mr. Anderson suffers from a similar affliction. Only his concern about an imposter makes me feel as if he may be dangerous."

Cassie's heart further softened toward the man. "How horrible!"

No matter what her feelings toward Harbury and Vivianne, now was not the time to indulge them. Now was the time to act. And, to properly understand what she could do to help, she had to set aside her upset.

"He must be found," she mused. "And quickly!"

"He has been," Miss Clapham responded. "Soon after my father left Mrs. Grant, he came across Anderson in the church, talking to one of the monuments. I was in the back doing some dusting."

"The most recent monument," Mrs. Townsend added with a significant glance. "The one of the duke's father. I went in after having heard the commotion from the street."

"My father has been able to keep Mr. Anderson there at present, but Mr. Anderson is, well…not right."

"I encouraged Miss Clapham to come to you."

"Not to Mrs. Grant?"

"No matter what Mrs. Grant believes, we aren't sure she has Mr. Anderson's best interests in mind," Miss Clapham explained.

"Or the duke's," Mrs. Townsend added.

"You see," Miss Clapham continued, "he says he will burn down the church if my father does not produce the duke—the real duke. He has the tinderbox, but so far, my father has been able to keep him calm by telling him he must wait for word."

A cold sense of premonition shivered over Cassie's skin. Not only was she concerned for Anderson, but also for the rector, as well as St. Margaret's, a jewel at the very heart of the Harbury estate. If she did not see this through in careful, deliberate, and precise steps, the day could end in an even greater disaster.

"I feel absolutely certain Mr. Anderson would listen to the old duke." Mrs. Townsend sadly shook her head. "If he were here."

She raised her gaze to the portrait of Harbury's father—high cheekbones, cleft chin, large dark eyes. She'd never noticed the stunning resemblance.

"Perhaps there is a way he can be," she said to the ladies.

She would need everyone's help, including—much as she

wished things were otherwise—Lady Pennington.

"Might you two be willing to sit with Lady Pennington? She is quite upset, as you might imagine."

"Certainly," Mrs. Townsend answered.

"Shouldn't we be getting back to the church?" asked Miss Clapham.

"Yes," Cassie agreed. "And you will, but not alone. My hope is that, after Lady Pennington has had a chance to calm herself, she will permit you to accompany her back to the church. I also intend to send our carriage, along with four footmen and, of course, the duke. If everything goes well, Mr. Anderson will have the direction he seeks, from the man he seeks."

Mrs. Townsend and Miss Clapham exchanged a confused glance. Then, Mrs. Townsend shifted in her seat. Just as Cassie had, she studied the prior duke's portrait.

"An inspired idea, Your Grace."

All three ladies rose.

"Now, if you will excuse me, I must make a few additional arrangements."

She bid them farewell and went to find Mrs. Pratt.

Mrs. Townsend and Miss Clapham had come to her because she was duchess, because they knew she would do whatever she could to protect her own.

She was still furious with her husband, and equally exasperated by the things Lady Pennington had said, but she set aside her anger and disappointment—*for now.*

Something greater than her heart was at stake.

❦

CHAPTER SIXTEEN

HARBURY TILTED HIS head, unsure he had properly heard his housekeeper. "Are you certain the duchess said she wanted Lady Pennington to wait in the parlor?"

"Quite," Mrs. Pratt replied. "As Miss Clapham and Mrs. Townsend have just come from the church, the duchess felt they might soothe the worst of Lady Pennington's fears and answer any questions while you prepare to speak with Mr. Anderson."

"I see," he said, though the details remained murky.

As far as he could understand, his wife expected him to confront his father's man, relieve Anderson of the tinderbox he'd threatened to use on St. Margaret's, order the steward to resign his post, and then deliver the man into the safekeeping of his daughter.

How he was going to accomplish these miracles while Anderson remained in a disordered state, believing him to be an imposter, he'd no idea.

His wife, on the other hand, appeared to have a plan.

Despite his present reservation, her counsel had not led him astray yet. The least he could do was offer her the benefit of the doubt. If she had a plan, he knew her well enough to understand she would have taken everyone's wellbeing into consideration, especially his own.

Even when upset—no, *furious*—with him.

So, he acceded to Cassandra's wishes and extended her invitation to Vivianne, who warily accepted.

"Lady Pennington," Harbury said as he ushered her into the parlor, "these two ladies, *whom you were so good as to point out to me when they arrived,* have come to let us know your father has been found and is currently with Miss Clapham's father at St. Margaret's."

Yes—his steady gaze implied—*the riff-raff you complained about came to offer their aid.*

"May I introduce them?"

"We are, I believe, already acquainted." Lady Pennington replied, with heightened color. "Mrs. Townsend." She nodded. "Miss Clapham. Thank you for bringing such welcome tidings. I cannot tell you how relieved I am."

"I will return shortly," he told them all, before leaving the room.

He hastened up the stairs and then opened the door to his chamber.

"Your Grace." Marsden inclined his head.

Harbury's gaze moved between his wife, his valet, and the assortment of clothes and fripperies covering both his dresser—a powdered wig, a pair of silk breeches in pink, a long coat with gold trim, and an elaborate waistcoat. He then focused on his father's pocket watch, which he usually kept in the very back of his top drawer.

"What's all this?" he asked.

"Marsden and I have been discussing what should be done," his wife replied.

His valet nodded in agreement.

"Mr. Anderson has been demanding to see your father," Cassandra continued, "we both feel, given Mr. Anderson's state, how you present yourself to him could make a great deal of difference."

He glanced back to the clothes. The collection of not-so-subtle symbols of wealth, of authority left him slightly nauseous. They conjured vivid memories. Memories of his father, barking orders from the table's head, scowling down at his disappointing son.

He swallowed. "You want to dress me up as my father."

"If you appear in a manner…more familiar to Anderson," Marsden gently suggested, "he will be more likely to calmly accept direction."

Anderson had always enjoyed the duke's confidence, but never his affection. He doubted his father would have put himself to this much trouble on behalf of anyone he employed.

In the same situation, his father would have been more likely to have disparaged the subservient class's weak minds before ordering Anderson escorted off the estate without even speaking to the man at all.

And his father would have been dead wrong.

Not, he realized, for the first time.

His wife's idea, though unusual and downright disagreeable, had merit.

In the guise of his father, he could not only persuade the steward with less effort, but also put the man's mind at ease. If the ruse worked, Anderson would feel free to relinquish his post while maintaining his employer's admiration and goodwill.

Moreover, Anderson—and Vivianne—would be out of their lives for good.

"I've also asked for the coach to be readied," Cassandra explained. "Four footmen are to join you, just in case Mr. Anderson cannot be convinced."

"You're a treasure, Cassie. I couldn't have asked for a better duchess."

"I only want what we all want—Mr. Anderson's safe return." Her gaze dropped to his collar, a collar still damp with her tears. "People are waiting on you, depending on you."

Is that *all* you want? His unasked question lodged in his throat. "Will you come with me?"

"No." She shook her head. "My presence could only confuse Anderson."

"I hate that I must do this. I hate that I must leave you."

"This will be hard, I know." Briefly—too briefly—she touched his shoulder.

For a time, he would become his father. To do so, however, would mean more than just donning old clothes. To be convincing, he would also have to adopt an air he'd never been able to master. An air that, since he'd embraced his softer side, had since become abhorrent to him.

Perhaps it was better she was not there when he did so. "You said you'd be here when I returned," he reminded. "Does that promise stand?"

She nodded, unable to meet his gaze. "Take care."

"I will," he assured.

She made her way back to her bedchamber and gently closed the door behind her.

"Well," he turned to Marsden. "Do your worst."

Piece by piece, he donned his father's clothes. When Marsden had finished, Harbury looked into the mirror, and an altogether different man gazed back.

He wouldn't have thought it possible, but the wig's warmth, the grayish curls brushing across his shoulder blades, the brocade jacket's weight, the silk breeches' slide across his thighs encouraged a sense of noble authority, a license to do as he pleased.

But doing only as he pleased, without consideration of how his actions affected others, was not how he wanted to live.

Harshly wielded power worked by invoking fear. His father had known exactly how to manipulate that sword. He, on the other hand, would have to approximate.

A leader strove to better conditions for all, but fear didn't bring out the best in people. Not like patience, inquiry, and mutually assured commitment.

Secure in the knowledge who he was on the inside could not be changed by how he was dressed, he faced his unfamiliar, distasteful reflection without shrinking. What he was about to do was not a resurrection, but a kindness. A kindness his father would never have been capable of performing.

A kindness Harbury might not have been willing to perform, had he not been made wiser by the pain of one love lost and the miracle of another, truer love found.

A love that, when this was over, he desperately hoped he could save.

He kept that hope burning in his heart as he applied himself to his mission. A short while later, he followed Lady Pennington's carriage to the church. The ladies went inside first, and the footmen positioned themselves, two outside of the front entrance, two in the back. When Mrs. Townsend gave the signal, Harbury strode into the church with a lifted gaze.

He spotted Anderson, who was standing at the base of his father's monument, clutching the flint and powder to his chest. The Rector, Miss Clapham and Lady Pennington were each speaking to him in turn.

"No," Anderson said to Lady Pennington. "I won't go with you."

Harbury approached, staring down his nose. He kept his expression haughty, his eyes cold. Lady Pennington turned.

"Your Grace." She dipped into a curtsey and then took a step backwards.

"Clapham, you are excused," he said to the rector. "As are the rest of you."

Anderson immediately rose to his feet.

"Not you. Nor the"—he added a touch of disgust—"*lady*."

Moving closer to her father, Lady Pennington nodded. The rest of the room cleared.

"Anderson, you've done well."

Anderson's hold on the flint box tightened. "I have?"

"The imposter has been removed." He nodded regally. "Exactly as I would have wished."

"I knew," Anderson whispered. "I knew you wouldn't want the imposter in your seat. In your study. Going through your accounts. Not to mention reveling in those books of...of..." Anderson's face darkened.

"Filth," Harbury said, hating that he must disparage the collection of tomes that had so increased his and Cassandra's pleasure.

But filth was how his rigid father would have described them.

"Filth." Anderson nodded. "And degradation."

Degradation. What a word for an act that was essentially the most powerful way of communicating love, the genesis of life itself.

"Just so." Keeping his chin raised, he held out his hand. "As there is no longer any threat to myself, I should like the flint box."

Anderson blinked down. "Yes," he said slowly. "Yes, you should have it."

Harbury received the box. "And now I have an even more important mission for you."

"Yes?" Anderson queried hopefully.

"Your daughter must be kept safe. I want you to go with her. Watch over her."

Anderson frowned.

"She is the only one besides us who knows, who understands," Harbury improvised.

"B-But what of you?" Anderson asked.

"Must I remind you?" Harbury narrowed his gaze. "I do not, as you know, tolerate any question of my authority."

"Of course." Anderson bowed. "I am grateful to be of service."

"Come." Lady Pennington put her arm around her father's shoulders. "Let me take you home."

Anderson nodded, looking as weary as Harbury felt. Then, he and Lady Pennington slowly made their way down the center aisle before exiting the church.

ALONE IN THE church, Harbury let the silence around him gather.

Becoming his father had been far more difficult than he'd anticipated. The weight of their combined mistakes weighed on his shoulders as he stared up at his father's likeness.

Echoes of their past arguments rang in his head. But his experience of those memories had fundamentally shifted. He no longer felt as if he'd been in the wrong on every subject.

And perhaps the thought that had occurred to him back in the vault was true—his father's rigidity had been, in part, a reaction to his grandfather's excesses.

What a strange familial chain successive generations wove.

Then, Harbury did something he'd never done to the real man—he touched his father's face. He had to reach up to do so, too. Had the stone statue been built to his father's accurate height, they would have stood nose to nose. His father had ordered his monument to be taller.

Ruefully, he shook his head. "How like you," he spoke to the statue.

For the first time, he was glad he hadn't ever "earned" the man's approbation. He exhaled, yanking off the ridiculous hat and wig. He didn't belong in the past. He wanted to get home to his future.

He made his way back to the hall and then promptly submitted himself to Marsden. Only after his valet had removed every trace of the old duke, did he cross over to Cassandra's door.

Bracing himself for whatever was to come, he knocked.

"Enter," she bid.

Tentatively, he peered into the room. She'd changed into her nightclothes, but she was not in bed. Resting on the mattress were two packed valises. A third, still open, sat on the other side of the room.

His heartbeat slowed. His limbs grew heavy. Some part of him had known she would be preparing to leave.

"Sally," she said, "would you please have these collected? And tell the coachman to be ready to leave at first light." She dismissed her maid, then asked, "Is Mr. Anderson safe?"

"Yes. Lady Pennington has taken him back to Rose Cottage."

She closed her eyes and sighed. "I'm glad."

"I should have acted sooner," he said.

"I know," she replied.

"I didn't see the changes in him because I didn't want to see the changes in him."

"I know that, too."

She turned away from him and went over to study the contents of the open valise on the chair in front of her dressing table. The table where he'd brushed her hair. The table where she'd been seated when he'd placed a necklace around her neck.

Had that only been this morning?

"You're leaving me." His voice rasped as he spoke. "Aren't you?"

"Taradiddle," she replied without looking up.

"Pardon?"

"Taradiddle. Something I say with Eliza, or, rather, when we hear nonsense, I say taradiddle and she answers twaddle, if the nonsense is particularly egregious, we add bilgewater." She paused and shook her head. "Something you would know about me...if you had courted me properly."

She was paler than she'd been before. Her mouth tight.

"Eliza," he echoed.

"You remember Eliza. My sister. My twin. Whom I miss. Desperately. Yes, I'm leaving. But I am not necessarily leaving you. I am going to visit Eliza."

"You're still angry...and you are placing your things into a valise. Pardon my confusion, but such things make it *look* as if you are leaving *me*."

She placed her brush carefully into the valise.

"Well?" he prompted. "Chastise me if you must. Just tell me what I can do to make you stay."

"There's nothing you can do." She flashed him a pointed glance. "You wouldn't challenge a clearly incompetent man because he's your—"

"—Because he was my father's man," he interrupted. "And also due my regard."

"Don't even try to convince me your failure to act had nothing to do with his relationship to Lady Pennington. To *Viv*."

"Very well, you're right. But only in part. I hesitated because my father had relied on him, and I didn't yet trust my own judgment. But, yes, I did feel a debt to him. And, yes, having him here kept a distant connection to Lady Pennington."

Admitting as much was painful even to himself. He'd been so damn foolish.

She stared at him long and hard. "I am not sure what you expect me to do."

"I want you to stay."

She shook her head. "I'm exhausted, Harbury. More than exhausted. Shattered. I don't even know what I want anymore." Tears shimmered in her eyes. "The only thing I can think of that would give me some small measure of peace is to go to my sister."

He could demand she stay, forbid her to travel. He could keep her here physically. He'd every right. By law, she belonged to him. But he couldn't make her *want* to stay any more than his father had been able to remake him in his own image.

No. He didn't want her to be here against her will.

He wanted her voluntarily present, not just in body, but in soul. And he sensed that, if he forced the former, he'd forever lose the latter. An awful paradox…if he truly wanted to keep her, he had to let her go. And this time, he felt like he was losing not just a rib, but an entire arm.

"I'll set things to rights here," he promised. "When you come back, things will be very different."

Bleakly, she met his gaze in the mirror.

He came up behind her. "But before you go, kiss me."

She appeared to deflate.

"Please," he added. "Just a kiss, I swear."

She bit her lips, studying him doubtfully. "Kissing me won't make me stay."

"I'm not trying to make you stay."

Slowly, she turned around. "You aren't?"

Ah, Cassie. Why hadn't he appreciated what he had found in her sooner?

He took her hand into his. "I'm only trying to remind you of the reasons you should plan to come back."

She stared up into his eyes, a weary, helpless expression on her face. But the softness he'd glimpsed once or twice before remained, if dimmed. In that softness he read a message he should have understood long before. One he might have responded to if he'd been open, if he had not believed his heart had been given to someone else.

She loved him.

He swayed back on his feet, moved by the realization's power.

Possibly against her will.

Bittersweet revelation, considering. But something he could hold onto in the coming days.

Gently, he bent his head and brushed his lips lightly over hers. Even brief contact kindled an invigorating rush, a sudden awareness of the wonder of being truly and fully alive. He wanted to linger, to deepen it, to hold her tight. But this wasn't a kiss of passion.

This was a kiss of promise.

He kept his eyes closed as he pulled back. Eventually, he must open them, but for now, he wanted to savor her taste.

She turned away and then resumed packing.

"Will you be taking Mercy?" he asked.

"He's not mine to take, is he?"

He couldn't answer.

His time at the Church and at the cottage had been so tense, so chaotic, he'd completely forgotten to discuss the pup with Viv, or, rather, Lady Pennington.

He would only think of her thusly from now on, he resolved.

He looked down into Mercy's sweet face.

One way or another, he would make sure they were able to keep their dog.

"Cassie?"

She turned.

"I promise we'll both be here when you return."

"Don't make promises you aren't sure you can keep."

"I intend to keep every vow I ever made to you…especially the 'til death do we part."

He scooped Mercy up from the bed, then buried his fingers into his fur. He'd thought watching her walk away had been the hardest thing he'd ever done.

Voluntarily walking away from her was far worse.

CASSIE ARRIVED AT Ravenswood Hall only to discover that Eliza, Adrian, her sisters, and their guests, Lord Neville and Lord Asquith, who remained guardian to her younger sisters, had all gone to dine at a neighbor's home.

Her sister's housekeeper, however, delivered her to a suite of chambers, exclaiming all the while at the remarkable resemblance between her and Lady Redver. Her cheeks hurt from maintaining a false smile throughout the conversation. Alone again, she opened her valise, looked down at her hairbrush, and only just managed to hold back a sob.

And then, the door flew open.

"Cassie! The porter told me you'd come and come alone, but I didn't believe him. Where is…"

Cassie turned.

Eliza raised her hand to her mouth.

"Oh, *dearest!*" Eliza exclaimed between her fingers.

The familiar sound of Eliza's voice—her twin sister's voice— nearly reopened the floodgates.

Cassie held up her hand. "Don't."

Eliza closed the door behind her and then held out her arms. "Come here."

Cassie stepped quietly into the welcome circle of her sister's embrace. *"Don't* feel sorry for me," she warned. "And *don't* say I told you so."

"I would nev—" Eliza stopped herself. "Well, actually, I would absolutely say *I told you so.*"

Cassie snorted reluctantly. "You have done often enough."

"Yes, well, I couldn't in this case. Little more than a month of marriage is hardly enough time to make any sort of judgment about compatibility. Besides, you two make a handsome couple. And I've grown accustomed to saying *my sister, the Duchess* with an air of great importance."

Cassandra responded with a half-hearted chuckle.

"And with my husband as close as brothers to yours, we're sisters twice over," Eliza continued. "Plus, Harbury's estate is *huge.* And—"

"Stop trying to make me feel better!"

"What would you like me to do, then?"

Cassie wiped the damp from her eyes and glanced sheepishly through her lashes. "Hate him?"

"Oh, let's!" Eliza clapped her hands together. "Let's *hate* the Duke of Harbury."

Cassie chuckled half-heartedly.

"He's horrid. *Hideous!* On the inside, of course. To make a proper assessment, we will ignore, for the moment, his Adonis face. But there *must* be some evidence of perfidy on his person." Eliza squinted. "Did you get a look at his feet? I'd wager ten to one he's got cloven hooves instead of toes."

Cassie wrinkled her nose as Eliza mimicked the clip-clop of hooves with her hands.

"He *does!* Doesn't he? Oh, I'm certain Harbury is not human at all, but a right demon. Shouldn't be allowed to live!" Eliza folded her arms. "Oh, yes! Let's hate him!"

Cassie broke into a true laugh. "That's enough!"

Eliza lifted a brow. "I'm right about the cloven feet, aren't I?"

Cassie groaned. "He's got fine feet to go with a *very* fine figure. His looks have never been the problem."

Eliza extended her hand. "Come. Let's climb into bed, shall we? Just like we used to before we were old and married. And you can tell me all about what went wrong."

Together, they climbed up onto the bed. Cassie sighed as they huddled. Sitting so close—head to head, as they'd so often done—made her feel less unmoored.

"I can't *talk* about it, Eliza."

"Twaddle and bilgewater," Eliza dismissed her objection. "Was he simply arrogant? Or was he truly dastardly? I'll bet his cloven feet are terribly scratchy, too. Hoof lacerations would upset *anyone*."

"*Taradiddle*." Cassie chuckled half-heartedly. "No. And *no*."

"Then why are you here…alone?"

"I needed time away." Cassandra chewed on her lip. "I just can't *think* when he's near."

"You can't think? Or you can't be as mad at him as you would like to be?"

Cassie smiled reluctantly. "The latter, I suppose."

"I completely understand. Sometimes I could wring Adrian's neck, but then he smiles at me in his special, intimate way, and—" Eliza interrupted herself with a growl and then punctuated with an eyeroll.

"Evil!" Cassie said mockingly.

"I know!" Eliza nodded enthusiastically.

Cassie sighed. "I'm hopeless."

"Doubtful."

"Really? What if I told you I can't stop thinking about the moment he swept me onto the Almack's dance floor?" Again, the dizzying memory. The colors. The scents. The unbelievable thrill of being chosen by a young, handsome duke, followed by the absolute horror of humiliation when the patroness had ordered them out of the room.

Tears blurred Cassie's vision.

"Don't cry, Cassie." Eliza gripped her shoulders. "There's no need to relive that night." She shivered. "The gasps, the whispers, the way the women swept aside their skirts."

"The crowd's reaction came after the countess ordered the music to stop. And, to me, the gasps were *not* the most mortifying part. Not *at all*."

Eliza's brow wrinkled in question.

"At first, when he was walking toward me with a look so full of determination," Cassie explained, "I thought he'd chosen me *on purpose*."

"Oh, Cassie."

"I thought—I was stupid enough to think—the handsomest, most powerful man in the whole room had chosen *me*."

The room blurred even more, and she covered her face with her hands.

"Oh, my poor sweet girl. How did I never suspect you had true feelings for him?"

"I never wanted you to suspect."

Eliza rubbed her back. "Love at first sight?"

Cassie sniffed. "Attraction at first sight, at least."

"Maybe he *did* choose you on purpose," soothed Eliza. "Only he just didn't fully know his own mind at the time."

Cassie laughed bitterly. "Have you forgotten what he said to me before he swept me out onto the dance floor?"

"I remember." Her sister shuddered.

"*You'll do,*" she repeated the hurtful words aloud. "Eliza, I think something in me shattered at Almack's, only I didn't know yet. I held everything together...until today." She put her hand to her head. "It just became too much."

"Do you want to talk about what happened that sent you running off?"

She shook her head no. "Not yet."

"Well, he doesn't know how lucky he is." Eliza chewed her

lip. "I *hate* him and his cloven hooves!"

"I know what you're trying to do," Cassie said. "But I already *know* hating him is overwrought."

"*Do* you hate him?"

Cassie didn't answer.

"When he was pretending to court you, you liked him," Eliza reminded. "You called him gentlemanly."

"Gentlemanly," she sighed. He had been. Even though he'd been forced to court her, he'd been thoughtful in small, unnecessary ways, just as he'd been these early weeks of their marriage. "Harbury *is* gentlemanly."

"See? Your voice softened! You *don't* hate him after all."

No, she didn't. "It doesn't matter how I feel about him. I *want* to be sweet and nice, understanding and accommodating, but when I try to turn my good intentions into action, I feel a silent roar in my chest."

"What did he do to make you flee?"

"I didn't *flee*. I left him for a time. And not because of something he did, but something he didn't do. He didn't tell me the woman he swore he'd love forever had been his sister's governess."

Eliza winced.

"Eliza! You knew, too?!"

She nodded. "Adrian told me everything after he and I saw Lady Pennington at the Royal Academy. And, if you remember, I tried to talk you out of marrying him by revealing his infatuation, but you told me you already knew all about his first love."

Cassie scowled. "Apparently he forgot to tell me a few essential details."

"What did he do when you found out?"

"He held me. He let me cry." Cassie's shoulders slumped. "He repeatedly told me I knew him better than she ever had."

Eliza's eyes went soft. "The fiend."

"Not you, too!"

"You must admit it's romantic."

"He's romantic. And thoughtful. And when he smiles"—she jabbed her finger into her cheek—"he has a stupid dent right here that makes me want to kiss him."

Eliza nodded knowingly. "*Clearly* evil."

"I'm so, *so* angry. I feel like the anger will never end."

Eliza gazed at her with sympathy. "Maybe the anger you are feeling is not only about Harbury. Maybe your anger has something to do with Mama's unhappiness, too?" Eliza held her breath as she studied Cassie. "Maybe," she continued, "you're just a little bit angry that following her example of sacrifice hasn't worked?"

Cassie grabbed a fistful of her skirts and twisted. "*You're* the angry sister, not me!"

"Yes, I know." Eliza half-smiled as she gently worked the fabric out of Cassie's hand. "Millie and I rebelled. Lenora became a changeling, disappearing into fantasy, while Nettie favors sweets and larks. But you—you chose Mother's example."

Had she?

"Mother," Eliza continued, "made herself the martyr who suffers an absolute monster of a husband in silence. You simply believed your role, too, was to take every blow without complaint."

For a moment, every muscle in her body seemed to scream. Then, the pain passed, and she became numb to everything but the slide of a cool tear down her hot cheek.

"Don't think we all didn't notice."

"Well," Cassie replied, "you might have said something before."

"Things have been unsettled for us all for a long time. And, before Adrian, I hadn't truly understood how different marriage can be when both husband and wife have a mutual regard, so I don't think I understood how much we were all influenced." Eliza squeezed her hand. "As the oldest, we're the ones who best remember Mother before Father's unreasonable demands and infrequent visits silenced her and broke her heart."

Cassie gazed bleakly at Eliza. "Are you trying to tell me I'm desperately afraid of becoming our mother—devoted to a man who will never love her back?"

Eliza grimaced, then gave a reluctant nod.

Cassie forced herself to swallow. "But Harbury isn't a monster."

"He's not?" Eliza asked.

"No." Cassie turned over the last few weeks in her mind, dwelling longest on the times Harbury had asked questions to draw her out and listened deeply to her answers. "He's nothing at all like our father."

"After witnessing how uncaring he was of your feelings after the Almack's debacle, how he thought only of his own, I own I believed Harbury as meanspirited as our father. But Adrian insisted I give him a chance. And I agreed, because he and Adrian have been close since they were children, and any man who has kept up a true friendship for that long must have *some* redeeming qualities."

"A few," Cassie admitted.

Her sister patted Cassie's hand. "If anyone can bring them to the surface, you can."

"But I don't want to bring out his good qualities!"

Eliza sat back, giving Cassie a considering look. "What do you want, then?"

"I want him to value his own good qualities."

"Good. But what do you want…for *you*?"

Last night, she'd simply wanted the comfort of her sister's presence. But she couldn't remain here forever. Eventually she'd have to face Harbury again. And, when she did, what did she hope would happen?

"I want him to want me," she started carefully. But she already knew he did. "I want him to *need* me." No, *need* wasn't quite right, either. She wanted to be more than just a source of comfort. Which left only… "I want him to love me."

She closed her eyes, trying to rein in the sudden swell of inner longing.

"I want him to love me as completely, as desperately, as I love him."

"Oh, Cass. I want that for you, too." For a few, long, silent minutes, Eliza stroked Cassie's hair. "You know," she mused, "I was so angry I could have shot Harbury for what he did to you at Almack's."

Cassie's partial giggle ended in a sniff. "Instead, you headed out to a gaming hell and got yourself mixed up with Adrian."

"Did I ever tell you what the owner of that hell told me about my anger? She told me to use the rage I felt to make change."

"*Use* your anger?" Cassie repeated, mulling. Yes, she supposed one could. She would never have worked up the courage to come to Eliza's if anger hadn't bolstered her strength and certainty. But she didn't *want* to feel this awful way. "Easier for you than me, I think. You've always been a little angry. And somehow displaying such unladylike emotion never made *you* feel ashamed."

"As opposed to you, perhaps. You've always been the perfect daughter. Maybe it's time to use the voice I know you have."

"You mean you *want* me to give in to these horrible impulses? To blurt out every horrible thing that comes into my mind?"

"No. I want you to treat the angry part of you as you would treat me when I'm upset—*listen to it.*"

Cassie sat and *listened.*

But the warring voices in her head had gone silent.

She sensed, however, a wide range of possibilities between either making her husband's life grotesquely uncomfortable or silencing the parts of herself that had needs and made demands.

"But if I gave up sacrificing my happiness….?" Her eyes filled and she shook her head.

"Oh, Cassie—you don't have to be perfect to be loved. Lord knows how far I am from perfection, and yet Adrian and I—"

"—are perfect for each other," Cassie finished her sentence.

Eliza nodded. "Just remember, whatever happens, Millie, Lenora, Nettie, and I will be here for you. If you honor your anger, yet still give him a chance, and he continues to make you unhappy, we can go back to hating him." She leaned forward. "I imagine there are hundreds of devious ways determined sisters can make a duke pay."

Cassie snorted.

"We'll bring the whole family in on the fun," Eliza continued. "Millie can draw caricatures more distorted than any political sketches. Lenora can mimic and mock him. And Nettie... Ah, I know! Nettie can bake him a poisoned apple tart."

"*Can* Nettie bake now? I mean, I know she's always wanted to learn but father forbade it, and Lady Asquith's cook had no time or interest."

"Well, *I* saw no reason to prevent Nettie from learning something that gave her joy. And Cook's delighted to teach. Nettie is ever so happy."

"I'm so glad," Cassie sighed. "As for Harbury"—she flashed Eliza a significant look—"murder might be a bit much."

"No hasty decisions," Eliza replied. "Sleep on the matter first."

Sleep she would.

Though without Harbury, she doubted sleep would come easy.

CHAPTER SEVENTEEN

HARBURY ANGLED HIS way through the three horseless carts in Rose Cottage's courtyard, each of them in various stages of being filled. Sturdy men begged his pardon as they passed him, traipsing in and out of the house carrying all manner of boxes, bags, and carefully wrapped furniture.

Though he could truthfully say he hadn't had a moment to spare in the past week, he'd been avoiding this visit, afraid of what he might feel when he saw the place emptied of memories. He needn't have worried. Relief was the only sentiment that washed over him.

And relief was certainly a welcome change.

Eight days without Cassandra, and every one of them had added increasing weight to his shoulders. His burdens felt literal, as if he were carrying a Sisyphean rock that drained triumph of joy and robbed repose of rest. Fatigue infected every tissue straight down to his bone marrow.

So far, however, for the sake of his promise to Cassandra, he hadn't allowed an ounce of distress to show. He'd simply soldiered on.

He had wrongs to right and an estate to set straight.

The morning after Cassandra had left, he'd begun exactly where he thought she would have wanted, by meeting with Townsend and his son. The younger Townsend proved knowledgeable, skilled, and more than eager to take on the position of steward.

Each day since, Harbury and Townsend-the-younger had gone over every lease, statement, and letter in his files. One by one, they compared terms, output, and improvements Anderson had already paid for or promised, as well as improvements suggested but not yet attempted.

Yesterday, they had held a meeting.

The public room in Upper Harfield had been filled to the brim with anxious men. Though the meeting started out hostile, when Harbury took the floor, they listened to his plan, point by point.

Mr. Anderson was to be pensioned, Townsend's son to take over his responsibilities. More importantly, rent due, for the remainder of this slump in prices, could be offset by the submission of any receipts for improvements made. Additionally, if there was need, rent could also be delayed from Michaelmas to Lady Day, so long as an improvement plan had been submitted and approved.

As Harbury spoke, the grumbling lessened. And, by the time he finished, the sentiments of those present had transformed from hostility to grudging regard. He was still a long way from trust, but he'd made progress.

Solid progress.

And he'd done so not by becoming more like his father, but by trusting his instinct, and the counsel of his wife and of his chosen advisors. But only time would prove his sincere interest in his tenants' well-being. For now, he'd shown he could be effective without being rigid.

His father's way was not the only way.

As he'd suspected, Cassandra's love hadn't made him weak. Her love had been an impetus, an inspiration. And if he could prove he could be the leader the estate needed, perhaps he could also prove he could be the husband Cassandra deserved.

But first, he had to get through this visit.

Lady Pennington greeted him awkwardly, before inviting him in for tea and leading him into a half-empty parlor.

"How is your father?" he asked, once they had been seated and served.

"Calmer now." She spoke with her head down, gazing into the dark liquid inside her cup. "He genuinely believes your father gave him a mission. Whenever he starts to fret about all he is leaving behind, I assure him his life's work is in good hands." She glanced up. "Am I telling the truth?"

"I've always cared deeply for the land and its people."

"I know." She hesitated. "Mrs. Grant, however, says you will never earn the tenants' trust."

"Mrs. Grant is prejudiced."

She smiled a slight, knowing smile. "If you mean my father and I have her loyalty, then yes. She always behaved toward me in a motherly fashion." She sighed. "Will you hire a new steward?"

"I already have. The estate's largest tenant, Mr. Townsend, has a solicitor son who has managed several smaller properties for a London firm. At my request, he has taken the position. Having grown up here, he is familiar with the land. Furthermore, he is eager, knowledgeable, and competent. I told him he may move into Rose Cottage after Michaelmas."

"How…efficient." She cocked her head and blinked, as if she weren't certain she believed he was capable of having executed all of the above in such a short time.

She didn't have any faith in his abilities at all, did she? She never had.

No wonder his father had so easily convinced her of his betrayal.

"At least the place will not stand empty." Her gaze moved around the room. "Has Mr. Townsend a family?"

"He's got a wife, a strapping young lad, and a little girl who is but a babe in arms."

"How nice to think of children enlivening the cottage once again."

"Indeed."

The conversation fell silent.

Not, he realized, because there were things they could not say, but because they'd already exhausted every topic of polite conversation they had in common. Further proof they shared a past, but not the present.

"Edward—"

"Harbury," he corrected. "…Lady Pennington."

"Just as well, I suppose." She tilted her head. "You've changed."

"I know," he replied. Marriage had changed him, first. Then, love. He was, he hoped, becoming the man he'd always wanted to be.

"Harbury," she started again, "before I go, I want you—and, more importantly, the duchess—to know I am sorry for how I acted the other day. I should not have gone out of my way to antagonize either of you."

Grateful for her gesture, he inclined his head. "She will appreciate your apology."

"And despite what I said, I don't blame you for the way things ended. What you said in your letter was right. Our elopement would have brought shame on your family. I knew how much you longed for your father's good opinion. I was mad to think you would have crossed him to marry me."

He contemplated telling her the truth, that he hadn't written the note his father had delivered on his behalf, that his father had deceived them both.

But what good would such revelations do, especially now that he had finally come to know his own heart? Gazing at Lady Pennington now, he felt as if he were looking at a stranger.

When Cassandra returned—he could not bring himself to say *if*, even in the privacy of his own mind—he would not only tell her but also show her he returned her love with all his heart.

"I am sorry," he told Lady Pennington sincerely, "for any harm I caused, too."

She ran her finger along her cup's edge. "Well, you weren't

wrong to end things, you know."

"What do you mean?"

"I cared for you." She shifted as if uncomfortable. "But perhaps not as much as I allowed you to believe."

"How….honest." A few months ago, her admission would have devastated him.

Now, he simply shook his head.

"My father's first thought was always of your father, of the estate." she went on. "*Always.* I resented that he placed the well-being of your family over his own. When I realized you cared for me. I…" Again, she shrugged. "I went after what I thought I could get."

"We were both young."

She laughed ruefully. "*You* were young. *I* was foolish."

In his opinion, they'd *both* shown an appalling lack of sense. "You are happy now," he gently reminded.

"With Pennington?" Her face went soft. "Yes. And you? You love your duchess, don't you?"

"With all my heart." His answer came readily and with ease.

"That's good." She looked away. "Well, we had our day," she said with a sigh. "You were a lovely distraction from drudgery."

"A distraction," Harbury repeated, with a half-smile…then a snort, then an ironic chuckle.

She'd thought of *him* as a distraction.

As his laugh deepened, she raised her brows and shook her head as if she didn't understand him at all.

"I can't explain." He inhaled deeply and shook his head, suppressing his appreciation of the irony. "It's just…I have some experience with distractions."

She raised her brows. "Apparently."

"Be happy," he offered.

"I intend to." Her smile broadened. "Penny finds me fascinating, you know."

"That, you are."

"What does your lady think of you?"

He considered. "I hope she finds me…" What was the opposite of a distraction? "As essential to her as she is to me."

Lady Pennington nodded as if she approved. "I also want to let you know how much I appreciate what you did for my father."

"The duchess put the plan in motion. I only played a part… For *his* sake." Another awkward silence. "What will you do about him?"

"Take him home with me. Take care of him. Make sure that, if nothing else, he understands he is safe."

"He will receive a full pension from the estate."

She shook her head. "I don't want your money."

"A little late to be noble?"

She inclined her head. "Perhaps, but I must insist. I *want* to care for him."

"Be the better person?"

"Rise above my resentments, yes."

"I wish you both well, then." He took a deep, cleansing breath. "And as…enlightening as our conversation has been, the past is not the reason I came over here today."

"No?"

"I came to talk with you about the pup. My wife rescued him. And I'd like to keep him."

She assessed him critically. "He was my litter's best. If I hadn't gifted him to my father, he would have fetched a nice price."

"I'm not asking for a gift. I am willing to pay. And"—he leaned forward—"I can assure you the duchess and I are sincerely attached to Mercy."

"Mercy?" The corner of her mouth turned up.

"As in, '*Mercy,* what have you gotten into this time!?'"

She laughed lightly. "I can see you are sincerely attached to him."

They negotiated a price. He didn't haggle hard. The important thing was to make sure the pup remained with him.

Mercy belonged at Harbury Hall. Just as Cassandra belonged with him.

He only hoped she'd come to her senses and return soon.

He took his leave with a lighter heart than he'd had when he arrived. And, as he mounted the steps to Harbury hall, he heard the sound of wild barking. As soon as he crossed the threshold, Mercy—ears flopping and claws rat-a-tatting against marble—circled him in ever more exuberant rings. Harbury glanced down with affection. The dog was thrilled, but also anxious.

Ever since Cassie left, he'd had taken up a place at the door.

"As soon as she comes home," he said as he scooped up the pup, "we will tell her how much we missed her, won't we?"

"If you had half a brain, you wouldn't wait. You'd be at Ravenswood, on your knees."

Harbury swiveled toward the voice. "Adrian!"

Adrian stood with his boots crossed at the ankle, leaning against the balustrade as if he hadn't a care in the world. But, Harbury noted, he was still wearing his greatcoat. As they exchanged a hearty handshake, Mercy sniffed at Adrian as if he weren't quite certain if the man were friend or foe.

"Oh, now that your protector has returned, you're brave enough to sniff me." Adrian tickled behind Mercy's ear, settling the matter in Adrian's favor—*friend*. "I've heard about you. Insufferably adorable, just as reported." He transferred his gaze to Harbury. "You, on the other hand, look like the devil."

"No doubt." He kept hold of the dog, just in case. He might need comforting, depending on what Adrian had to say. "I'm surprised you could tear yourself away from Eliza. To what to I owe the pleasure?"

"On horseback, the ride is no more than a few hours. Besides, I came at my wife's behest."

Adrian had come because Eliza had asked him to do so? "Has *my* wife sent a message, too?"

"*Cassie* doesn't know I'm here."

Cassie.

He tamped down an irrational flare of jealousy. Of course, Adrian was on family terms with his wife. He was her brother-in-law.

"But before we discuss Cassie, there's something else I'd like to know." Adrian leveled his gaze. "I heard Lady Pennington is on the estate, is that true?"

"Lady Pennington is staying at Rose Cottage," he confirmed, resenting the implication in Adrian's tone.

Only he hadn't any more cause for his resentment than he'd had for his jealousy. Adrian hadn't been with him over the last few weeks. As far as Adrian knew, the last time Harbury had seen Lady Pennington, Harbury had lost his head.

"As a matter of fact," Harbury continued, "I've just come from there. I went over there to secure our Mercy." He hefted the dog and tilted his head. "Do you hear that?" He spoke directly to the spaniel. "I've bought you fair and square. You belong to Cassandra and me for good."

Mercy yipped, lifting his head to snuggle beneath Harbury's chin.

"Mutt negotiations?" Adrian lifted his brows and shook his head. "That's *all* you discussed?"

"We discussed the past, too. Briefly."

"Briefly?" Adrian's eyes narrowed. "Would you have me believe you reminisced with Lady Pennington and felt nothing?"

"I wouldn't say *nothing*." He rolled his shoulder to ease his discomfort. "Seeing her will always be, oh, I don't know…like witnessing a memory come to life. No longer painful, merely distant. And, before you even ask, no, I wouldn't have gone over there if I hadn't wanted to make clear my intention to keep Mercy. He was Lady Pennington's by right, but he's stolen Cassie's heart."

Adrian raised his brows. "I'm glad you were able to settle the matter. But are you actually saying you've finally realized I was right all along where Viv is concerned?"

Harbury snorted. "You never did like Lady Pennington."

"No. I didn't like *you* when you were *with* Vivianne."

Harbury cocked his head. Harsh words. Painful, too.

"Oh, don't look so hurt." Adrian elbowed him. "You know very well once you set Viv on a nonpareil's pedestal, you had no choice but to become her rabid, growling guard—a guard who would nip and snarl at anyone who threatened to topple her, especially your father."

Adrian had placed a thumb against a scale Harbury had already abandoned.

But he wasn't wrong.

"Frankly," Adrian continued, "you were exhausting."

Harbury frowned as different scenes from over the years flashed through his head. Yes, he'd repeatedly made a fool of himself for Lady Pennington. And some of that may have had to do with rebellion.

"I don't think I liked myself much then, either," Harbury said finally.

His younger self had wanted what he'd thought he'd found in Lady Pennington—an idol to worship. Perfection to admire. When his wrung-out rag of a heart had lost the will to worship, he'd chosen pretty dutiful, sweet Cassie as an alternative.

But, even then, there'd been the glimmer of something more, hadn't there?

A diamond no one else could see, sparkling in the corner of his eye.

Marriage had been his aim. An ornamental duchess. But marriage, he'd since discovered, was not just a state of being, but the melding of lives. And Cassandra was not a decoration, but a lady with needs and desires, too.

A lady he loved.

And a lady he'd deeply disappointed.

"I miss her, Adrian. And I'm not sure I can make amends."

Adrian scoffed. "Don't be an ass."

"I'm not being overly indulgent! I really am uncertain. I've bungled everything from the start...not that I expect you to understand. You and Eliza communicate so easily, you hardly need words."

"A good thing, too, as, unlike you, we've had little time to ourselves since we wed. Not that I'm complaining. Between my sister and Wainwright ladies, the house has never been so full of chatter. You of all people understand what a drastic change that makes from the home I remember."

Harbury nodded. "I'm glad. But how *did* the two of you form so quick and easy a bond?"

Adrian chuckled. "Even if I told you the whole story—which I am *not* at liberty to do—you wouldn't believe me." He smiled an enigmatic smile. "We are simply meant for one another."

"*Simply meant for one another* isn't much help."

Adrian snorted. "For a romantic, you don't know much about romance, do you?"

No. Harbury feared he did not.

Oh, he knew all about nurturing pain, wallowing in disappointment. But to save his home and his marriage, he would have to learn another way to be.

And learn fast.

"If I went back with you now, would she see me?"

"See you?" Adrian rolled his eyes. "*Of course,* she will see you. And if we leave now, we could be back at Ravenswood by nightfall."

"I'll get my coat." He glanced down at Mercy. "And a satchel."

CASSIE STOOD AT the window, part of the whole and yet separate, alone, listening to the sounds of Eliza's guests as they laughed and mingled behind her, a sound she'd come to think of as bittersweet.

At first, being with her sisters had brought her comfort, but with every passing hour, she became increasingly aware of a growing emptiness within, a hollow only Harbury could fill.

She missed quiet breakfasts with her husband, the exchange of pleasant nothings that had quickly come to flavor her days. With Adrian's sister Emily, Lord Asquith, and Harbury's cousin Lord Neville in residence at Ravenswood, breakfasts here were far louder and more boisterous, as boisterous, in fact, as the present gathering in the parlor.

A gathering minus one. Adrian had taken himself off before the morning meal. And, since Eliza hadn't seemed concerned in the least when Adrian had not returned for tea, she suspected his destination had been Harbury Hall.

Would he come back alone? Or was she soon to be reunited with her husband?

She stared down at a miniature Harbury had given her just after they'd agreed to wed. In the tiny painting, Harbury's hair was darker than the shade she could vividly imagine running through her fingers. His brow was slightly cocked, and his look was entirely raffish. He appeared, in fact, exactly as she'd pictured the scoundrel from her favorite book.

"Harbury looks particularly dashing in that portrait."

Cassie hadn't noticed her sister Eliza glancing over her shoulder.

"Doesn't he just?" Cassie resisted the urge to rub her finger across the protective glass. "He reminds me of a character from *Sense and Sensibility*. The one Marianne fell for first."

"Willoughby?" Eliza cocked her head as she studied the miniature. "Perhaps. Harbury not only looks the part of a romantic rogue, but he's also proven he can *be* a rogue, too."

Cassie nodded in agreement. "Clearly, he is capable of falsehoods." And of binding an innocent's heart to his own, of carelessly breaking that heart in service of his own best interests.

Eliza sighed. "Too bad Harbury hasn't suffered a similar punishment for his flaws."

"Punishment?" Cassie frowned.

"Willoughby had to marry a jealous heiress, while Harbury—though equally undeserving—got you, one of the finest ladies I know."

Cassie sent her sister a grateful smile.

"Elinor reminds me of you, you know."

"Longsuffering?" Cassie chuckled half-heartedly. "Committed to duty above all else?"

"No," Eliza drew out the single syllable. "Capable of deep and lasting happiness with a man who, eventually, proves himself worthy of her love."

Cassie blinked away the sudden water in her eyes.

"Harbury will realize what he lost." Eliza snaked an arm around her waist. "And soon. ...If he knows what's good for him," she added under her breath.

"Will he?" Cassie asked rhetorically. She wasn't sure.

She hadn't left him in order to be chased, but she had expected to hear from him by now. For the last four days, she'd inquired about the post. And, though a packet had arrived all the way from London for Adrian—one dated after she'd left Harbury Hall—she'd received nothing.

Deep in her heart, she was starting to lose faith.

"Oh, heavens!" Eliza leaned toward the window.

"What's wrong?" Cassie followed Eliza's gaze. "I don't see anything amiss."

"Over there. Just outside the yew hedge."

Cassie squinted, trying to identify the figures partially hidden behind branches. "Is that Lenora and...*Asquith*?"

Lenora, they both knew, had harbored unrequited feelings for her guardian and their godmother's son for years.

Asquith, for his part, appeared oblivious. But he had never, to Cassie's knowledge, allowed himself to be alone with Lenora. Millie, yes...Eliza, too, as both had enjoyed riding as much as he did, but never Lenora.

Cassie didn't think he held Lenora in contempt; she'd assumed he was being cautious.

She might have assumed wrong.

Eliza stepped closer to the sash. "What *is* she doing?"

"I don't know," Cassie replied. "Is it me? Or does Asquith look particularly harassed?"

Just then, both figures disappeared fully into the maze.

"Who is looking harassed?" queried Millie from behind them. "And what has the two of you looking so intent?"

Both Cassie and Eliza turned. Behind them Millie stood arm-in-arm with Lady Emily, Adrian's sister, and their youngest sister Nettie, all of them with wide-eyed expressions of curious innocence.

"Where is Lenora?" whispered Eliza.

"Headache," Nettie replied, at the same moment Millie said, "Resting."

"Lenora," Lady Emily clarified, "is resting because she has a headache."

Vigorous, simultaneous nods followed.

Eliza folded her arms. "And the two pairs of shoes visible beneath the yew?"

Nettie stood on her toes. "I don't see any shoes."

"Lenora," Millie murmured her sister's name like a curse. "I *told* her to go all the way into the maze."

"A much better place to—" Emily stopped herself. "Converse," she finished with a guilty blush.

"Millie, what's going on?" Cassie demanded.

"Nothing," they answered in unison.

While Cassie and Eliza exchanged a glance, Neville sauntered over to the group.

"Why is it," he asked Millie, "you always appear to be up to something?"

Millie cast him a withering gaze. "What you perceive as 'up to something,' Little Lordling, is, in fact, the exercise of wit and imagination." She smiled sweetly. "Two things beyond your experience."

Lady Emily snickered. Nettie bit her lips as she did whenever she wanted to keep from smiling. Cassie and Eliza sent Millie identical warning glances.

"Lacking in imagination, am I? Well…" Neville cast his gaze about the room. "Asquith is missing. As is Lenora." He turned his gaze back to the sisters, looking from one to the other. "I can imagine a few reasons why that might be so."

"Lenora has a headache," Nettie repeated.

"And has gone—"

"And," Cassie interrupted Millie, "has gone out with Asquith to take a turn about the garden, in hopes a little air would help improve her condition."

Cassie ignored the young ladies' mutinous glares.

But what could she have done? Neville's too-perceptive gaze had landed in the general direction of the visible shoes. To be caught in a blatant lie was worse than whatever game they had decided to play.

Or so Cassie hoped.

"Should they be alone outside?" Neville glanced at Eliza. "Is that proper?"

Millie glanced heavenward. "He's their godmother's son. And our legal guardian."

"We've known him all our lives," Nettie added.

"They are in full view of the house, too," Lady Emily pointed out, although that wasn't quite true at present.

Neville's gaze narrowed. "I don't trust you…any of you. I'm going out there." He headed toward the door muttering something about Wainwright wiles.

"Oh dear," Nettie breathed.

"Don't worry," Millie whispered back. "I'll catch him before he catches them."

Eliza's hand shot out, preventing Nettie and Lady Emily from following Millie. "*Four* people wandering the garden is quite enough."

Nettie pouted. "You *never* let me have any adventures."

"Speaking of adventure, how did you and my brother first

meet?" Lady Emily asked, her voice deceptively light. "I've always been a little bit curious about the speed of your engagement."

"Fair enough," Eliza replied. "Just be sensible. I don't want Lenora to get hurt."

"You don't have to worry," Nettie replied. "Truly."

"Very well." Eliza's expression remained skeptical. "But remember—Cassie didn't sacrifice herself only for her younger sisters to raise scandals of their own."

Sacrifice.

Cassie felt rather than heard the word. She had never felt marrying Harbury was a *sacrifice*. But if he didn't write soon…

"Nora just wanted to talk to him," Lady Emily replied.

Cassie turned toward her sister, and they exchanged a speaking glance. Then, behind Cassie, the door opened. Cassie knew from the way Eliza's face lit, *her* husband had returned. Her own heartbeat sped, but she couldn't bring herself to see if Harbury had come with him.

"Perhaps Nettie, Emily and I should go for a walk after all," Cassie suggested.

"I don't think you'll want to leave," Eliza whispered, with an elbow nudge to her ribs.

Cassie turned, and everything else faded away. She was so blind, she hardly noticed the room empty of guests. All she could see was Harbury—somewhat worse for wear, but present. And looking at her as if she were a cool glass of ale after a long, hard, and dusty ride.

He came toward her with outstretched hands.

"Please—"

His voice made her heart sing.

"—Stay."

Yes, she would stay. She could hardly trust her legs to walk, after all.

But her weak knees weren't the only reason she would not be running away.

One smile and two outstretched hands were proof enough.

He was the husband she desired. She was the wife he needed. And, even if he had not come with the express intention to take her home, for once in her life, she intended to fight for him.

❦❧

CHAPTER EIGHTEEN

B ELATEDLY, HARBURY REALIZED the room had emptied of people. While he welcomed a moment of privacy, he didn't care if they had witnesses or not. Either way, he was going to tell his wife everything he should have told her from the start.

"Cassie," Harbury caught up both his wife's hands and gathered them against his lips. "Good G—" He stopped himself from cursing. He sighed. "I've missed you, love."

"At present, I wouldn't mind an oath." She smiled shyly. "Because I'm...*devilish* glad to see you, too."

He didn't know how long he stood there with a silly, stupid grin on his face.

He couldn't help himself.

He heard the door open for a short moment before closing again. And then, a small bundle of fur bounded into the space between them with a deliriously happy bark.

"Mercy!" she exclaimed.

"You left a few things behind." His voice was rough, unsteady. "Two things, to be precise. Two things belonging to you."

"But I thought Mercy belonged to Lady Penningt—"

"Lady Pennington," he interrupted, "forfeited her claim."

From her expression, she had not missed his double meaning.

She bent down, picked up the dog, and buried her face in his fur.

"Come." He placed his arm around her waist and led her to the settee.

They sat down together, as close as two people could be.

Her presence at his side felt like a miracle. He took in her warmth, her scent, and those things worked to mend his inner, broken places.

"The pup," he continued, "had been a gift from Lady Pennington to her father. But instead of soothing Anderson, the pup increased his agitation. They were on their way to town in her carriage when he abruptly tossed Mercy out the window."

"Oh! You poor thing." Cassie kissed the pup on the forehead. "That tumble must have been horrid for you."

"As with some of Anderson's other actions," Harbury continued, "I don't think he understood the harm he would cause."

"That man wasn't well," Cassie translated to Mercy. "But we'll take good care of you from now on. You may place your full trust in us." She turned her gaze on Harbury. "Can't he?"

The ease, the total conviction, with which she'd said the word *us* caused Harbury's throat to thicken. "I've already promised him the same. Repeatedly."

Together, they cooed over the puppy.

And somehow, though he'd been leaning toward Mercy, Harbury's head ended up resting on his wife's shoulder. He closed his eyes, savoring her closeness.

She turned her face, pressed her cheek against his curls and inhaled.

"Did you just *sniff* me?" he asked.

"Yes." She giggled. "I missed your scent."

"Lucky thing Adrian and I washed before coming into the parlor, then." Could it be his scent gave her the same reassuring sense of solace as hers gave him? "What do I smell like?"

"Like home," she replied with a soft smile.

He sat up, taking her hand in his. "Does that mean you are ready to come home with me?"

"I'd like to." Her smile faltered. "Oh, Harbury, I *want* to..."

"What can I do to convince you?"

"It's not a matter of convincing. But, before I return, there *is* something I need to know."

He braced for her question. "Ask me anything you wish. I will answer honestly."

She kept her gaze, not on him, but on Mercy. "After you realized I would be upset, why didn't you tell me that Vivianne had been Sarah's governess?"

"Because"—he lifted her face so that he could look fully into her eyes—"you were growing more important to me by the day...by the hour, even. I didn't want you to leave me." Ruefully, he twisted his lips. "As happens more frequently than not, my own actions caused my deepest fear to come true."

"I didn't leave you for good. I—I was just worn out."

"I know," he said cupping her cheek. "Terms or no, marriage is more complex than either of us expected."

"*I'll* say," she enthusiastically agreed.

"But when you proposed, you placed the most significant wager of your life." He brought his lips against her brow. "You were the first—the only person—to vest full faith in me. Tell me, *please* tell me I haven't fully squandered that faith."

"Oh, Harbury. Of course you haven't. And, by coming to get me, you've only increased it. I've been *wretched* without you. Why didn't you write?"

He drew back. The pain in her eyes broke his heart all over again.

Could she have actually been doubting his love when, at the same time, he'd been fearing, despite her promise, she would never return to him?

"You could have saved me *so* much fretting," she scolded.

Tenderly, he tucked a stray curl back behind her ear. "The night you left, you said you needed to see your sisters. You said you didn't know what you wanted anymore. I never imagined you *wanted* to hear from me."

She shook her head, once again freeing the curl. "Oh, you senseless, thickheaded man."

He didn't mind the insults...not when she was smiling up at

him with her unspoken love shining out from her eyes.

God, the sight was beautiful.

A sight he'd thought he might never see again.

"Cassie…" He paused until the thick feeling in his throat passed. "I love you."

She closed her eyes and pursed her lips. She looked as if she were also holding back tears.

"I love you, too," she whispered.

He wrapped his arm around her shoulder and pulled her in close.

They remained that way, his mouth against her hair, her face turned into his neck until Mercy let it be known that he didn't find the position tolerable at all.

She sat up and adjusted her cap. "How are things on the estate?"

"I promised you I would set things to rights, and I have. I've taken your suggestion and hired Townsend's son as steward. He and his young family are to take up residence after the Harvest festival. I hope you don't mind that I didn't wait for you to return to engage him."

"Not at all," she replied. "I'm glad."

"Anderson really did believe I was an imposter, you know."

"Poor man."

"He's been better, so I've been told. Or, perhaps, the right word is calmer. I don't think his condition will reverse. But at least he will be with Lady Pennington, where he will have care and plenty of rest."

She frowned.

"What thought troubled your brow just then? You should know that, while I did visit her, I only visited to discuss Mercy."

"That's not it." Cassie shook her head. "I knew you would have to speak with her."

"What I told you in the carriage was true. You do know me better than she ever will."

"I don't doubt you. Not anymore. It's just that…Lady Pennington called you Edward." She glanced up through her lashes. "But you've never given *me* leave to call you anything other than Harbury."

"Not even Adrian calls me Edward." He threaded his fingers through hers. "And, you should know that on that visit, I rescinded permission for Lady Pennington to do so."

"You did?"

He nodded. "My Christian name should only be used by someone with whom I'm intimately connected."

"Like me?"

He nodded. "The first night of our marriage—"

"I was furious," she interrupted. "Furious and frightened."

"And I *ached* for you to call me Edward. Only, for years, I'd rejected every part of me 'Edward' embodied. You changed that. You made me understand I could take the best parts of the boy I had been and use them to become a better man."

Her features went soft. "The *best* of men."

"Please, call me Edward. Call me anything you wish."

She laughed. "Even thickheaded?"

"Especially thickheaded." He ran his thumb back and forth across her hand. "I cannot wait to take you home. But there isn't time to return to the Hall today."

"No," she agreed. "We should wait at least until tomorrow."

"I didn't bring much, but I did throw a few necessities into a satchel." He glanced up. "Should I have my things sent up to your room?"

She wrinkled her nose.

"What?" He raised his hand to his chin. "Do I have something on my face?"

"No." Her grin widened. "But you were making the same face Mercy makes when he wants his belly tickled."

"Are my attempts to influence you working?"

"Perhaps."

He leaned forward, then lowered his voice. "I wouldn't *object* to having my belly tickled, either."

She pretended to consider. "Perhaps…so long as you agree to page 57."

He groaned. "I will *always* agree to page 57."

"Then, yes," she said primly. "You may send your things up to my room."

He kissed her softly, lingeringly.

"Come, Edward," she said with a wide smile. "Be with my family."

And, perhaps for the first time in his life, Harbury felt as if he were exactly where he belonged.

A FEW DAYS later, Cassie stood in Ravenswood's drive a few yards away from where her husband and Adrian were having a good natured argument while overseeing the packing of her carriage. Asquith and Neville had left the day before.

With hushed voices, she and her sisters bid farewell. The familiar, five-person hug had grown larger by one—Adrian's sister Emily.

"I'll miss you all," she said.

"In a few more weeks we'll be together again in London," Eliza reminded.

"I'm glad you came," Millie said.

"Millie didn't like Harbury," Nettie whispered.

"Nettie," Emily scolded under her breath, "you never tell a lady anyone dislikes her husband."

"Not *dislikes*," Millie replied. "*Disliked*. Past tense."

"He has been different these past few days," Emily agreed. "I've known him all my life, and I hardly recognize him."

Lenora sighed. "Because Cassie has softened his edges."

"I do believe I have." Cassie stepped back and settled her gaze on her husband. "Marriage does that."

Millie rolled her eyes. "Don't you start talking about *marriage of minds.* We've heard enough of that drivel from Lady Asquith."

"Perhaps it is only true if one is married to the right person," Nettie offered. "Mother never changed Mr. Wainwright."

"Must we mention Mr. Wainwright?" quipped Millie.

Cassie sent Millie a sympathetic glance. The pain in her tone suggested she had not yet come to peace with their parents' memories.

"Well, Harbury is the right person," she said to Lenora. "The right person, at least, for me."

She smiled as she watched him croon to the dog, who, by leaping back into his arms from the carriage seat, had just made clear he *would not* be riding inside the carriage.

"Weather's fine," the coachman said to her husband. "I can take him up here with me."

Harbury handed up first the basket and then the dog. The coachman settled the basket between his legs and Mercy propped his feet up on the footboard and yelped excitedly.

Harbury turned and caught her gaze. He smiled wide, and her already full heart expanded.

"Ready?" he asked.

"Yes," she replied, taking his hand and stepping up into the carriage.

Harbury raised his brow. "A little room, please?"

"I thought you would ride alongside the carriage."

"I'm leaving my horse here. Adrian will bring him down on his way to London."

"Is Moses injured?" she asked.

"No." He winked. "I just want to serve as your pillow."

He made an excellent pillow, too. And, since they hadn't had much sleep the prior night, she spent most of the journey in a contented, dreamless slumber.

All her dreams, after all, had already come true.

Many hours and several stops later, she yawned and stretched as the carriage passed through the toll gate that led to Harbury lands. In the distance, she could see the gables of Rose Cottage.

There were workmen on the roof.

"Have Mr. Anderson and Lady Pennington gone, then?" she asked.

"Looks like they have. Mr. Emmit Townsend was only to begin alterations after Mr. Anderson had fully vacated."

She assessed her husband. "Are you sorry?"

"I feel only sympathy and regret that Mr. Anderson is so ill. He was always such a strong presence in my life." For a pensive moment, he gazed in the direction of the cottage. "I believe feeling he had done his duty made a great difference in his willingness to move on. I have you to thank, too. I never would have thought to dress like my father."

"You weren't just dressed as him." Cassie shivered. "Everything about you was different. Your posture. Your voice."

He grimaced. "I didn't want you to witness that."

"I only saw you from the window. From what little I could see, I don't think I would have liked your father."

"He was widely admired, but I doubt anyone ever referred to him as aimable. Or kind-hearted. Or well-meaning."

She cupped his cheek. "Not like you, you mean."

He turned his face further into the cradle of her palm. For a long moment, he held that position.

"My father was…" She searched for a word. "mean-spirited, too."

"I'm sorry," he said sincerely. "I thought that might have been the case when you referred to him as Mr. Wainwright."

"At his command," she sighed. "The times he wasn't at Willowhurst were the happiest. Promise me we will raise our own children differently."

"I swear our children will know they are loved."

She sighed, placing her head back against his shoulder only to raise it again when the coach slowed. They came to a stop next to a very familiar clearing.

"Why are we stopping?" she asked.

"I'll tell you, but first, may I ask a delicate question?" Harbury ventured.

"Yes," she cautiously replied.

"It's important to me that you feel at home on the estate. Everywhere on the estate. That you understand, that, while I may occasionally see something that reminds me of Lady Pennington, that she does not linger here. Not any longer."

She frowned. "I didn't hear a question."

"Are the priory ruins forever spoiled for you?"

She studied his face. "Why did you take me there?"

"Truthfully?" He visibly swallowed. "In the moment, I was thinking only of you. I thought they would make you smile. I'd completely forgotten everything that had come before."

She sighed. "Then I, too, promise to forget."

"May I take you there?"

"Now?"

He nodded. "I have something I'd like to show you. Something new."

"Something new?" She cocked her head. "In a ruin?"

He smiled enigmatically. "Yes."

"Very well, then," she replied.

Hand in hand, they made their way to the site. Cassie hadn't any idea what to expect, but she couldn't immediately discern anything different as they passed under the former chapel's arch and made their way to the stairs. Then she saw it, a little monument in rose marble, just to the side of the stairs.

"Go over," he urged. "Read it."

She approached the stone and knelt down, shading her eyes from the afternoon sun.

C+E had been carved inside the shape of a heart. And just underneath the heart's point, the words *Our place. Always.*

Her heart spasmed in the best of ways. She bit her lip as she traced over the carving, and then she rose to her feet. "Edward,"—she turned—"I—"

He had gone down on one knee.

"Cassandra…Cassie…love," he said. "I've never properly

asked." He reached out and grasped her hand. "Would you do me the honor of becoming my wife?"

She blinked. Rapidly. And she sniffed to hold back her tears. "I'm already your wife."

"But would you marry me again? Now? Right here in this chapel?"

"Without a clergyman?" She smiled. "Without a *roof*?"

"The only thing that truly matters is the vow before God."

"Why?" She whispered.

"Because…" He cleared his throat. "Because I want to promise again to love you, to comfort, honor, and keep you, in sickness and in health, and truly and completely, forsaking all others."

"Harbury—*Edward*—do you mean it?" She couldn't keep herself from adding, "You really don't love her anymore?"

"I thought that was clear."

"No…I mean, I know you love me, but I feared, perhaps, you still loved her, too."

He shook his head. "I know now what I felt for Lady Pennington wasn't love. Only a kind of idolatry." He squeezed her hand. "I know because I know what love—a deep, abiding, strengthening love—feels like."

Cassie had wished for his affection. And she'd hoped for—and received—his passion. She had decided to try to become first in his heart, but she never truly believed she would fully win him.

"Tell me again," she whispered.

"I love you, Cassandra. And I promise to keep myself only for you." He brought her hand to his lips. "As long as we both shall live."

She knelt. Facing him, she took his other hand.

"I have a secret, too."

"Oh?"

"From the moment I saw you, I wanted you. And since then, you've come to mean so much to me, I'm sometimes afraid."

"You've loved me? From the start?"

"Not just loved you. I've been mad for you. Jealous, too."

"There's no need—"

"But there is. The other ladies you've been with…" her voice faded.

He winced. "There's something else I should have told you. I've always believed chastity before marriage a virtue. A virtue that should be practiced by all."

She jerked back. "Are you telling me I am the only woman you've ever taken to bed?"

"Yes," he said solemnly. "I've only known that kind of intimacy with you."

She searched his gaze, finding no sign of falsehood. She saw only love, vulnerability, and the deepest of commitments.

He was hers—entirely hers—in a way she'd never expected.

She cupped his face and smiled her softest, tenderest smile.

"Harbury…Edward. What a gift you've just given me."

He smiled in a teasing fashion. "If you're incredulous, I must have done something right."

"I love you." She ran her finger down his face. "And I will marry you again. Edward, I give my heart into your keeping, in sickness and in health, forsaking all others"—her sigh was long and heart-felt—"as long as we both shall live."

They kissed as the sun slanted through what had once been the altar window, bathing them both in light. Then, Cassie heard a distant, indignant yip.

"Mercy," he breathed.

She giggled.

"Time to go home?" he asked.

"Time to go home," she answered.

Together, they turned back toward Harbury Hall.

EPILOGUE

"**S**HE'S BETRAYED US," Millie whispered to her sister Lenora as they watched Cassie and Harbury waltz around the Almack's dance floor at the start of the next Season.

"You said you liked Harbury, now," Lenora pointed out.

"I like him well enough," Millie shot back. "But she's *mooning* over him. *Here*. In Public."

"That she is." Lenora sighed happily. "And you thought nothing could be worse than Eliza and Adrian."

"You're *all* mad—you with Asquith, Nettie with Blackwell, Eliza with Adrian and"—she waved her hand in the direction of the dancing couple—"that abomination over there."

Briefly, Lenora glanced in Asquith's direction. Then, she turned back to her sister. "Cassie has too loving a nature to ever be called an *abomination*."

"Ugh." Millie groaned. "The way her feelings for her husband spill out of her eyes! It is almost worse than having our under-things out on a line to dry where everyone can see."

"Sst," Lenora hissed. "You can't say"—she mouthed *under-things*—"at Almack's. Are you trying to get *our* vouchers revoked, too?"

"The patronesses wouldn't dare." Millie tossed her head. "Not only has Lady Asquith taken us under her wing, we've both a marquess and a duke for brothers-in-law."

"Well, I'd rather stay on Lady Asquith's good side," Lenora said under her breath. "If everything goes well, I will need her approval."

Millie's gaze came to rest on Asquith. She'd no objection to their guardian, but he was deep in conversation with the man she thought of as *the little lordling*, or, as Asquith's mother might say, *that Neville*. "How are things going?"

"Nothing to report." Lenora blinked innocently. Too innocently. "*Yet.*"

Millie narrowed her gaze. "Nothing since the hedge?"

Lenora blushed. "I told you I don't want to talk about the hedge."

"Very well." Millie had her own reasons for not wanting to think about the afternoon she and Neville had followed Asquith and Lenora into the yew maze at Ravenswood.

"These things must be done slowly," Lenora added. "*Carefully.*"

Millie made a dismissive noise.

"You just carry on with your plan to test the limits of Society's outrage," Lenora said. "But don't go as far as to ruin my chances—or Nettie's. Or Emily's, for that matter."

"I gave up on you and Nettie a long time ago. *Love. Love. Love.* That's all you and she ever want to discuss."

"To be fair"—Lenora raised her brows—"Nettie talks about pastries quite a bit."

"Well, Lady Emily, at least, is no more interested in finding a husband than I am." While not strictly a Wainwright, Emily had become part of the family circle.

Lenora frowned. "Did Emily tell you she had no interest in marriage?"

Millie shrugged. "Why else would she have delayed her debut another year?"

"So she might come out with Nettie, of course."

"Well, anyone who places their security in something as fickle as love is, in my opinion, mad. *I'd* rather be notorious than leg-shackled!"

"Notorious?" Lenora chuckled. "Well, that dress of yours is a nice start."

Millie's smile broadened. "Isn't it just?"

TO AMBROSE AUGUSTUS Merriweather, better known as Lord Neville, this Wednesday night at Almack's was even more painful than the last. Every stratagem he could think of to keep his gaze from repeatedly straying to Millicent Wainwright had failed. In his defense, she was, by far, the most beautiful young lady in the room.

Pity she was also the most infuriating.

Little lordling, she'd taken to calling him. And every time she did so, he wanted to—Well, perhaps he should just say he could think of any number of ways to put her lips to better use. He closed his eyes, shook the thought right out of his mind and then reopened them.

Unfortunately, she was still directly within his line of sight.

The pale purple hue of the silk gown she'd chosen may have been appropriate, but the closely fitted cut was drawing too many pairs of eyes. Male eyes. Including his own. He sent his friends Lord Asquith and Lord Blackwood a sidelong glance. *Of course*, they were staring in her direction, too.

"She's outdone herself tonight." Lord Blackwood folded his hands behind his back as he shook his head. "What a spectacle!"

"If you mean Miss Millicent"—Neville used the excuse to prolong his study—"Then, yes, I wholeheartedly agree."

"Actually, I was speaking of Duchess of Harbury." Blackwell smirked. "And, for that matter the duke."

"I don't see anything untoward in *his* behavior." Neville replied.

The duke and duchess were dancing too close, of course. But Harbury was his cousin. If Neville was anything, he was loyal.

Blackwell turned to Asquith. "Even your mother and her

fellow battle-axe dowagers are over there sighing."

"I know," Asquith replied darkly. "My mother has a soft spot for all the Wainwright ladies. Only the twins are her godchildren, but, since I inherited their guardianship from my father, she's taken the younger three under her wing, too." Asquith's gaze followed the couple as they took another turn. "I cannot believe how hard Harbury has fallen for Cassie! Redver for Eliza, too. Clearly, the Wainwrights pose significant danger to any unmarried man."

"Do I detect a hint of fear?" Blackwell took his friend's measure. "Fear, perhaps, you may be the next to succumb to the siren call of a Willful Wainwright?"

"Don't be ridiculous," Neville cut in. "Asquith would never do anything so untoward as to fall for one of his wards."

"Untoward," Asquith repeated under his breath. "Yes, very." He gave himself a subtle shake. "A marital alliance is out of the question—not that I'd want one."

"What do you think is their secret?" Blackwell asked.

Asquith shrugged. "Well, Eliza is a firebrand. Cassie is sweet. Nettie has a bright and curious mind. And Millie…" He frowned. "Well, clearly every man present has taken note of that dress. Every man other than myself, that is. Millie has been like a hoydenish little sister to me."

"You see?" Neville said to Blackwell. "If he fears anything, it's failing to marry them off in a timely fashion."

"Ah," Blackwell replied. "Then I suppose desperation to marry them off is why, when the Wainwright ladies were living with your mother and you moved into the Albany, you begged us to come along with you whenever you were invited to dine?"

"I asked you to come because you adore the tarts my mother's pastry chef is so fond of creating." His gaze met Neville's. "Him, I invited because he's a paragon."

"I asked him because he's a paragon. An absolute model of propriety."

"I see," Blackwell responded at length. "No one could accuse either of us of having nefarious intentions toward the ladies with a bishop's nephew at our side."

"Glad to be of service," Neville said dryly.

Blackwell cocked his head and frowned. "Neville, am I mistaken, or did Asquith forget to mention Miss Lenora when describing the Misses Wainwright?"

"*Lenora.*" Asquith said under his breath. "I could never forget Lenora."

Neville frowned.

Last summer, Asquith, who'd always taken care to keep his distance from the youngest Misses Wainwright, had disappeared into a maze with Miss Lenora. Goaded on by Miss Millicent, Neville had plunged into the maze, intent on finding the pair before any damage was done.

Then, Miss Millicent had burst upon him, and then…

Well, he'd rather not think about *and then*.

"Asquith," Blackwell said with an edge of disappointment. "Have you, perhaps, been using us as a shield?"

"How lovely Millie looks…" Asquith changed the subject.

She did that. *The minx.*

"…Hard to believe she's the same cheeky chit that stole my breeches so she could practice riding astride."

Neville felt as if someone had punched his gut.

Asquith chuckled nervously, clearly hoping that a shocking *on dit* would permanently alter the conversation.

Neville's frown deepened.

Which was worse—the *yew incident* or the indecent picture that arose in his mind of Millicent in breeches? Again, he shuttered his thoughts. While he might find his natural, ah, appreciation for her form difficult to suppress, he'd no desire at all to be intimately acquainted with the lady.

She *was* a hoyden, through and through.

But—my God—how had she gotten Asquith's breeches up over those hips?

Hips that had, for a few indescribable moments, accidentally fit against his own as they'd tumbled backward into dark branches.

He closed his eyes, again, reminding himself his interest could only ever be *familial* in nature. Her sister Cassie—the very sister dreamily circling the room—had married his cousin.

Which, in a way, made Millicent part of his family, now. And as part of the family, didn't he have a responsibility toward her?

The two eldest Wainwrights had, by a mere hair's breadth, skirted scandal. *Someone* needed to keep an eye on Miss Millicent, lest she tumble into the same.

Tumble.

He cleared his throat. Poor choice of words.

"Breeches you say?" Blackwell cocked his head. "Can't imagine…"

Neville lifted a brow. Blackwell had better not try to imagine!

"…Though, I must admit, she is the most dashing and statuesque of this year's crop. My interest, of course, is purely academic," Blackwell clarified. "I've no taste for scandal, and ten to one Millie will embroil herself in one before the little Season is done."

"*Please* don't make that bet," Asquith sighed.

"Shame on you both," Neville snapped. "Especially you, Asquith. Her protection is your responsibility. If you're worried, you *should* be devising a plan to keep her safe." His gaze moved to Blackwell. "And you, at the very least, should be refraining from gossip about your good friend's wards."

Blackwell blinked innocently. "If you're so keen to protect, Millie, why don't *you* volunteer?"

"Me?" Neville felt his cheeks heat. "I have neither feeling nor responsibility for any of the Misses Wainwright, especially Miss Millicent."

Blackwell exchanged a glance with Asquith. "*Especially,*" he repeated.

Neville did, however, have a keen sense of impending disaster. "I was merely pointing out that young ladies are in want of protection."

"I beg your pardon," Asquith replied. "After last Season's Almack's catastrophe, I made sure Harbury at least pretended to court Cassie, and I had to threaten him to do so. I shudder to think what further misadventures lie in store for me. Then again…" He turned a speculative gaze on Neville. "Blackwell might have a point."

"What point?"

"You." He lifted his brows. "And Millie."

"Don't be absurd," Neville scoffed. "Besides, *you* owe *me*, not the other way around. I didn't have to volunteer to serve as your second in case Harbury accepted your challenge, especially since your challenge was to my own cousin."

"*Please*," Asquith replied. "You only came because you were afraid of the damage his actions could do to your family name. We both knew Harbury wouldn't agree to a duel. He just needed a little nudge to act."

Neville folded his arms. "Yes, well, that's beside the point."

Blackwell reached into his pocket and drew out a pen knife. "Asquith, your fob chain, if you will."

Hesitantly, Asquith handed over the chain. Then, he and Neville watched as Blackwell cut a string off the tassel.

"Hey!" Asquith exclaimed.

"Frayed," Blackwell said apologetically. "Been driving me mad all night. Do have a word with your valet."

Asquith scowled down at the tassel. "*He's* likely to want a word with *me*, thanks to you."

Blackwell turned away. When he turned back, he held out his fist, which contained three lengths of gold string.

"I have cut the string into three parts. One piece is shorter than the other two. Time to take lots, gentlemen. The person who pulls the smallest string from my hand must keep watch over Millicent Wainwright, either until the Season's end, or until she is properly betrothed, whichever comes first. Neville, as you seemed the most concerned, you go… begin."

Neville eyed his friend with suspicion, then glanced to Asquith.

Asquith shrugged. "I'm willing to abide by the result. And I'm willing to lend my flintlock to the poor sod who draws the smallest string."

"None of us would turn a pistol on a lady!"

Asquith snorted. "What if the lady drew first? Millie is a crack shot, you know."

Neville knew Millicent could be outrageous. She rather thrived on the condition. But a crack shot? Just how mad was she? He glanced over his shoulder, easily spotting the indecent frock. He had to admit, the effect was rather like staring down the barrel of a gun, and not just because of the dress.

That hair—brown, yes, but, in the right light, with an intriguing reddish hue. That statuesque, *arresting* figure. That slim waist. That...*ample* bosom. And that fire glowing in her green eyes...

That was a blaze which could well become an inferno, if not properly tended. Untended, she was a danger to humanity. *Someone* needed to tame her and that someone would be doing humanity a great service.

"Very well."

As he reached for one of the tassels in Blackwell's fist, his heart beat more rapidly than the situation should have called for. A second later, drawing a string less than a half inch long felt like fate.

"Well," Blackwell said, "there's no point in continuing. Clearly, you've drawn the shortest string."

Neville stared at the tiny slash of gold between his thumb and forefinger.

A great service.

A sacrifice for the good of all mankind.

He tucked the thing into his waistcoat pocket and adjusted his cravat. "If you'll excuse me, I will see to my duty."

"What do you intend to do?" Blackwell asked.

"Ask her to dance," he said. "Of course."

Amused, his friends watched him march away.

"Seems *he's* fallen hard, too," Asquith commented.

"And he has *no idea*." Blackwell chuckled. "This should be entertaining."

"I'm just glad he drew the short thread," Asquith said. "I've enough on my hands with…other matters."

"There was never any danger of him drawing the larger."

"What do you mean?"

Blackwell shrugged. "All three lengths were the same size."

"Blackwell, you fiend!"

"A fiend who not only took a headache off your hands, but one who has just acquired a front row seat to what is bound to be the Season's best entertainment."

"You know, Blackwell, your youthful face belies terrible cunning."

"Oh, I know." Blackwell straightened his jacket. "That's why no young lady will ever get the better of me."

"Nor of me," Asquith agreed, intentionally avoiding any public acknowledgment of Lenora, now gazing speculatively in his direction.

THE END

Author's Note

A few years ago, a good friend of mine developed Lewy Body Dementia; this book is, in part dedicated to her. Marilyn was kind, delighted by antiques, children, flora, insects, and anything having to do with a holiday. Over two decades and many family-and-friend gatherings, we shared photographs, extensive philosophical conversations, stories from the past, and a great many laughs. She was one of the few people I've known who retained childlike wonder throughout her life.

The disease progressed over a period of a few years, during which she lost all understanding, but never her kind heart. She was devotedly attended by her husband Henry, and it was his careful, tender care and support of her that inspired my inclusion of the disease in this novel.

It takes great patience and strength to remain with a loved one where they are and to reassure them they are safe and they are loved even as they understand less and less of the world around them. This is what Henry gave Marilyn, and this is what I envisioned the fictional Mr. Anderson will receive from his fictional daughter, even though Anderson played the part of an unintentional villain in the early part of the story.

As for the second part of the dedication, Mercy's history and likeness is a nod to my dear friend Richard P's fur baby, Monty. Monty was a truly special dog. His soulful, loving gaze could melt an iron heart. He greeted every scratch and snuggle with transports of joy, but he saved his greatest adoration for the man who rescued him.

I enjoyed every moment spent with you and your beautiful

boy, Richard.

Cassie and Harbury's puppy name, Mercy, came from Blevenda J's suggestion in a contest I ran during the February 2025 Cozy Socks and Cocoa party on https://www.facebook. com/groups/historicalromanceloversgroup.

She wrote, "For a name for the pup wrecking havoc I'm going to suggest 'Mercy' only because that was the name of my beloved companion who passed away September of 2024. He got his name when I brought home thirteen years ago and my husband proclaimed "Lord, have MERCY not another dog!"

Thank you Blevenda for agreeing to let me use the name of your beloved fur baby.

ABOUT THE AUTHOR

Historical Romance author Wendy LaCapra writes award-winning books reviewers describe as 'heart-pounding, entrancing', 'lusciously romantic and sparkling with wit.' As a teen, Wendy discovered spine-tingling gothics in her local public library, inspiring her to craft her own seductive tales full of secrets and scandal. She lives with her husband in a quirky, historic building in NYC and loves a girls' night in. For new release, sale alerts and other news, sign up at http://bit.ly/GetWendyNews.

Email: wlacapra@wendylacapra.com
Newsletter: http://bit.ly/GetWendyNews
Website: www.wendylacapra.com
Facebook: WendyLaCapraAuthor
Instagram: wendylacapra
TikTok: @wendy.lacapra
Goodreads: WendyLaCapra
Bookbub: bookbub.com/authors/wendy-lacapra
Amazon: https://amzn.to/48PCpIX

www.ingramcontent.com/pod-product-compliance
Lightning Source LLC
Chambersburg PA
CBHW051553030726
47592CB00001B/271